Murder
on the Matterhorn

An Abercrombie Lewker mystery

by Glyn Carr

The Rue Morgue Press
Lyons / Boulder

Murder on the Matterhorn
© 1951, 1953 by The Estate of Glyn Carr
New material
© 2010 by The Rue Morgue Press
87 Lone Tree Lane
Lyons CO 80540
www.ruemorguepress.com

ISBN: 978-1-60187-047-6

PRINTED IN THE UNITED STATES OF AMERICA

Cast of Characters

Abercrombie "Filthy" Lewker. The noted Shakespearean actor-manager and mountaineer, also a gifted amateur detective.

Léon Jacot. Formerly a leader of the French resistance, now a celebrated sportsman and one of the richest men in France, about to launch a new career in politics.

Deborah Waveney Jacot. His tall, graceful wife, a former stage star.

John Waveney. Deborah's devoted twin brother, also a former actor and a former fighter pilot, now employed in the aviation industry.

The Comte de Goursac (Paul). A passionate Alpinist with an otherwise stolid and impassive personality.

The Comtesse de Goursac (Camille). His wife, a volatile Junoesque brunette.

Bernard Bryce. A veteran climber and novelist, badly smitten with Deborah Jacot.

Mrs. Beatrix Fillingham. An imposing, outspoken, and seemingly foolish woman, known as Aunty Bec to her friends.

Margaret (Margot) Kemp. Her shy, dark-haired niece, expected by her aunt to marry Bernard Bryce.

Dr. Lawrence Greatorex. A bearded physician and experienced mountaineer who has climbed with Lewker in the past.

Heinrich Taugwalder. A weathered guide who is an old friend of Lewker's.

Lisse Taugwalder. His flaxen-haired daughter, betrothed to young Franz Imboden but enamored of Léon Jacot, much to her father's displeasure.

Franz Imboden. An innkeeper's son and friend to John Waveney.

Baptiste Frey. A young physics lecturer and member of the Flambeaux, a French anti-Communist group.

Julius Simler. The discreet proprietor of the Hotel Obergabelhorn in Zermatt.

Herr Schultz. The pompous, arrogant, and usually wrong-headed Kriminal Kommissar of the Swiss Criminal Bureau.

Adolf Venetz. A cheerful young Swiss professor and temporary hut warden.

Sir Frederick Claybury. Chief of Department Seven, British Secret Service.

Bertrand. An observant waiter at the Hotel Obergabelhorn.

Plus assorted guides, villagers, assistants, police officers, innkeepers, etc.

The Abercrombie Lewker novels

The Detective Novels

Death on Milestone Buttress (1951)*
Murder on the Matterhorn (1951)*
The Youth Hostel Murders (1952)*
The Corpse in the Crevasse (1952)
Death Under Snowdon (1952)*
A Corpse at Camp Two (1954)
Murder of an Owl (1956)
The Ice Axe Murders (1958)
Swing Away, Climber (1959)
Holiday with Murder (1960)
Death Finds a Foothold (1961)*
Lewker in Norway (1963)
Death of a Weirdy (1965)
Lewker in Tirol (1967)
Fat Man's Agony (1969)

The Spy Novels

Traitor's Mountain (1945)
Kidnap Castle (1947)
Hammer Island (1947)

*Reprinted by The Rue Morgue Press

About Glyn Carr

Glyn Carr was born Showell Styles in Four Oaks, Warwickshire, England, in 1908 and died at his longtime home in Wales in 2005. He did his first mountain trek at the age of three and spent the rest of his life scrambling on rocks, snow, ice and mountains. During World War II Styles used his shore leave from the Royal Navy to pioneer new ascents in North Africa and Malta. After he was discharged, Styles led two exploring and climbing expeditions to the Lyngen Peninsula, 250 miles from the Arctic Circle, where he climbed seven virgin peaks. In 1954, he led an expedition to the Himalayas to attempt a 22,000-foot peak in the Manaslu range in Nepal. He published numerous books on climbing as well as young adult fiction. If you look upon a mountain climb as taking place in a large, open-air locked room, then Showell Styles was right to choose Glyn Carr as his pseudonym for fifteen detective novels featuring Abercrombie Lewker, all of which concern murders committed among the crags and slopes of peaks scattered around the world. There's no doubt that John Dickson Carr, the king of the locked room mystery, would have agreed that Styles managed to find a way to lock the door of a room that had no walls and only the sky for a ceiling. In fact, it was while Styles was climbing a pitch on the classic Milestone Buttress on Tryfan in Wales that it struck him "how easy it would be to arrange an undetectable murder in that place, and by way of experiment I worked out the system and wove a thinnish plot around it." That book was, of course, *Death on Milestone Buttress*, which first appeared in 1951 and was published for the first time in the United States by the Rue Morgue Press in 2000. Upon its original publication Styles' English publisher, Geoffrey Bles, immediately asked for more climbing mysteries. Over the next eighteen years, Styles produced another fourteen Lewker books (fifteen, counting one last, currently lost unpublished manuscript) before he halted the series, having run out "of ways of slaughtering people on steep rock-faces."

CHAPTER ONE

MR. LEWKER IS CAJOLED

Mr. Abercrombie Lewker sat upon the floor of his very nice sitting room in Cleveland Row. Around him on the big Ispahan carpet were spread ropes, boots, maps, timetables. On his bald head a dilapidated woolen helmet was perched askew, on his large and pouchy countenance an expression of the utmost beatification hovered like morning sunlight on the face of a Buddha. He was polishing the steel head of an ice-axe. To him entered Rosa the maid.

"Sir Frederick Claybury to see—" she began; and then, catching sight of her employer, emitted an explosive sound and withdrew.

The lean gray man she had admitted stepped lithely forward and paused, gloved hands resting on stick, to wag his head sorrowfully over the figure on the floor.

"Celebrated actor-manager attains second childhood," he murmured. "My dear Filthy, forgive me. I didn't know. I would have bought you a nice puff-puff—"

"Rarely, rarely comest thou, spirit of delight," boomed Mr. Lewker, casting the ice-axe from him and rising to his feet. "Sit down, Chief. I will order tea."

Only when he spoke could one understand how this bald and bulbous-nosed gentleman, five-foot eight and broad out of all proportion, had become the finest Shakespearean actor of his day. His voice filled the room like the music of a double-bass, and yet every word was perfectly pronounced and given its full value. He took a small bell from a side table and rang it before sitting down beside Sir Frederick on a long divan.

"Tea," sighed his visitor, "is the only good thing London in August has to offer. How I wish I were going with you to Zinal!"

"How did you know I was going to Zinal?"

Sir Frederick looked wise. "It is our business to know things."

"Traditional retort, by chief of Department Seven, British Secret Service," grunted Mr. Lewker, eyeing him suspiciously. "Your spies, of course, are everywhere."

"They are not. That's exactly my trouble. Look here, Filthy—"

The door opened and Rosa came in.

"Tea for two, Rosa, please," said Lewker.

Rosa struggled with speech, nodded, and fled with a singular hissing sound.

"I cannot imagine," complained the actor-manager, "why an otherwise efficient girl should respond to a simple request by imitating a soda-water siphon."

"Perhaps if you took off that extraordinary woolen hat," suggested Sir Frederick, "Rosa might be able—by the way, what *is* it?"

Mr. Lewker swore and flung the offending headgear to the floor.

"An article of mountaineering equipment," he replied, "known to British climbers as a balaclava and to the French as a *passe-montagne*. Its associations are not comic, so far as I know. I had forgotten I was wearing it. But I still fail to see why Rosa—"

"It was hardly a tragedian's wear," remarked Sir Frederick. "You'd have brought the house down, on the halls." He caught Lewker's eye and went on hastily: "Of course, you're preoccupied with the prospect of a mountaineering holiday. I could have deduced that from the fact that the quotation with which you greeted me was not from the works of William Shakespeare."

"Georgina says I must cure myself of quoting him. I do essay the task."

"How is she? I hear she's staying with the Hazels while you go shinning up the Alps."

Mr. Lewker shifted his squat body and fixed his keen little eyes on the other's face.

"Now how did you hear that?" he demanded. "Chief, you are up to something. Why this interest in my holiday arrangements? Beshrew me, but I smell intrigue."

"I will admit," said Sir Frederick, "that I have taken some pains to put myself *au fait* with your projected movements."

"Oh, you have. And what, may I ask, have you discovered?"

Sir Frederick showed a slight embarrassment. He frowned and tapped a finger on his knee.

"It was merely routine, in connection with a little scheme we had in mind. We had no wish to inconvenience you in any way—"

"Charming of you. No doubt your myrmidons laid bare all, including the color of my holiday pajamas."

Sir Frederick's thin face changed its gravity for a schoolboy grin.

"Don't get wrathy, now," he begged. "After all, we got a lot of it from the papers. 'After the recent triumphant season of the Abercrombie Lewker Players, their popular founder and manager is to spend a well-earned vacation in the Swiss Alps. Although he is not far short of fifty, Mr. Lewker is still an active mountaineer.' Photo in adjacent column, showing distinct trace of double chin."

"We have seen mountaineers," boomed Mr. Lewker resentfully, "dewlapp'd like bulls—"

"Quite. Allow me to continue—I make a clean breast of our findings. You are going to Zinal, which is in the next valley to Zermatt, for three weeks' climbing. Your wife is staying with friends in Wales and you are going alone. You have engaged Heinrich Taugwalder, a Zermatt guide with whom you climbed some years ago, to meet you in Zinal. You intend, among other things, to traverse the Matterhorn from the Italian side to Zermatt. You propose to travel by the 9:50 from Waterloo on the day after tomorrow, via Newhaven and Dieppe. Correct?"

Mr. Lewker sat upright and screwed his large face into a ferocious scowl.

"Now by two-headed Janus," he fulminated, "this is too much! Is there no privacy left in this bedeviled country? Does the fact that I was once, by fortune of war, a member of your infernal Ogpu—"

"Tea, sir," announced Rosa, entering demurely with a tray.

Sir Frederick talked cricket until she had poured out two cups and departed. Then he began again.

"Perhaps you'll allow me to explain—"

"A child," interrupted Mr. Lewker, waving his cup, "a child could deduce that you have some proposition to make, some intrigue in which you think I could assist you. I warn you, Chief, that foul deeds and stratagems, cloak and dagger stuff, are not in my repertoire now. I am Benedick the married man."

"Nothing of that kind is contemplated. It is a perfectly safe diplomatic mission—"

"I am resolved to take a holiday. My rooms at Zinal are booked, my travel reservations are made, I am not a diplomatist, thank God, nor a secret agent. Furthermore "

"Will you be quiet, you noisy devil? Let me tell my story and you can rant afterwards."

"I resent the word 'rant'," said Mr. Lewker pompously. "However, say on. Cease this mystification, Chief, and deliver a plain unvarnish'd tale. You have our ear."

"That's something, anyway." Sir Frederick took a meditative drink of tea and set down his cup. "You remember Léon Jacot, of course?"

At mention of that name the actor-manager's memory jumped to a period that had been, for him, like a separate existence. For a second or two he was back in the turmoil of the war years, a lonely agent of Department Seven making his perilous way through Occupied France to contact the leaders of the Underground Resistance. Vividly he saw himself slinking into the Paris cellar where the hidden fighters of the French capital had their headquarters; saw the crowd of reckless youngsters gathered there under the smoky naphtha lamps, their eyes fixed in something that was almost adoration on the leader who harangued them; saw that leader, handsome, athletic, Gascon in gesture and speech, hauling the stout English secret agent on to the platform to embrace him amid enthusiastic cheering. The dark eager face with its flashing brown eyes, the extraordinary magnetism of the man—

"Yes," he said, returning to the present. "I remember Jacot. I saw him again two years ago, when he married Deborah Waveney, the theatrical star. Her twin brother John was in the profession for a while, with the Metropolitan Repertory Company."

"Exactly." Sir Frederick beamed upon him. "You see how nicely you link up."

"I see nothing of the kind. Have some more tea—and one of these cakes. You may then elucidate further."

Sir Frederick accepted the tea but preferred a cigarette to cake.

"Yes," he went on, exhaling a thin cloud of smoke, "Léon Jacot has done very well for himself since the Liberation. He is possibly the richest man in France, and one of the most popular. His wife is a very beautiful woman and a niece of Lord Pangbourne. He has captured half the amateur sporting trophies of the last three years. And now he has announced his intention of entering politics—of forming, in fact, a new party."

He paused and glanced at his companion as though expecting comment. Lewker's heavy features showed polite interest and nothing more.

"The English papers made little of it," he continued. "I don't suppose you noticed their paragraphs. But this decision of Jacot's is, or may be, of the very gravest importance to France and, in consequence, to England."

Lewker stirred impatiently. "I am aware of Jacot's record as a sportsman," he said. "I also know that he made a guideless traverse of the Dent Blanche two seasons ago. As a politician he is negligible, I should have said."

"That's because you don't know the state of things in France. Communism and Communist-influenced parties are much stronger there than is generally known. We—that is to say the Foreign Office—are watching the situation closely. We know, roughly, the strength of the various factions. But we don't know a thing about Léon Jacot's politics."

"He was a violent anti-Fascist when I knew him."

"Naturally. But that was eight years ago. Jacot calls this new party of his the New Republicans, but that may mean anything or nothing. The point is that the New Republicans are going to be extremely powerful in French politics."

Sir Frederick crushed his cigarette stub into an ashtray and leaned forward impressively.

"The young Frenchman of today is a worshipper of sport. Here's Jacot, who licked our best player at Wimbledon last year—who fought the American middleweight champion to a standstill in February—who holds the 1,000 meters cycling record. He's a brilliant member of the Groupe de Haute Montagne, a championship skier, and as handsome as Apollo. Add to that his almost legendary past, as the d'Artagnan of the Resistance Movement, and his extraordinarily compelling personality. And what do you get?"

"You," pointed out his audience, "are telling me."

"I am. You get a man who'll have every man and girl under thirty flocking to his political banner, irrespective of what motto it carries. You see how important it is that we should know on which side the weight of the New Republicans is going to be thrown in the next elections."

"Well," said Mr. Lewker reasonably, "why don't you ask the gentleman?"

"My dear Filthy, the gentleman has been asked by thousands of interested persons from newspapermen to ministers of state. The F.O. has tried to get a statement of policy from him. Department Seven has tried three different approaches. The man, in spite of his remarkable achievements, is like a child with a secret. He seems to have realized the power he can wield and takes delight in keeping everyone guessing. There's an odd touch of vanity in his makeup—and an almost phenomenal obstinacy." Sir Frederick paused, helped himself to a cigarette, and lit it before going on; his tone became lighter, more casual. "Léon Jacot, his wife, and a man called the Comte de Goursac arrived at Zermatt the day before yesterday."

The founder of the Abercrombie Lewker Players clapped one hand over his eyes and held the other aloft.

"Don't tell me!" he begged. "I am clairvoyant. I see it all. I am to take Jacot up the Matterhorn, dangle him over Italy on the end of a rope, and threaten to let go unless he tells me whether he favors Communism, Fascism, anarchism or government by, with, or from the people. Am I right, sir? That was your card, I believe? I thank you."

The other did not smile.

"To most people," he said slowly, "Léon Jacot's politics might not appear a particularly serious matter. I assure you the Foreign Office takes a different view. It is essential, at the present time, for us to have this knowledge, and to have it quickly. The man who could gain it for us would be doing a considerable service for his country. He—"

"Pray observe," interrupted Lewker loudly, "I have earned my holiday by hard, and I may say meritorious, work. I propose to take it among the eternal snows, where leading ladies cannot rouse me to murderous thoughts and politics will not lift their raucous voice. I want peace and quiet. I want fresh air and exercise. I do not propose to run round after enigmatic Frenchmen trying to dig secrets out of them. What reason have I to play cat's-paw for Department Seven?"

Sir Frederick flicked his half-smoked cigarette into the fireplace and rose to his feet.

"None whatever," he admitted sadly. "I had really no hope of persuading you. You must forgive me for troubling you, Filthy. Had my best men not failed me—"

"Even Carslake? I remember him as a first-rate man."

"Carslake was never in your class. He hasn't that unique intuition, that delicacy of observation, that gift for wriggling out of tight places, which I remember in yourself. Nor has he the advantage of having worked with Jacot in the past. I had hoped that you—but I quite see your point. And I must be going." Sir Frederick gathered up gloves and stick and held out his hand. "Good luck with your Alpine campaign, my dear Filthy. And thanks for the tea."

Mr. Lewker frowned at the outstretched hand but did not take it.

"Zermatt, you say," he murmured thoughtfully. "Which hotel are they staying at?"

"Hotel Obergabelhorn, I believe," replied Sir Frederick. He looked remarkably downcast; but there was, surprisingly, the suspicion of a twinkle in his eye.

"Obergabelhorn. An excellent house. I wonder if Simler still makes his own cream cakes?" Mr. Lewker cocked a calculating eye at his guest. "You would have required me to stay in Zermatt, I suppose?"

"It would have been preferable. The Hotel Obergabelhorn would naturally have been—but I must be going."

"Hm." The actor stretched out a detaining arm. "Sit down, Chief. Rest, rest, perturbèd spirit." Sir Frederick, concealing another twinkle, obeyed. "You realize, of course, that I have engaged a room in a Zinal hotel? That the guide Taugwalder is meeting me there by arrangement?"

"A cancellation could have been arranged quite easily. Department Seven would have borne all expenses."

"Ha. Another thing. I am not so well acquainted with John Waveney as you appear to imagine. I've met him once, at the Theatre Club, and I saw him act some time ago at the Court—a very mediocre performance."

"He left the stage, you know," said Sir Frederick abstractedly, "and took a job with the Finster Aircraft Company. He was a fighter pilot in the war, of course. But your acquaintance with him was only a secondary matter."

"Just as well. I am averse to starting this mission accredited with acquaintances I do not possess."

Sir Frederick's thin face registered incredulity. He leaned forward eagerly.

"You don't mean—you're not telling me you'll take the job on after all?" he stammered.

Lewker beamed upon him. "Beshrew me, Chief," he boomed, "but I fear I shall have to, if only to bring back the roses to those haggard cheeks."

"My dear fellow! I had scarcely hoped—you mean you'll place your undoubted talent at the disposal of Department Seven for the purpose of getting this important information?" persisted Sir Frederick, allowing relief to supersede dubiety on his usually expressionless face.

"I do." Mr. Lewker, radiating magnanimity, helped himself to a cake. "Provided I am allowed to climb a peak or two in my spare time, I will extract this Gallic oyster's secret for you."

"You've taken a great load from my mind, Filthy," said the other fervently. "You're probably the only man in England who could do it."

Mr. Lewker preened himself and munched cake.

"You'll have to go to work very casually, of course," continued Sir Frederick. "And don't let him bluff you. Make certain you've got his true intention. Better try and get a cross-check—Madame Jacot might provide you with that, or—"

"Leave it to me, Chief," said Mr. Lewker expansively. "Am I to bring this information back with me, or do I send it by wire?"

"Neither. Herr Schultz, of the Swiss Criminal Bureau in Basle, is spending the summer vacation with his parents in Visp. He is an old friend of mine. Visp is twenty-one miles from Zermatt by rail. Get your message to him in person—he knows what's afoot—and he'll see it gets safely to me. But you'll have to work quickly."

"Why so?"

"Because according to our information Jacot's only reason for visiting Zermatt is to climb the Matterhorn. Apparently it's one of the few peaks he hasn't bagged. Lord knows where he'll push off to when he's done it, for he's an unpredictable chap in every sense."

Lewker sat up, cake in hand.

"But observe, my ingenious plotter," he said with his mouth full. "He's been in Zermatt two days. With good weather, he may have bagged his peak already."

"Exactly. That's why I want you to get there tomorrow—by plane."

A crumb got in the way of Mr. Lewker's protest. He choked and spluttered helplessly while Sir Frederick solicitously thumped his massive back, talking rapidly the while.

"Young Waveney's flying over to Zermatt to see his sister. He's taking one of the new Finster Tourers on test—a two-seater. You'll meet him at London Airport tomorrow morning. You can take climbing kit and some clothes with you but the rest of your luggage will be sent on. We'll arrange that."

He stood up, smiling pleasantly at the still speechless actor-manager.

"You've to do nothing but finish your packing and wire Taugwalder to be in Zermatt instead of Zinal," he added. "I must be off—got to be at the F.O. before five. Believe me, Filthy, I am extremely grateful. And I'm sure you'll succeed."

He gripped the other's unresponsive fist and went with quick strides to the door. Mr. Lewker found his voice, or some of it.

"Train—hotel—booked," he managed to splutter.

Sir Frederick paused and looked a trifle embarrassed.

"You'll—er—find that will solve itself," he said soothingly.

"Oh, and you'll need this."

He took an envelope from his pocket and laid it on the table. Then he was gone.

Mr. Lewker, purple in the face, made as if to follow him; thought better of it; and picked up the envelope. It was addressed to himself, care of Sir Frederick Claybury. The letter inside thanked him for his kind booking and informed him that a room with bath was reserved from August 5th to August 24th for his esteemed use. It was signed "Julius Simler, proprietor Hotel Obergabelhorn, Zermatt."

CHAPTER TWO

BY AIR TO THE ALPS

Of Abercrombie Lewker it was said, by one of his less tolerant critics, that he combined the pomposity of an Irving and the vanity of a Tree with the shape of a pocket-flask. Many of his acquaintances would have agreed with this superficial judgment; and indeed Mr. Lewker himself might have beamed approval, for the part of an actor-manager should be played with pomp and vanity. There were friends, among them Sir Frederick Claybury, who knew that such a judgment was superficial to the point of falsity. And there had been enemies, the late Dr. Goebbels among them, who had discovered the same fact too late to save themselves. As for Mr. Lewker, he was content to be an actor; though at this particular moment, with Lac Leman eight thousand feet below him under the clouds, he was subconsciously a trifle puzzled as to which of three roles he should fill.

Was he (ran the undercurrent of his thoughts) the celebrated actor-manager on holiday, or the solid mountain-climber, or the astute secret agent? The first would be easy to play; the second—tweeds and taciturnity, with a grim set to the jaw and an occasional stare through narrowed eyelids at the challenging peaks; the third, catlike movements and of course an enigmatic smile. His subconscious mind, lulled by the subdued roar of the little Finster plane, toyed idly with this theme until the jolt of an air-pocket brought his non-theatrical self to the surface. Mr. Lewker laughed at himself, settled his broad thighs more comfortably on the well-sprung seat, and glanced out through the curved perspex of the little cabin.

The Finster, heading southeast, rode high in the clear air with the sun behind her. The cloud sea, like vast dazzling snow-hummocks, hid the earth, and she seemed to hang vibrating but motionless in a void of blue, the deep blue of an afternoon sky. They had left Paris at three; Mont Blanc, Mr. Lewker calculated, must lie a bare fifty miles to southward.

In the seat in front of him John Waveney's dark head, its untidy curls ridged by the headphone bands, was bent over the instrument panel. He was picking up the air forecast from the Swissair meteorological station. Mr. Lewker had been more favorably impressed by John Waveney the air pilot than by John Waveney the actor. The young man had called him "sir" when they had met at London Airport, and this had been soothing. Then he had waved aside the actor's fears that the baggage he had brought with him would be too heavy to take in the plane.

"Not a bit of it, sir. The little Finster's built to take holiday kit. Come and see."

He had demonstrated the sliding doors in the underside of the hull which gave access to a roomy luggage compartment running half the length of the plane, and shown his passenger how they could only be operated by a press button on the instrument panel. He had expatiated on the ease and simplicity of the controls and had even offered to let Mr. Lewker take over during the flight. He appeared, in fact, to be delighted to have a passenger with him.

"Wizard piece of luck for me, sir, your missing your boat," he remarked, as he bundled rope and ice-axe and bags into the luggage compartment. "Sir Frederick—great lad, isn't he?—asked me days ago if I'd be prepared to take a passenger, but I didn't expect a celebrity. How did he know you were going to miss your connection?"

"Sir Frederick has a remarkably intuitive mind," returned Mr. Lewker gravely. "Believe me, Mr. Waveney, I am greatly obliged—"

"Please don't mench." John grinned amiably down from his five inches of extra height. "Sir Fred did me more than one good turn when I was throwing Spits and Hurrys about in wartime. Wanted to come up with us once, after I'd got switched into bombers, but the wallahs up top wouldn't let him, in spite of my efforts. So I'm glad to take a pal of his to please him." He glanced at his wristwatch. "Well, we'd better *einsteigen,* sir."

"Have you made this trip before?" Mr. Lewker had enquired as he clambered into his seat.

"To Zermatt? Yes. We'll be in for tea, with luck. It'll be good to see Deb again—my sister, you know—married a French bloke."

"I remember her well. A very charming lady with distinct dramatic talent. Does her husband add flying to his other accomplishments?"

John had turned away to beckon to a mechanic who was approaching across the airfield. He answered without looking round.

"Who? Jacot? Not on your life. That fellow's scared stiff of planes. He'll risk his neck on mountains but not in the air. Come on, George, and give this prop a swing."

His tone as he spoke of Deborah's husband had been oddly bitter. Jacot's famous personal charm, it seemed, had not impressed his brother-in-law.

Six hours later, with the roar of the plane in his ears, Mr. Lewker felt the old familiar thrill of the mountaineer; he was approaching the tall peaks that had enchanted him in his youth. He beamed at John Waveney as the latter turned in his seat.

"Got the O.K., sir. The Rhone Valley's free from cloud. We'll make it nicely. We'd have had to land at Geneva if there'd been cloud over St. Niklaus."

For the first time Lewker realized that his destination lay in a gorge-like valley under thirteen-thousand-foot snow peaks.

"Is there anywhere to land at Zermatt?" he asked with some misgiving.

"Nary a spot," came the cheerful reply. "But there's a peach of a meadow near Täsch—that's four miles this side of Zermatt. Son of the innkeeper's a mechanic—pal of mine. He's fixed it for landing."

He bent to his controls for a moment and then turned again, surprising an apprehensive frown on his passenger's face.

"All perfectly downy, sir," he shouted reassuringly above the Finster's drone. "I could land this little lady on a suburban front lawn."

Mr. Lewker, remembering the great rock-walls that stood above the tiny chalets of Täsch, was not comforted.

"What about air currents?" he persisted.

"Don't you worry, sir. I've landed there before. Last year, with a crosswind. It'll be twice as easy with this southerly, so— Glory, look at that!"

He pointed through the perspex of the nose. Mr. Lewker followed the direction of his finger. Ahead of them the cloud sea ended, like the lid of a box pushed back. Beyond and above stood a rank of golden snow peaks, blueshadowed in the westering sun and lovely as a dream. Mr. Lewker gazed as a wanderer might gaze who comes after long years within sight of his home. He named them eagerly, as the same wanderer might name the family that awaits him on the threshold: Monte Rosa, Breithorn, Matterhorn, Dent Blanche. Surely the Matterhorn was whiter than it should be at this season? That great hooked finger of rock ought to be bare and brown in the midst of its white-robed companions. This southerly wind—that meant bad weather. The Matterhorn was snow-powdered, and probably unclimbable. It occurred to him that it had quite possibly been in bad condition for some days, so that Jacot would not have achieved his ambition; but the thought was a passing one, for the shapely splendor of that concourse of giants was a sight to make man impatient of mundane things. In his university days Mr. Lewker had once upheld in debate the thesis "That we are, at this present moment, in Heaven." He wondered, as he gazed, whether that thesis had been quite as ridiculous as it appeared.

John Waveney looked up from peering at the now visible earth.

" 'Nother fifteen minutes," he shouted over his shoulder. "Hope Deb's on top line. She wired she'd meet us at Täsch with the car."

The rank of giants marched slowly towards them. Beneath the plane black rock and white snow surged up and fell away again. A great trench opened in the earth—the Rhone Valley, with a twisted skein of river in its depths. The Finster began to lose height, dropping towards the mouth of a deep side valley on the south. As John flattened her out again the snow peaks seemed to slide down into view. They were enormous now, dazzling in the sun. The incredible shaft of the Matterhorn began to tower above them, dead ahead. Lewker craned his neck to peer at the valley of St. Niklaus, green meadows and dark pines reeling away underneath them. Even from above it looked quite hopeless to seek a landing-place there. He glanced up, to see mountain-walls level with the wings of the plane and apparently quite close. Suppose some side-current of wind blew them off their course, to one side—

"Safety-strap on!" shouted John without looking round. "May be a bump or two!"

Mr. Lewker obeyed with feverish speed. Below, and not far below now, a white road, a river, trees, chalets, people—even people, with upturned faces—streamed past like toys on an endless belt.

"There's Franz and his white sheet!" John exulted. "All clear below, sir. Stand by for the wallop!"

The cabin suddenly felt much warmer. The roar of the engine ceased. There was an unnerving buck, a succession of lessening jolts, and the Finster was down and taxiing to a standstill. Two minutes later Mr. Lewker, feeling hot and slightly shaken, was stretching his stiff legs in the sweet-scented air of a high Alpine valley.

The big meadow had recently been cut for hay. It was at one side of the valley, which here opened out to a fairly flat strath, and a quarter of a mile away, above a narrow belt of low trees which ran between meadow and road, the top-heavy steeple of Täsch village rose as though in imitation of the tremendous rock steeple of the Matterhorn at the valley's end. On a winding track at the far end of the field an open car glittered like an oblong mirror in the sun. A girl in crimson slacks and a yellow sweater was walking from the car with long unhurried strides towards the plane, and in front of her sprinted a crowd of small Swiss children.

John had been greeting Franz, the stalwart young man who had signaled the landing ground clear.

"Franz says we're damned lucky to strike a good day," he said, turning to Lewker as he stripped off his flying jacket. "Yesterday was cloudy, with snow higher up, and it's only been fine since this morning. Hullo—here comes Deb."

He dropped his jacket and went to meet the girl. Mr. Lewker, watching them, observed that brother and sister had the same grace of movement, the same upright carriage and poise of the head. Deborah Jacot was tall for a woman and as slim as her twin brother, but her uncovered head was very fair and its expensive coiffure contrasted with John's untidy thatch. The two greeted each other with evident affection. Deborah, with John's arm round her waist, drew him towards Mr. Lewker.

"It is!" she exclaimed, halting in front of him. "Abercrombie Lewker himself. John told me but I wouldn't believe him. Mr. Lewker, I'm thrilled to meet you."

She held out her hand, with a most attractive smile. She was, he saw, very like her brother; but John's rather angular good looks were rounded and piquant in his sister. Her beauty was not of the classic type, but she was extremely attractive in spite of a too-heavy layer of make-up. Mr. Lewker's keen glance noted the faint signs of worry at the corners of eyes and mouth.

"Madame," he returned gallantly, "my journey has been worth while."

"Prettily said," she laughed at him, "though I feel you might have kissed my hand. That's the best of the legit, you know. Teaches you the best manners in the world. We poor vaudevillists never acquire the poise of you tragedians."

"Poise," boomed Mr. Lewker, "is a thing which, at this moment, I feel I do not possess. Air travel leaves me 'as pale as any clout in the varsal world'."

"You look fairly robust," Deborah remarked. She looked at him with her head on one side, charmingly. "Did John fling you about in the Finster?"

"On the contrary. Your brother is an extremely skilful pilot—and I speak as one who has flown with some very good pilots."

John gave his sister a playful thump on the seat of her slacks. "There's for you, Deb. Thank you, sir, for those few kind words. May I suggest that what you need is a drink?"

"A wash would be almost more welcome. I am limp as an unwatered plant."

"You poor dear!" Deborah slid her arm through Mr. Lewker's. "Come and get into the car. Where are you staying?"

"The Hotel Obergabelhorn. My baggage—"

"The Obergabelhorn? But that's marvelous. We're staying there, you know, my husband and I and—oh, quite a lot of nice people. Come along—John will see to your belongings."

"Leave 'em to me," John said. "Franz here's got a sort of little hay truck, and the kids are just itching to load it up and tow it to the car. Carry on, sir."

Mr. Lewker allowed himself to be led away. Deborah chattered pleasantly, as they walked to the car, of theaters and theatrical personalities in London and Paris. He found it soothing to be thus welcomed and fell easily into the role of Celebrity Receiving Suitable Flattery. But the Astute Agent, bobbing up unasked, insisted on calling his attention to the slight but undeniable constraint that underlay Deborah's light manner. That the girl was concealing anxiety of some kind was fairly obvious. He felt a sympathetic concern— purely, of course, paternal.

They reached the car, a sports four seater of the newest streamlined design. One or two farmhands stood round it, stolidly appraising. Deborah unfastened the canvas cover that was stretched over the rear seat.

"John and the luggage can go in there," she said. "You'll sit by me, won't you?"

Mr. Lewker said he would be delighted. They settled themselves in the front seat and he allowed the Astute Agent to take the stage.

"I hear your husband is a great climber in addition to leading the way in almost every other sport, Madame. Has he made any ascents from Zermatt this season?"

"Not yet. We've only been here three days, and the weather's been all wrong or something. I don't know much about mountains—isn't there a special wind that makes them dangerous?"

"Yes. The Föhn wind." Mr. Lewker restrained himself with some difficulty from gazing through narrowed eyelids at the challenging peaks. "It comes from the south and softens the snow slopes. Sometimes it brings isolated snowstorms. I imagine the Matterhorn has been unclimbable, by the look of it."

Deborah made a little grimace. "It has. Poor old Léon! He likes to be frightfully dashing, you know, Mr. Lewker. His idea was to dash from Geneva to Zermatt, dash up the Matterhorn—by the Zmutt Ridge, I think—and dash on to Rome for the Swimming Olympiad. If he has to hang about here for days and days before he can do his climb, the gilt will be off the gingerbread."

"Patience, Madame, is the mountaineer's rarest and most valuable virtue," observed Mr. Lewker sententiously. "But I can appreciate your husband's feelings. No doubt he is finding inaction very galling."

"Oh, Léon always manages to amuse himself wherever he goes."

The words were lightly spoken, but Mr. Lewker's quick ear caught the slight flattening of her tone. As if she knew this, Deborah Jacot turned the disconcerting gaze of her wide blue eyes on her companion.

"But of course, you and Léon are old acquaintances," she went on. "You worked together during the war, didn't you? You were in the British Secret Service."

Mr. Lewker frowned. "That, Madame, is not supposed to be known. I am no longer—"

"Husbands have no secrets from their wives, you know. And anyhow, Léon didn't tell me any secrets. He just said you were the best agent the British had in Occupied France. And he told me you'd once done some rather clever detective work. Was that right?"

There was a suppressed eagerness in her voice. Mr. Lewker, who was not particularly proud of his one successful attempt to detect a murderer, was deprecating.

"Nowadays, Madame, I devote myself to the theater. It is not—"

A burst of shrill chatter cut short further conversation. It heralded the arrival of the baggage on Franz's little blue hay-truck, drawn by half a dozen sturdy brown-faced little boys. John and Franz assisted them to maneuver it alongside and its contents were transferred to the rear seat. John inserted himself between the bags and turned to give parting instructions to Franz.

"I'll leave you to peg her down securely, old boy. I'm going to take her for a flip round the Matterhorn if the weather holds."

"I see to her, Mr. Waveney—but you take care if you fly her up in the mountains." Franz, being a Swiss hotelkeeper's son, had been brought up to speak excellent English and French as well as his native tongue. He showed white teeth in a grin. "I will not come, me. I want to get married, next year."

"I know," Deborah chipped in. "It's Lisse Taugwalder, isn't it?"

Franz's broad bronzed face darkened. He avoided Deborah's glance and turned to her brother.

"She is all set for taking-off, your plane. You come when you like. If I am not here, you find this hay-truck in the little shed there, behind the trees. Tomorrow I bring juice and fill your tanks."

"Good man. I can put her into the air by myself, so you won't need to interrupt your courting, old boy. *Auf wiedersehen!*"

Deborah had pressed the starter. She let in the clutch and the car surged forward amid the shrill yells of the children. They rocketed out of the field and on to the main road. Täsch, a brief vision of quaint chalets and staring faces, shot past them and vanished behind in a cloud of dust. Mr. Lewker, gripping the side of the car convulsively, registered a silent vow that for the rest of his holiday he would use no other means of transport than his own two legs. The pine-clad walls of the valley closed in from left and right as the road ran close to the little railway line to squeeze into the narrows. The sunlight had left them now, and hung like a golden frieze along the steeps high above on their left. Deborah swung the powerful car round a corner hewn out of the rock of the gorge and called across her shoulder to her brother.

"Johnny! What's the matter with Franz? He wasn't very polite to me just now."

"Must be your S.A. that's ceased to function," John shouted back. He rested his arms on the back of the front seat and addressed Deborah and Lewker impartially. "Franz is all right. He's a wizard chap, really. Just done his service with the Swiss Army—they have to. He was in the Air Arm, took his pilot's ticket. He's a natty mechanic and I believe he could take the Finster up himself if he liked. Super brakes this crate's got," he added casually as the car checked with a suddenness that set all four tires screaming and all but projected Mr. Lewker through the windshield.

They had come tearing round a blind corner to find the road blocked from side to side by a dense crowd of goats. This was at a place where the road was separated from the furious white torrent of the Visp, thirty feet below on the left, by a line of small white stones; on the right the rock from which the road had been carved fell almost sheer. There was, however, a shallow alcove, a small quarry with a sidetrack a few yards long leading off the main roadway at a slight angle. On to this track Deborah, applying all her brakes, had twisted the car a split second before it would have smashed into the herd. It came to rest with its front tires six inches from the rock of the quarry wall.

"Sorry," Deborah said lightly to her passengers. "Nearly provided us with a goat's-meat supper. Look at them—aren't they darlings?"

The goats surged past, a mass of tossing horns and tinkling bells.

"That was deft handling," observed Mr. Lewker, recovering from his fright.

"Oh, that was me, sir," said John, reaching over to grip his sister's shoulder. "I put the 'fluence on her."

Deborah laughed. "It's quite right, Mr. Lewker. We're twins, you see. When we're together we act as one entity. It was like that when we were children."

She patted the hand that lay on her shoulder.

Perhaps because of the shock, this incident, as Mr. Lewker afterwards found, impressed itself clearly on his mind, so that, later, it fell into its place with certain other matters which at first seemed of little importance.

The goats had almost gone by. The goatherd, a gnarled old fellow whose straggling white beard might have been copied from one of his charges, came past the car with a lame kid in his arms. Beside him walked a youngish man in a blue shirt and plus fours, with a rucksack on his back and an ice-axe under his arm. He threw a cursory glance at the occupants of the car, and Lewker caught a glimpse of a sallow humorless face, brilliant eyes deep-set under a brow that overhung like a crag. At the same moment he became aware of Deborah Jacot's hand clutching his knee with almost painful tightness. She was staring after the sallow tourist, whose long stride had by now taken him a dozen yards past them, and on her face an expression of fear was frozen.

"Hullo!" said John suddenly from behind. "D'you know that chap, Deb?"

The hand was quickly withdrawn from Lewker's knee. He heard her draw a long quivering breath.

"No. No, Johnny. I thought at first it was a man I met in Paris—but it wasn't."

"Looked French all right. They love colored breeks. Well, press on, old girl—I want my grub."

Deborah backed the car and turned it on to the road again.

"You'll have to wait, my lad," she told him with a laugh that to Mr. Lewker's ear sounded forced. "We don't dine for another two hours."

"That be damned for a tale," grumbled John. "I'll be chewing my braces before then. Cream cakes and tea for me."

The car sped on, unraveling the twists of the climbing road. Quite suddenly, framed in the massive walls of the gorge, the enormous obelisk of the Matterhorn swam into view. Poised above the shadowed valley, it flamed and dazzled in the sun of late afternoon, a pyramidal tower of which the two visible sides were sharply differentiated by sun and shadow, throwing the soaring Hörnli ridge which descended towards them into bold relief.

"By gum, that's wizard!" exclaimed John.

"It is," agreed his sister. "But you won't get Léon to say so. He just growls 'Look at the new snow' and swears, poor dear."

Mr. Lewker said nothing. The sight of that stupendous mass of rock rearing between earth and sky gripped him as it had first done years ago with its combination of beauty and ferocity. It drove from his mind the lingering effects of the shock of a narrowly avoided collision, and erased the memory of the fear on Deborah Jacot's face.

The valley walls fell back. Zermatt, a jumble of large hotels and ancient chalets crouched under pine-dotted slopes, lay before them. The car swung into an urban-looking street of shops and gay awnings, doubled up a side street, and halted before the carved wooden porch of the Hotel Obergabelhorn, where old Julius Simler waited to receive his guests. His toothless grin and gentle brown eyes were exactly as Lewker remembered them a dozen years ago; nor had his little hotel lost its pride of hospitality. In three minutes Mr. Lewker, having left John to go in search of cream cakes and tea, was stripping off his outer garments in a delightful paneled bedchamber smelling of hay.

The knowledgeable few who preferred the Hotel Obergabelhorn to the larger Zermatt hotels did not expect dance-floors, electric lifts, or views from their bedroom windows; the Obergabelhorn excelled in its table, service and comfort, and was content to leave the less essential trimmings to its neighbors. Mr. Lewker having cleansed himself of travel (Simler always had hot water in his taps), put his head out of the window and was pleased to find that the upper portion of the Matterhorn was in view, framed in the wooden gables of the old chalets, dark with age, that filled most of the outlook from his first-floor room. The growl of a car engine filled the narrow cobbled alley, and Deborah Jacot passed beneath him in the sports car. The projecting balcony of the room next to his hid her from view as she drove up the alley, but he presumed that the hotel garage was at its farther end.

Mr. Lewker withdrew himself from the window, and his eye fell on the bed. It was an inviting sort of bed, suggesting repose. By way of experiment he lay down upon it, and was asleep in ten seconds. When he woke it was to find the room darker and the air full of the chill freshness of evening at five thousand feet above the sea. His watch told him it was twenty minutes to eight; dinner, he knew, was at eight o'clock. He got up reluctantly and took from his suitcase a gray lounge suit. At the Obergabelhorn one does not dress for dinner. He had donned the trousers and was tying his tie before the mirror when there was a light double-knock on the bedroom door.

"Come in!" he boomed.

Deborah Jacot came in quickly and closed the door behind her. She looked extremely attractive in a black velvet gown cleverly tailored to accentuate her not very obvious curves. She stood with her back to the door and her bare arms pressed against it—an attitude that recalled to the actor-manager her theatrical past. Her white teeth indented the redness of her lower lip and her blue eyes were worried.

"Mr. Lewker," she said hurriedly, "I've come to ask your help. I'm afraid. I'm afraid for my husband."

CHAPTER THREE

IMPRESSIONS OF AN ASTUTE AGENT

Mr. Lewker regarded his visitor attentively, but said nothing. She seemed a little embarrassed by his gaze.

"I know it must seem odd, my bursting into your room like this when we only met two or three hours ago," she said quickly, "but you see I'm very worried about Léon."

"Allow me," said Mr. Lewker. He put on his coat. "Now, Madame, I am at your service. Will you sit down?"

"I'd rather stand." She took a few paces across the carpet and back again, her gown swinging to her graceful movements. "It won't take long, and anyway they'll be serving dinner soon and you'll need yours."

"I beg that you will ignore my needs, my dear, and tell me your trouble," said the actor-manager paternally.

Deborah took an impulsive step towards him. Her slim hands clasped themselves round his arm.

"I don't want Léon to know I've told you," she said urgently. "He mustn't know—he'd never forgive me. Please promise you'll say nothing about it to him."

Mr. Lewker, very conscious of her nearness, permitted himself to pat one of the hands.

"Of course. But if it is against your husband's wishes—"

"He's so terribly against police protection or anything of that sort, Mr. Lewker. He's had more than one threatening letter since he started with politics—he doesn't tell me about them, but I found out—and he just laughs at them." She dropped her hands from his arm and turned away towards the window. "I told you this afternoon we had no secrets from each other. It wasn't true. Léon and I don't hit it off together. He's a brute to me sometimes. But I don't want him to be murdered."

"Murdered!" repeated Mr. Lewker involuntarily. He was startled. "My dear Madame Jacot, surely you are taking this too seriously. All men who make their way into the forefront of public life receive threatening letters. You know the saying, that threatened men live long. You must not suppose—"

"Wait." She faced him again, a little screw of paper in her hand. "You haven't heard everything yet. And—there's this."

She held it out to him. He took it and unfolded it. It was a half-sheet of common blue notepaper with two lines of typing on it. The words were in English, and he read them aloud:

"The path you are treading is a dangerous path. One more step, and you will not live to take another."

Deborah drew in her breath sharply. "You see? Léon received that yesterday morning, only two days after we got here. It came with the other letters."

"Hum. It is somewhat oracular. Do you know what it means?"

"I can guess," she told him, twisting her fingers agitatedly. "You know about Léon's new political party, of course—the New Republicans?"

Lewker nodded. "Also that it is not known whether Monsieur Jacot intends to influence his followers to back the present government or to swing over to the extreme left."

"That's just it—nobody knows. I, his wife, don't know. But there are people in France who are trying their hardest to find out, and someone may have done so. Mr. Lewker—have you ever heard of the Flambeaux?"

"No, Madame."

"Not many people have, even in France. They're a small political group, violent anti-Communists. That's all I know about them, except—that they've threatened Léon before."

"Before? You think, then, that this note comes from them?"

Deborah nodded. Fear showed in her lovely eyes.

"I'll tell you why in a moment. I know political murder sounds ridiculous to an Englishman, but in France politics are a kind of war. I haven't learned much since I've lived in France—I can't even speak French, except a few words—but I have learned that. And these Flambeaux people are like the Mafia. They don't hesitate to strike and they never get caught. I know," she added with the ghost of a smile, "that it sounds terribly like fiction."

"I have heard stranger truths in my time," he reassured her. "But if these people have threatened your husband before, without any unpleasant result, why should you now be afraid of this further threat? After all, it implies that the fatal step has yet to be taken."

"It wasn't until this afternoon that I was really afraid," she replied in a low voice.

Mr. Lewker remembered something. "It was the man who was walking behind the goats?"

"You guessed that? Yes, it was the sight of that man. I've seen him once before. It was in Geneva. We were getting out of our car to go into the hotel. That man was standing in the shadow by the door—Léon didn't see him, but I did. He dodged away somewhere out of sight and I thought nothing more about it until we saw him on the road from Täsch. Doesn't it look as if he followed us here from Geneva? And then this note—"

She paused, watching him anxiously.

"You had not seen this man before Geneva?" he asked.

Deborah hesitated. "I can't be sure. There was a man very much like him who came once to visit Léon in Paris. I remember Léon was in a very bad temper when he'd gone."

"I see. So you think this man is an agent of the Flambeaux, who have, presumably, learned in some way that your husband is turning towards Communism, and that he is here in this valley to implement the threat contained in the note. And what, Madame, do you want me to do?"

She reached a slim hand towards him hesitantly. The blue eyes pleaded for his sympathy.

"Only to watch, to help me to guard against what might happen. It's a worry I can't bear alone—why, just because he hasn't come in yet to get ready for dinner I'm all nerves. Please, please—"

Mr. Lewker took the hand and pressed it reassuringly. It was time for the Astute Agent to take the stage.

"I shall do everything I can to help you, Madame," he boomed. "And now—about this note. It came by post?"

"No. It was in an unstamped envelope addressed with my husband's name only."

"How did you obtain the note?"

"Léon and I breakfasted in our room yesterday morning. The maid brought our mail to us. I took it and gave Léon his—that's how I saw the unstamped envelope. I was reading my own letters when I heard Léon give one of his jeering laughs. I looked up and saw him crumpling a piece of paper angrily. He threw it into the wastebasket, and I didn't say anything. But afterwards I went to look for it—and it was that note."

"You kept the envelope?"

"No. Ought I to have done? The wastebasket will have been emptied by now."

"Hum. Well, the prime inference is that the writer of this note is, or was, somewhere in this district. But we must remember that it could have been sent under cover to someone who would deliver it on behalf of the writer." Lewker was getting into his part. "The case has—er—possibilities. It should not be difficult to discover, by making enquiry—"

"No—no enquiries, please." Deborah clutched his arm in instant concern. "Léon would be sure to find out, and that mustn't happen. Just to know that you'll be on the lookout—that's all I want."

Mr. Lewker pocketed the typewritten note and beamed at her.

"Very well, my dear," he boomed. "And you are to stop this worrying. I still think this is an empty threat. It is, at all events, not important enough to bring anxiety to one so charming."

Deborah smiled at him and stepped back to curtsy playfully. "Thank you, kind sir. And now—will you take me down to dinner, please?"

Mr. Lewker signified his pleasure and offered his arm. They walked along the well-carpeted corridor and down a wide staircase to the hall, where old Simler stood bowing benevolently to his patrons as they entered the dining room. Deborah paused to speak to him.

"Oh, Mr. Simler—my husband hasn't come in yet. I'd like Mr. Lewker to sit at my table. Is that all right?"

"Parfaitement, Madame, si vous le voulez."

"He will talk to me in French because I've got a French surname," whispered Deborah laughingly as they entered the dining room. "I don't understand half of it."

The *speisezimmer* of the Hotel Obergabelhorn was a very long room divided into several smaller ones by wide-arched wooden doors beautifully carved and polished. Each of these semiprivate rooms contained two large tables, one by a window and the other on the inner side of the room, so that a good thoroughfare for Simler's fleet-footed waiters passed between them for the whole length of the *speisezimmer*. The Jacots' table was a window table, and two people were already seated at it. Mr. Lewker found himself being introduced to the Comte and Comtesse de Goursac, the former a heavily-built man in the middle forties who looked like a caricature of a Prussian, his wife a Junoesque brunette with expressive eyes. Mme de Goursac turned the full force of her warm brown stare on the new arrival.

"But this is most nice!" she exclaimed in a musical contralto. "Abercrombie Lewkair! The man who bring Shakespeare to the people—we have hear' of you in Paris, Monsieur—have we not, Paul?"

Her husband grunted and made a slight inclination of his bullet head without taking his gaze from Mr. Lewker's face. He had a face like a ham, with a ham's lack of expression. The Comtesse turned to Deborah.

"Where then is Léon?" she demanded. "We have not see him all the afternoon."

Deborah did not seem to hear her. She was smiling at a rather bulky man in tweeds, one of a party of four who were taking their places at the other table. He returned her smile very briefly. He had a brown, mustached face under smooth fair hair, and his heavy jaw looked sullen and obstinate. He turned away from them to speak to his companion, a man as tall as himself but considerably thinner and with most of his face hidden under a bristle of black beard. With them at their table were a rather pretty dark girl and a large middle-aged lady of the type that clings determinedly to its youth.

"Deb! *Dites-moi, chérie*—where have you hidden my Léon?" insisted the Comtesse loudly. "I shall tell him, me, that Monsieur Bryce makes big eyes at you when he is not here."

Deborah's smile did not conceal the angry glitter in her eyes. The back of the fair-haired man's neck (he had seated himself facing away from their table) reddened noticeably. Mr. Lewker, slightly embarrassed by this byplay, addressed himself to the Comte, whose expressionless gaze had shifted itself to his wife.

"You are a mountaineer, I understand, Monsieur. I fear you are having bad luck with the weather?"

De Goursac looked at him, but was silent for so long that Lewker was about to repeat his remark in French, thinking he had not understood it, when he replied in excellent English:

"That is so, Monsieur."

"Paul is always unlucky, Monsieur Lewkair," broke in his wife volubly.

"He is what you call a Jonah—*la chance* passes him by."

"It did not do so on his wedding day," said Lewker with ponderous gallantry.

The remark was received without enthusiasm. There was what might have been the shadow of a sneer on the Comte's hamlike countenance; the Comtesse, after flashing an automatic smile at the actor-manager, compressed her full lips and shot a sideways glance at Deborah, who was abstractedly crumbling a piece of bread. But Lewker had scarcely time to become aware of the moment of tension before John Waveney, arriving simultaneously with the soup, restored normality. John, it appeared, was already acquainted with the de Goursacs. He greeted them cheerfully and apologized for being late.

"Been prowling round the village and got lost," he explained. "Saw Léon, Deb, though he didn't see me."

"Where did you see him?" Deborah's voice was quite casual.

"In that café place—Hoffman's, isn't it?—in the main street. Saw him through the window. I was rushing to get back here, so I didn't go in. Besides, he seemed to be—well, busy."

"With the pretty blonde waitress," murmured the Comte unexpectedly. His head turned slowly until he was staring at his wife. Mme de Goursac laughed shrilly. John seemed unconscious of this byplay.

"She was a smooth piece of work," he agreed. "Wizard complexions these Swiss misses have. Talking of pretty girls, Deb," he added in a lower tone, "who's the dark damsel at the other table?"

"Her name's Margaret Kemp," she told him rather shortly. "She's with her aunt, Mrs. Fillingham."

"Is that the boiling-piece with dyed hair? No wonder Margaret looks a bit browned off. But she's easy on the eye, is Margaret, very easy."

The Comtesse, who was sitting next to him, gave him an admonitory nudge. *"Ah, méchant!"* she whispered loudly. "Take care, *alors*. Margaret, she is to marry Monsieur Bryce. Her aunt tell me so."

"Mrs. Fillingham does a good deal of wishful thinking, Camille," said Deborah sweetly.

"Per'aps she is not alone in that," rejoined Mme. de Goursac, with equal sweetness.

Mr. Lewker, who had just finished dealing with Herr Simler's excellent soup, chose this moment to enter the conversation.

"Bryce—I know the name," he boomed. "There was a Bernard Bryce on the last Himalayan expedition to Nanga Parbat."

"This Mr. Bryce's name is Bernard," Deborah said. "I'm told he's a very good climber. He writes books."

"Both Monsieur Bryce and his comrade Dr. Greatorex are expert Alpinists," put in de Goursac with something approaching animation. "In the Groupe de Haute Montagne we know of them."

Mr. Lewker threw another glance at the second table. The black-bearded man caught his eye, grinned, and raised a hand in salute. The actor returned the gesture.

"Hullo," remarked John. "Friend of yours?"

"Now that I have his name I recognize him. The enrich'd panoply of his visage put me off. I took Lawrence Greatorex on his first big Alpine climb fifteen years ago—the Teufelsgrat."

John shrugged. "Means nothing to me, being no mountaineer. Where is it?"

"It is a most difficult ridge of the Täschhorn," de Goursac explained. He turned to Lewker. "I did not know you were so accomplished an Alpinist, Monsieur."

"I assure you I am far from accomplished. Once I had some little skill, but now I am declined into the vale of years."

"Bah!" The Comte waved this aside. "You make the meiosis, as is the fashion of your countrymen. The Teufelsgrat, that is a good climb. It was two seasons ago that Charlet and I traversed it. You remember doubtless, the *rappel* on the upper part of the *arête*? There is an overhang, *très formidable*, eh? Ah, you recollect. *Eh bien*, Monsieur, this overhang—"

Once fairly launched, there was no pause in the Comte's flow of mountaineering reminiscence. "L'Alpinisme," as he called it, appeared to be his one passion; certainly it unlocked his tongue. Mr. Lewker was not averse to indulging in a bout of mountaineering shop, and John Waveney and the two women were left more or less to their own conversational devices for the rest of the meal. During some of de Goursac's more lengthy reminiscences, the actor-manager allowed his thoughts to stray a little (a really Astute Agent should always be able to talk about one thing and think about another simultaneously) and among his mental comments was the reflection that no one seemed to expect Léon Jacot to come in to dinner, although he was only a few score yards away at Hoffman's. The inference was—and it confirmed all that he remembered or had heard of the man—that Deborah's husband was a man who did exactly as he pleased.

It is the custom at the Hotel Obergabelhorn for coffee to be served in the big lounge after dinner. The lounge (Herr Simler calls it, with pride, his *besuchszimmer*) is long and low, beautifully panelled and carpeted, but retaining something of its antique dignity from the days when it was the parliament-house of the canton. The one concession Simler has permitted himself to the taste for imitation antiquity is here—electric lights disguised as great hanging lanterns. The thirty or forty guests gathered chattering over their coffee-cups were mostly either English or American, or so Mr. Lewker assessed them; there was no sign of Léon Jacot, or of the man of whom Deborah had been afraid. Not that he had expected to see either of them. But the keen observation which was, as Sir Frederick Claybury had remarked, one of his hidden talents had been put on its mettle by Deborah Jacot's appeal, and he noted almost automatically every detail on which his little eyes chanced to fall: John Waveney persuading his sister to introduce him to Margaret Kemp; Miss Kemp's swift sidelong glance at Deborah as the latter, having performed the introduction, monopolized the willing attention of Bernard Bryce; the skill with which Dr. Lawrence Greatorex was edging away from the little circle which Mrs. Fillingham, by sheer force of conversation, had collected round her.

The Comte de Goursac, who had been listening to his wife's whisperings with an expressionless countenance, begged Mr. Lewker to excuse them. Madame was a little indisposed and wished to retire early. They had scarcely taken their departure when Greatorex came across the room and gripped Lewker's hand.

"Filthy Lewker, by George! The world, as Shakespeare ought to have said, is a devilish small place." He grinned down at the other. "I wondered if you'd recognize me behind the whiskers."

Mr. Lewker, studying the square-cut, tanned face with its beak-like nose and mane of black hair, still found himself unable to link the features with the scraggy medical student whom he had taken up the Teufelsgrat. There were deep-graven lines in the broad forehead and round the eyes, and the bristling beard scarcely hid the furrows beside his mouth.

"You have changed, indeed," he said. "But after all, fifteen years will have their way. Ay, past all surgery."

Dr. Greatorex chuckled. "Still quoting Shakespeare, I see. I remember how you shouted to us on the Teufelsgrat when that damned blizzard began—'The storm is up, and all is on the hazard.' Gad, that was a climb."

"You have done harder climbs since then. By the way, what became of that young Frenchman who was with us that day? He was a friend of yours, if I remember."

Greatorex's face hardened. "He was my closet friend. René Lescaut. He was killed in the Alps two years ago."

"I am sorry. A climbing accident?"

"The papers called it an accident." He stopped short and abruptly changed the subject. "You're here for some climbing? I saw the newspaper reports, vacation for famous actor and so forth. The weather's playing ducks and drakes with our plans—Bernard's and mine."

"I had intended to bag an easy peak or two," said Mr. Lewker cautiously. "I understand the Matterhorn is in bad condition."

"It is. Even the Hörnli route is dangerous. According to the guides it won't be safe for two days at least, even if the Föhn clears off. I'm off tomorrow to cross the Théodule, to see if there's better weather in Italy. Bernard won't come—seems to have found attractions in Zermatt. I suppose you wouldn't care to join me?"

Mr. Lewker was almost tempted. He would have liked nothing better if he had been free to go. Reluctantly he declined, pleading that he had still to make contact with the guide he had booked.

"Pity," said Greatorex. "We might have exercised our phalanges on the rocks of Jumeaux. Look here," he added impatiently, "let's go for a stroll outside. This mob's getting on my nerves."

He took the older man's arm and steered him through the crowd to the door. As they passed out of the porch and down the steps into the lamplit street the night air placed a cool invigorating robe about them. Greatorex sniffed the darkness and grunted approvingly.

"The Föhn's going. We'll be on decent snow in a couple of days, up aloft."

They walked slowly along the narrow street and out into the wider main thoroughfare. High above the lit windows and shadowy roofs, peering down above the looming shoulder of the Untergabelhorn that rose blackly over the village, the glimmering snows of the Matterhorn hung ghostly in the zenith among the stars, like another planet hovering above the earth.

"Moon won't be up for another two hours," Greatorex remarked, staring up at the vision. "Still beautiful by starlight, eh, Filthy?"

" 'A peace above all earthly dignities,' " quoted Mr. Lewker softly.

They crossed the street slowly. Few people were abroad, but several of the shops were still open. From a restaurant whose red-curtained windows bore the name "Hoffman" in curly script black against the glow came the faint thrumming of dance music. As they gained the opposite side of the street the door of the restaurant opened and two figures, a man and a woman, came out and stood silhouetted against the red-lit windows. The two silhouettes melted into one for a long moment. Then the woman, a slight short-skirted figure, went back into the restaurant. The man remained to light his cigarette before striding away in the direction of the Hotel Obergabelhorn. By the flare of the match-flame Lewker recognized the face of Léon Jacot; and as he did so he became aware that Greatorex had come to a halt and was staring after the man, his broad shoulders hunched oddly. Some trick of darkness and lamp-light made the doctor's attitude seem bestial, the poise of a great animal stalking its prey. The fancy passed, but it left Mr. Lewker uneasy. He spoke to dispel the feeling.

"That was Monsieur Jacot, I think."

Greatorex turned slowly.

"What? Oh, yes. I need clean air in my lungs. Brisk walk down the road to the station and back, Filthy. Then I must turn in—four o'clock call in the morning for me. Right?"

Mr. Lewker agreed. By the time they reached the hotel porch again he was conscious that he was badly out of form and also inclined for bed himself.

"I suppose," he panted, coming up with his companion as the doctor turned in at the door, "I suppose that unconscionable speed was necessary for some therapeutic purpose, such as ridding the bloodstream of impurities."

"And the mind," added Greatorex quietly, "of murderous thoughts. Good night."

CHAPTER FOUR

TROUBLES OF A GUIDE

For all its noise and sophistication, there lingers about air travel some aura of the marvelous, something faintly Arabian-nightish. Not that the bone-shaking racket of a plane has anything in common with the presumably smooth flight of a magic carpet; but the very speed with which one is machine-handled from one country and climate into another imparts a dreamlike quality to the first sights and sounds of the place of arrival. As though, thought Mr. Lewker, one's body had arrived rather in advance of one's mind.

He was thinking these idle thoughts in bed on the morning after his arrival in Zermatt, and wondering whether they were a sign that he was getting elderly and old-fashioned. He was quite unable to imagine John Waveney thinking them. At any rate, he had gone to bed (early, and without meeting Léon Jacot) feeling that he had fallen in with a slightly odd and not particularly pleasant lot of people; he woke, with the clangor of church bells in his ears, convinced that this feeling had been merely the result of traveling too fast. His mind, restored to normal, told him that these were ordinary folk enough, with ordinary folk's oddities and nothing more. Even the typewritten warning Deborah Jacot had shown him had slipped into its proper place as one of those empty threats which all public men receive from time to time. As for certain odd phrases he remembered hearing, they were only words after all. It was Sunday morning, and he was among his beloved mountains.

Mr. Lewker had been wakened some hours earlier. There had been footsteps in the passage outside his room, footsteps at once heavy and stealthy. Something had been dropped with a clatter, and a man's voice had growled a curse. That would have been Dr. Greatorex setting out for his crossing of the

Théodule Pass. Mr. Lewker lay remembering the many times he had turned out into the dark and cold of early morning to stumble bad-temperedly up a path and on to the crisp starlit snow of a glacier. Then, with a start, he realized that it was nearly eight o'clock of a fine morning. He scrambled out of bed, hastily shaved and dressed, and went downstairs. Two or three people were consuming coffee and rolls in the *speisezimmer,* but none of his acquaintances of yesterday were among them. Mr. Lewker tried his German on the pleasant-faced maid who brought his breakfast.

"Where shall I find my mail, Fräulein, when it arrives?" he asked.

"Herr Simler sorts it with his own hands," she told him, "and it is laid out on the big table in the hall."

"The table opposite the doorway?"

"Yes, *mein Herr.*"

He thanked her. He had noticed that the big door leading out to the street, which was closed at dinnertime when the hall became a sort of anteroom, was flung wide this morning. It would be no difficult feat for any passerby to stroll in and drop an envelope on the table unobserved. Having thus perfunctorily salved his conscience in the matter of Deborah Jacot's appeal, by establishing that the anonymous letter could have come from outside the hotel, he finished his breakfast and went out into the invigorating air.

As yet the sun had not reached the valley bottom. The Matterhorn's eastern precipice caught the golden light on bare reddish rock and dazzling ribbons of snow, but the village and its surrounding pastures were in blue shadow. A few men and women in decent black were on their way to morning service. Mr. Lewker, un-Sabbatically attired in baggy climbing breeches and a windproof jacket, made his way to the bridge over the gray-green Visp and thence along the lane on the right bank of the river. Presently he took a well-worn path leading up the hillside between scattered Arolla pines which soon became a wood, and emerging on a cleared slope of the hill met the sunlight as it poured over a shoulder of the snowy Breithorn. The chalet of Heinrich Taugwalder, for which he was making, was still half a mile away. He sat down with his back against a tree and got out his pipe.

It was a good spot from which to contemplate both the valley five hundred feet below and the mountain eight thousand feet above. From here the Matterhorn showed its apparent symmetry; the two immense precipices made a sharp angle with each other like the covers of a partly open book, the eastern face falling unbroken to the Furggen Glacier on the left, the shadowed northern face sweeping down to the Matterhorn Glacier on the right. The Northeast Ridge, which forms the narrow spine between the two, looked impossibly steep from this foreshortening angle. Small wonder, meditated Mr. Lewker, that Edward Whymper, the first man to climb that awesome and devil-ridden peak, should have made all his early attempts from the other side. That very ridge had in the end proved the easiest way to the top; and up there, on the snow-cased "shoulder" below the final peak, had occurred the famous accident when Hadow, Hudson, Lord Francis Douglas and the guide Michel Croz had fallen to death on the Matterhorn Glacier four thousand feet below. The ascent from Zermatt had become the most hackneyed in the Alps since that tragic day in 1865, but still the great mountain claimed at intervals its human life or lives, overwhelming its victims with falling stone or sudden treacherous storm, or seizing upon incompetence and inexperience with its inexorable hand. Even a good mountaineer might not tackle that ridge when, as now, the new snow lay glistening on its shelving sides. Two more fine days such as this, and the guides would once again swarm with their charges on the ascent.

Mr. Lewker was disturbed in his sun-warmed solitude by the sound of footsteps on the ascending path below him. The newcomer panted into view a score of yards away and waved a hand skittishly at him.

"Oy!" she shouted. "I thought it was you. Followed your spoor, ha-ha!"

It was Mrs. Fillingham. She wore a blue-and-yellow check shirt from the short sleeves of which large sun-blistered arms emerged. From her massive haunches swung a very short skirt, and there were yellow ankle socks turned down over the tops of her immense nailed boots. Frizzy hair of an incredible gold stuck out beneath a blue beret. She was fearfully and wonderfully made-up.

"Don't get up," she roared as she approached with elephantine tread. "Be pally, that's my motto. Mind if I squattay?"

She plumbed herself down beside him without waiting for a reply. Mr. Lewker averted pained eyes from a display of reddened thigh; John Waveney's remark about boiling-pieces recurred to him, and involuntarily he thought of underdone steak. He opened his mouth to make some conventional remark but the lady easily talked him down.

"I know we haven't been introduced and all that guff, but I know you. I'm Bee Fillingham. Bee short for Beatrix. Widder-woman. When I saw you walk in I said, Bee, I said, you *are* among the nobs, you are. What with Monsieur Jacot and Abercrombie Lewker in the same hotel you'll find yourself in the *Tatler* yet—'and friend,' ha-ha. Seen you act, of course. What's it like being in the limelight and spouting to thousands?"

Mr. Lewker, repressing a groan, felt that some reply was needed. He did not yet know Mrs. Fillingham.

"Well, my dear lady," he began, "it is—"

"Ah, you artists! Doesn't do to pop questions about your art. On holiday, too. Weren't at the Obergabelhorn last year, were you? I've been three years running. Brought Margot with me last year—brother-in-law's niece. Nice girl. Young Bryce fell for her then. You seem to know his pal Larry Greatorex.

Nice chap. He's climbed with Léon Jacot once or twice. Deb's sweet, isn't she? Haven't met her brother before, but my pal Mona Smith saw him once when he was on the stage. He tried variety, you know. She says he took off film stars jolly well—Charles Boyer and so forth. Going up to the Riffel? I am. Sabbath day's journey for your Aunty Bee."

She paused for breath. Mr. Lewker, scenting a possibility, managed to squeeze in a question.

"Monsieur Jacot, I hear, is a new force in French politics," he boomed hastily. "One wonders whether he will favor the Left wing or the Right."

He had no great hope of acquiring from his companion any useful information on this point, but it seemed a pity not to utilize her determined frankness; somewhere in the spate there might be a hint.

"*One* wonders!" repeated Mrs. Fillingham, amused. "My dear man, we all do. I've asked him. He won't tell, even when he's half tight as he was last night. Well, a quarter tight, anyway. You weren't there, of course. Had us in fits. Nice chap, and pally when he's got the drink taken, as the Irish say. Handsome as they make 'em, too. A lad with the wenches, believe me. Sorry for Deb. But he was on about the Matterhorn last night. Said he was going to be the first man to cycle up it. Laugh! I nearly died—but he talked about climbing it tomorrow whether or not." She jerked her frizzy head at the mountain. "Looks good, eh? I like mountains. Don't climb 'em, of course—just like 'em. They're unconventional, like your Aunty Bee. No use for convention. That's why I like the Obergabelhorn. No silly fuss about dressing for dinner—"

She rattled on. Mr. Lewker ceased to listen. Already he was planning various desperate ways of shaking off the widow. He was not averse to a flow of conversation, but this cataract gave him a submerged feeling. Mrs. Fillingham, however, provided him with an easy escape.

"Great Godfrey!" she ejaculated, cutting herself off in mid-sentence to glance at her wristwatch. "Nearly ten! And me not halfway to the Riffel." She hauled herself to her feet. "Come on. You did say you were bound for the Riffel, didn't you?"

Mr. Lewker got up. "I fear I am not so energetic—this is the limit of my morning walk," he lied without compunction. "I shall descend."

"Oh. Well, it's Excelsior for your Aunty Bee. Nice to have had a chat. See you later—*au reservoir*, ha-ha!"

She set off up the path at a tremendous rate, sending the stones flying under her great boots. Mr. Lewker gave her five minutes' start and then followed more slowly. He came to an open alp where creamy cattle grazed beside the path and a small neat chalet, with scarlet geraniums on its windowsills, stood close to a mossy boulder larger than itself. On a wooden bench against the front wall of the chalet a man was sitting, puffing at a big curved pipe. He stood up as Mr. Lewker approached, and taking his pipe from his mouth raised it in wordless greeting.

" '*Morgen*, Heinrich," beamed his visitor, and gripped the sinewy hand of the guide. "Twelve years is a long time, but you have not changed."

Indeed, the hard, strong face, keen as though chiseled from freestone, and the drooping yellow mustaches, were exactly as Lewker remembered them from that last Alpine season in the summer before the war. There was a trace of gray in the lank fair hair, but the eyes beneath the fiercely sprouting brows were bright and adventurous as ever.

"Belieben Sie, mein Herr," said Heinrich, getting up and indicating the bench. "I get you some milk."

Mr. Lewker detained him. "No, thank you, my friend. Sit down again and tell me how you are and what you have been doing."

The guide complied, crossing one long leg over the other and drawing unhurriedly at his pipe.

"It was fortunate for me, *mein Herr*," he said at last in his careful English, "that you changed your plan of meeting in Zinal. There are things here in Zermatt I must attend to."

"I am glad the alteration did not inconvenience you. But you are ready for some climbing, I hope?"

"*Ja, ja*—I climb with you, when the mountains are in good condition again. Perhaps the day after tomorrow we go up to a hut, if you wish."

"Good. I had thought of something easy to begin with. The Breithorn, for example."

Heinrich nodded. "I myself am out of practice a little. I think perhaps tomorrow I get up *sehr früh* and make a training walk."

Mr. Lewker recognized this as a gentle hint.

"I also," he said, "shall go for a long tramp tomorrow. Like Hamlet, I am fat and scant of breath."

"Today also is a fine day for a walk," Heinrich added, with a sidelong glance at his employer's paunch.

The actor chuckled. "I see. Well, you may be right. I will walk up to the Gorner Grat and lunch there."

"Gut."

They talked for a while of peaks, climbs and climbers, while the sun rose higher and the scents of hay and flowers, intermingled with the homely odor of cows, came soothingly to their nostrils. Presently, the conversation having come round to Zermatt and its intricately related families, Lewker remembered something.

"By the way, Heinrich, what has become of that little daughter of yours?" he asked. "Last time we met she was just about the height of an ice-axe."

"Lisse is a woman grown now," responded Heinrich shortly.

"Of course—Lisse was her name. Lisse Taugwalder—and I heard some news of her at Täsch yesterday. She is to marry Franz, the son of the hotel proprietor. I felicitate you, my friend. Franz seems a fine upstanding young man."

Heinrich bent to tap the ashes from his pipe. His bushy brows were drawn together so that they quite obscured his eyes. He made no reply to Lewker's remark. When he straightened up again he jerked his head at the Matterhorn.

"You think of climbing him this season, *mein Herr?*"

Mr. Lewker accepted this change of topic, not without surprise. Lisse had been the object of her widowed father's adoration when last he had seen them together. He wondered if Heinrich disapproved of his daughter's choice.

"A traverse from the Italian side was in my program," he replied. "When the mountain is safe again, of course."

"It will be safe in forty-eight hours if tomorrow is fine like today," said the guide. "Not before then."

"One of the guests at the Hotel Obergabelhorn talks of doing it tomorrow."

"Then he is a *Dummkopf*. He will get no guide to take him, unless he is a very good climber—as good as a guide. Was it perhaps the Herr Doktor Greatorex who spoke of it? There is one who might well do it in safety."

"No. It was a Frenchman—Monsieur Jacot. I understand he—*achtung*, Heinrich!"

The guide had let his pipe slip from his fingers to the ground. Mr. Lewker rescued it in two pieces, but these proved to be stem and bowl separated and unbroken. He restored it to Heinrich, who muttered his thanks and proceeded to refill it with fingers that were not quite steady.

"Yes," he said presently, "the Herr Doktor, he is safe anywhere, that one." He accepted a match from Mr. Lewker. "The other, the Frenchman, he is also good. I have heard of him."

"I know you've climbed with Greatorex. You have not climbed with Jacot, then?"

Heinrich blew out a long cloud of smoke. "*Nein*," he said with quiet emphasis. "I shall not climb with that gentleman. I do not like his kind."

Mr. Lewker looked surprised.

"He seems to be an all-round sportsman of an unusual skill," he observed. "I should have thought—"

"If you please," interrupted the Swiss gravely and without offense, "we shall not speak of him. Please, *mein Herr*, let us talk of peaks. The Lyskamm, now—"

For a further ten minutes they ranged on the wings of reminiscence over the delights that Zermatt offers to the mountaineer. Heinrich was in the middle of a detailed description of the alterations that had taken place in the ridge of the Zinal Rothhorn since 1939 when he stopped suddenly, his keen glance going beyond his companion to the path. He laid down his pipe and stood up, frowning.

"It is my daughter who comes from church," he said.

The girl who swung up the path towards the chalet was as good to look at as a ripe apple. There was, thought Mr. Lewker, something of an apple's shapely roundness and glowing color about her. She had very fair hair charmingly braided round her head, and the hat that was perched on top of it had certainly come from farther afield than Zermatt. Her face, pretty above the ordinary in a country where pretty faces are far from rare, had exquisite coloring and a small nose tip-tilted impudently; but her red mouth was both sulky and petulant, and there was a palpable defiance in her blue eyes. For all her prettiness, there was nothing ultra-feminine about Lisse Taugwalder's trim figure. She was as sturdy as a daughter of the mountains should be.

Lisse had a dimpling smile and a prettily spoken greeting for Mr. Lewker, whom she pretended to remember. She spoke a little English, but had not her father's fluency. Heinrich Taugwalder stood woodenly by while the actor-manager ran through his stock of German compliments, and then politely begged his visitor to excuse them. Father and daughter went up the worn steps into the chalet, whence in a moment or two Lisse's voice emerged, angrily raised in German.

"Of course I have been to church—where else should I go?"

An unintelligible mutter from Heinrich followed, and then the girl spoke again in an access of temper.

"I have not seen him, I tell you! But I would if I'd wanted to—so there!"

A door banged, shaking the wooden wall against which Mr. Lewker was leaning. The guide could be heard banging on the door and calling wrathfully. Mr. Lewker got up and strolled a few yards away across the sunlit turf. A goat, appearing suddenly from behind the chalet, came and nuzzled his pockets in search of food. He bent and rubbed his knuckles across its bony skull, but his thoughts were elsewhere. Two and two were easily put together and he didn't like the answer; but it was not bound to be the right one, and he could check it. It was, perhaps, no business of his, except that Heinrich was an old acquaintance and a guide who loved mountains for their own sakes rather than for the living he got by their aid. Between mountaineers there is almost a family bond. Mr. Lewker was concerned for the happiness of the Taugwalder family.

Heinrich came slowly down the chalet steps and loosed a Zermatt oath at the goat, which shook its horns and stalked away with a hurt expression on its odd countenance.

"Well, my friend," said Mr. Lewker cheerfully, "if I am to lunch at the Gornergrat I must be going. The day after tomorrow we go up to the Gandegg Hut, eh? You will call for me at the hotel, I take it?"

The guide hesitated, frowning. There was reluctance in his curt reply.

"*Ja, mein Herr*. At two o'clock, after lunch."

"Good. I will see to the food. That is a fine strong daughter of yours, Heinrich. She looks like a mountaineer."

Heinrich's face brightened a little. "I have taken her up Breithorn, Nadelhorn—*ja*, and she climb the Matterhorn Couloir on the Riffelhorn. She is a good climber." The frown returned. "But she is very *eigensinnig*."

"Pretty girls are often wilful, my friend. She works in Zermatt, I understand?"

"*Ja.*"

"At a restaurant?" persisted Mr. Lewker.

"At Hoffman's," said Heinrich shortly.

"Ah. Well, I must jog on the footpath way. *Auf wiedersehen*."

He left Heinrich puffing at his pipe and staring out over the green valley depths to the stark precipices of the Matterhorn. For a while Mr. Lewker's pleasure in the immense views which opened out as he toiled upward was obscured by his thoughts. Two and two did indeed make an unpleasant four. It was one of the oldest situations in drama; pretty self-willed daughter, handsome undesirable lover, angry and impotent father. Even the honest suitor was there in the background. But Heinrich was somehow not the comic figure a dramatist would make of him. Five minutes after Mr. Lewker had left the chalet he had looked back, to see the guide still standing there motionless, gazing at the Matterhorn as though the mountain held the solution to his problem.

That erect brooding figure intruded itself upon his mind as he trudged up the rough track. But in another hour, with the sweat running into his eyes and the sun striking down from a gentian-blue sky, there was one vision, and one only, that hovered before Mr. Lewker: the tall, cool glass of lager that awaited him in the Riffelberg Hotel at the end of his ascent.

CHAPTER FIVE

LÉON JACOT UNDERTAKES A FEAT

"*Sangdieu!*" laughed Léon Jacot. "It was not guns and planes that put an end to Schickelgruber and his crew, but the unconquerable alliance of Lewker and Jacot—eh, *mon vieux?*"

Dinner was over and they were standing round the small semicircular bar which occupied a corner of the hall. Jacot had one hand on Mr. Lewker's shoulder and a glass of cognac in the other. John Waveney and Margaret Kemp, Mrs. Fillingham and Camille de Goursac, were grouped round the pair; at a nearby table Bryce and Deborah were talking in low voices. A few other people were in the hall, but the majority had gone out to admire the afterglow that still lingered on the snow peaks.

"So I have always thought," boomed Mr. Lewker gravely. "However, I learn from a book I have just read that despite the treachery and obstruction of the indolent Capitalist allies the gallant Red Army, alone and unsupported, crushed the might of Germany. The book," he added, "was written by a Russian historian."

"Guff!" ejaculated Mrs. Fillingham angrily. "They were pally enough at first. I suppose they've forgotten they were on Hitler's side to start with. My pal Mona Smith knew a Russian who—"

"Ah, *ces bons Russes!*" Jacot said, interrupting her with an ease that compelled Mr. Lewker's admiration. "They have much to learn, I fear—except in the art of turning a blind eye to facts." He drained his glass and gestured to the barman to replenish any others that needed it. "Listen, *mes amis*. I will tell you of a thing that happened eight years ago. You shall judge if the late Hitler had any chance of winning when two such men as Monsieur Abercrombie Lewker and myself were arrayed against him."

He launched with much dramatic gesture into an anecdote of wartime doings in France of the Occupation. Mr. Lewker, who felt that such tales were better left untold, had to admit to himself that the Frenchman told it well. His dynamic figure dominated the little group as naturally as it dominated any company in which he happened to be. Standing a head and shoulders above the actor-manager, he used his expressive eyes and very masculine good looks as an experienced actor uses his, yet without any touch of theatricality. The slight exaggeration of every gesture, every smile, every flourish of the strong brown hands, would in another man have been ridiculous; in Léon Jacot it was merely a projection of his forceful, magnetic personality. A musketeer swagger enhances the attraction of a D'Artagnan, and to D'Artagnan Jacot had often been compared by his admirers; a fact of which he was evidently well aware, since he made a practice of using the picturesque oaths current in the days of Richelieu.

Mr. Lewker, sipping his grenadine (he had eschewed stronger liquors, regarding himself as being in training for the Breithorn) watched the tall Frenchman and his audience with a keen but casual eye. He noticed that all the women in the hall were looking, either covertly or openly, at Jacot, whether they were near enough to hear what he was saying or not—with one exception. Deborah Jacot continued to look at Bernard Bryce, although the latter was listening, with a somewhat scornful expression on his tanned face, to her husband's story. Margaret Kemp appeared to listen attentively, but the observant Lewker had a shrewd idea that her dainty ears were tuned to catch any conversation that might reach them from the table where Deborah sat. He had been introduced to Margaret before dinner; she was, as John Waveney had observed, easy on the eye, but he suspected hidden fires beneath her shy self-possession.

As for the Comtesse de Goursac, it was obvious to the most casual eye that for her there was only one person worth looking at or listening to. At dinner he had learned that her husband, after vainly endeavoring to persuade Jacot to accompany him, had set out alone to walk up to the Swiss Alpine Club hut at the Schönbuhl, above the Zmutt Glacier, intending to spend the night there and return next day by way of the Schwarzsee. Freed from the sardonic regard of the Comte, Camille de Goursac set herself almost blatantly to capture Jacot's entire attention. Mr. Lewker, observant of the way she hung upon the man's lips, her brown eyes fixed beseechingly upon him, was reminded unpleasantly of a spaniel begging for cake. The woman positively glowed with pleasure whenever he threw her a word or a glance. Yet—and this was odd—Léon Jacot did not seem to respond. Rather he seemed to evade her gaze, to be embarrassed by her flattering attentions. To Mr. Lewker's critical mind this appeared out of character.

Jacot was finishing his story.

"—and those six Boche spies, Goebbels' pet agents, walked straight into the cellar where we were waiting for them. And who, *mes amis*, set this most ingenious trap? Why, *vertudieu!* Who but Monsieur Abercrombie Lewker, the cunning one!"

He slapped the actor-manager on the back amid laughter and applause.

"Ah, *mais quelle bravoure!*" exclaimed Mme de Goursac, languishing at Lewker. "I could kiss him for it," she added, with a hopeful glance at Jacot.

"I assure you, Madame, that Monsieur Jacot exaggerates my part," said Mr. Lewker hastily. "I am in reality neither ingenious nor cunning. Do I look it?"

"You don't," Mrs. Fillingham shouted. "But looks aren't everything. Remember? 'Who would have thought the old man had so much blood in him?' "

She hooted with laughter. After all, she had put away four gin-and-lemons, thought Mr. Lewker tolerantly. He let her off with a compliment.

"You yourself, dear lady," he boomed urbanely, "testify to the misleading nature of appearances. Who would see in the exquisitely-gowned Beatrice of tonight the adventurous Rosalind I had the pleasure of meeting this morning?"

Margaret was overcome by a fit of coughing and had to be patted on the back by John Waveney. Mrs. Fillingham positively blushed beneath her paint, and, smoothing her vivid crimson dress, was for once silent for lack of words. John looked up from his ministrations, his lean face blandly obtuse.

"Look here, sir, come clean," he begged. "Who's this Rosalind you met? It wasn't by any chance that bunchy little blonde from Hoffman's? She looks adventurous, if you like."

Involuntarily Lewker's glance went to Jacot. For a second the Frenchman's eyes looked murder. Then he was laughing loudly.

"My poor *beau-frère!*" he said derisively. "You squash Monsieur Lewker's pretty compliment under your blundering boots."

"Oh. Sorry if I trod on any corns," said John. But the little smile at the corner of his mouth was not apologetic.

Mrs. Fillingham won Lewker's respect, and made him feel slightly ashamed of himself, by her next speech.

"All right—I can take it," she said, grinning at him. "Mine's a good stout leg to pull, as my pal Mona Smith's always telling me."

"My dear lady," protested Mr. Lewker lamely. "I assure you I—"

"Rubbish." She dug him in the ribs. "All between pals. What about drinks all round, folks? On your Aunty Bee?"

The barman came out from behind his counter and began to collect glasses and orders. Margaret Kemp bent her black brows at Mrs. Fillingham's "same again, George."

"I thought you were going into training, Aunty," she remarked reprovingly.

"So I am, Margot. Perhaps you're right." She peered into Lewker's glass. "What's that? Grenadine? George! Make mine grenadine. D'you drink the stuff because you like it, or are you in training for something, Mr. Lewker?"

The actor-manager modestly explained his plan to start his climbing holiday by going up the Breithorn.

"Well!" hooted Mrs. Fillingham. "You kept very quiet about it. I never guessed you were a climber."

"Aha!" said Jacot, wagging a finger at her. "With *le bon* Lewker you never know what he is up to. Did I not tell you he is a cunning one? You noticed, perhaps, how he made a sarcasm about Soviet historians a few moments ago. Do you know why? Because he wished to see whether I would agree or take the Russian side. *Le vieux renard!*" He poked the finger into Mr. Lewker's waistcoat. "He fishes for my political sentiments, like everyone else. Eh, *mon vieux*? Have I caught you?"

'Touché,' acknowledged the Astute Agent sadly. "However," he added, making the best of it, "you admitted that the Russians have much to learn, which is what no Communist ever admits."

Jacot laughed loudly, a little too loudly. He had disposed of a good deal of wine at dinner, and the cognac was taking effect.

"Can I not dissemble as well as you, *monsieur l'espion*?" he demanded. "Or shall I tell you the truth?" He picked up the glass which the barman had placed at his elbow, smiling derisively at the actor. "The truth, then. *Vive la France!*" He tossed the cognac down his throat and set the glass down with a flourish. "There, *mes amis*, are the political sentiments of Léon Jacot."

Mr. Lewker became aware that Deborah Jacot, with Bryce just behind her, was standing at his side.

"Don't be so theatrical, Léon," she admonished in her level voice.

Jacot bowed to her mockingly. "I must leave that to my lovely vaudeville artiste, I suppose."

"It would be better, until you are sober," she riposted.

"*Sangdieu!*" He spread his hands in derisive appeal. "Have I then had my allowance of cognac for tonight, *chérie?*"

"You've had enough to float you up the Matterhorn tomorrow, I should think," said Deborah lightly.

"Day after tomorrow, you mean," cut in her brother. "Not that I know a thing about this mountaineering game, but a bloke I was talking to, a knowledgeable sort of cove, said the guides weren't taking anyone up tomorrow."

Jacot turned and leaned with his back against the bar, facing his brother-in-law with a curl of his sensual lips.

"*C'est formidable*, this reliance of the layman upon any chance opinion in matters he does not understand," he drawled. "The guides will not take any-one up the Matterhorn tomorrow—that is true. They are wise. For commonly their charges are novices or poor climbers who must be dragged up and low-ered down. For such the mountain is still dangerous. It is not dangerous for Léon Jacot."

"Léon!" Camille de Goursac moved swiftly to his side and laid scarlet-nailed fingers on his sleeve. "*Tu ne feras pas cet ascension! C'est une blague—n'est-ce pas?*"

"*Pas du tout, Madame,*" he answered her shortly. "I am quite serious. Did I not tell Paul I intended to climb the Matterhorn, at luncheon today?"

He took her hand and removed it from his sleeve, dropping it as though it had been a piece of inanimate matter that had fallen there by accident. The Comtesse looked round her piteously.

"But we thought you were joking," she murmured. "It is not safe—"

"Don't play the fool, Léon," interrupted Deborah sharply. "You were boast-ing as usual, of course."

Jacot's handsome face darkened angrily and for a moment it seemed as though he would retort with an outburst. Then he controlled himself, shrugged, and spoke in his usual musical drawl.

"I flatter myself, *chérie*, that I have no need of boasting. But you make too much of the affair. The guides wait until it is quite certain the mountain is safe for *les maladroites*. In my opinion it will be in good condition by tomorrow. If there is still a little ice on the rocks, it will take me a little longer, that is all."

"But look here, old boy, you're surely not going up that Godawful thing on your own?" said John Waveney incredulously.

"Bernard—do tell him to be sensible," said Deborah.

Bernard Bryce nodded. He stood with his hands thrust into his pockets and his broad shoulders hunched, regarding the Frenchman with rather obvious contempt. The posture gave him an almost apelike appearance, thought Mr. Lewker; at least, he looked very unlike the popular conception of a novelist.

"You ought to know better, Jacot," he said somewhat overbearingly. "You're supposed to be a mountaineer. Solo climbing's a mug's game, anyway. And Deb doesn't like it."

The other laughed unpleasantly. Mr. Lewker, who agreed with Bryce, put in his word.

"For the Matterhorn by the Northeast Ridge," he boomed placatingly, "you would surely have to go up to the hut tonight. That is the usual procedure, and the hut is a four hours' climb from here."

Jacot, regaining some of his good humor, clapped him on the shoulder.

"Aha—the usual procedure. *C'est entendu.* For me, I do the unusual. I climb the Matterhorn in one day from Zermatt!"

"Bosh!" said Bernard Bryce loudly. Jacot turned upon him swiftly.

"You think so, eh? *Ecoutez donc.* I shall start from here at two o'clock tomorrow morning. By three o'clock tomorrow afternoon I shall be back again, here in the hotel, having climbed the Matterhorn. What do you say to that, Monsieur Bryce?"

"Can't be done."

"No?" He turned abruptly to Lewker. "Tell us, *mon vieux*, what says the guidebook of the times on the mountain?"

Mr. Lewker, who began to like this business less and less, answered him reluctantly.

"From the hut to the summit, six hours. Four hours for the descent. That is for a party of three, including halts."

"*Merci.* You are a veritable Baedeker." Jacot faced Bryce again. "I shall take at most four hours up and three down. That is seven. From here to the hut I do easily in three hours and back in two. Total, twelve hours. One hour I allow for rest and food. *Voilà!*"

"Still say it can't be done," growled Bryce. "You'd be a fool to attempt it."

The Frenchman stood erect and deliberately flexed his splendid muscles, smiling wickedly the while at Bryce.

"*Vraiment?* Monsieur would not be such a fool as to back his opinion with a wager, of course."

"I don't bet on mountaineering," Bryce said curtly.

Jacot showed white teeth. *"Naturellement.* You only bet on certainties, doubtless."

The other's jaw tightened. He made a slight movement, instantly arrested. The atmosphere round the little bar had for some time held a noticeable but indefinable tension, and in the little pause that followed Léon Jacot's words the tension grew. Before the situation could develop further, however, John Waveney had broken in with blundering good intent.

"Pack it up, old boy, pack it up," he advised his brother-in-law. "Beats me why you want to walk up the damned thing anyway. I was going to suggest we flip round the Matterhorn in my little Finster tomorrow. See the sunrise, if you like. How about it?"

"You could parachute on to the summit," shouted Mrs. Fillingham inanely. "That'd make a record, ha-ha!"

There was some slightly relieved laughter from the rest. Bryce stopped scowling at Jacot and abruptly enquired what everyone was drinking.

"For me, nothing, thank you," Jacot said. He glanced at his wristwatch. "I must go to bed. I shall need a few hours' sleep."

"But look here," persisted John, "I meant that about a flight tomorrow. Call it a reccy flight and do the big assault day after tomorrow."

"Léon—please put your climb off until then." Deborah's voice trembled slightly, and her eyes were fixed appealingly on her husband. "To please me."

"Dîtes que vous n'allez pas demain," whispered the Comtesse, her hand once more on Jacot's sleeve.

He shook it off in a sudden access of temper.

"Sangdieu!" he exploded. "I have had enough of this *bouffonnerie!* I tell you I shall climb the mountain tomorrow. I have arranged to be called at two. One would think I was intending suicide! Good night!"

He pushed his way unceremoniously between Lewker and Deborah and went with long strides towards the foot of the stairs. As he reached it Simler was coming down. Mr. Lewker, whose frowning gaze had followed the Frenchman, saw him stop the proprietor and detain him while he scribbled something in a small notebook. He tore out the leaf, folded it, and gave it to Simler, who took it without altering his benign expression and went on his way through the hall. Jacot continued up the stairs without looking round.

Bernard Bryce, who had been occupying himself with the ordering of drinks, was distributing them efficiently and unconcernedly. Camille de Goursac took hers from him, looked round her rather wildly, and put it down on the nearest table.

"I—I think I go to bed also," she said hurriedly; and without another word went quickly up the stairs after Jacot.

"Well!" exclaimed Mrs. Fillingham. "I must say! Of all the—"

Her somewhat uncertain eye fell on Deborah Jacot and she stopped short.

"The woman's a fool," Deborah said quietly. She accepted the drink Bryce was holding out to her and sank into a chair. "She'll only make him more determined, if that were possible."

"After all," said Margaret Kemp practically, "is there so much to worry about? Your husband's a very good climber, isn't he?"

Deborah appeared not to hear the question. Bryce was bending over her and she was smiling up into his eyes. Margaret, with an extra tinge of color on her cheeks, turned to Mr. Lewker.

"Is it really so dangerous for a good climber like Monsieur Jacot?" she asked.

"It is not so much a question of skill, Miss Kemp, as of chance," he explained. "He is breaking two of the rules of the game, and he ought to know better. A good mountaineer does not climb alone, nor does he tackle a route that is known to be in bad condition. The short spell of bad weather will have left patches of treacherous snow, ice on the rocks, stones ready to come down at a touch."

"But won't all this sun have altered that?"

"It may have done so. But another day of it would make sure, as the guides know well."

"Let's hope he doesn't break his neck," said Mrs. Fillingham. She put down her empty glass. "Great Godfrey! It's a rare old fug in here. Margot, come for a bresh of freth air—well, you know what I mean. Get your Aunty Bee sobered up, ha-ha!"

"All right," said Margaret obediently.

"I say, look here," protested John Waveney. "I'm still keen on taking the Finster up tomorrow. I suppose—er—Margaret, you wouldn't by any chance care to have a flip round the Matterhorn with me?"

"No, thank you," she smiled at him. "I'm always sick in a plane."

"Come on, Margot!" shouted Mrs. Fillingham from the door.

The girl, with a brief glance at Deborah and Bryce, hastened to join her aunt and they went out together. John wagged his head dolefully.

"Always sick in a plane," he repeated with a grimace. "That girl ought to soar like a bird. She's got to get air-minded some time. What about you, sir—coming up with me tomorrow?"

"I fear I must decline," boomed Mr. Lewker. "Some other time I will like a dewdrop from the lion's mane be shook to air. Tomorrow I use a more primitive form of locomotion."

Deborah stood up and came to stand by her brother.

"I'll come with you, Johnny," she said. "Can we get up early and fly into the dawn?"

"We can and will," he told her enthusiastically. "Up at five, eh? Drive down to Täsch and away. If the air currents aren't too tricky we could flip down pretty close to this ridge your obstinate spouse is going to climb, and see how he's getting on."

"No aerobatics, Johnny—I don't like them." She linked her arm in his. "Come for a stroll and then I'm going to turn in. Good night, Bernard. Sweet dreams, Mr. Lewker."

Brother and sister went to the door and out into the starlight. Bryce followed them with his eyes until they had gone. Left alone with him, Mr. Lewker essayed conversation.

"I gather that you, like myself, do not intend to rise with the lark, Mr. Bryce."

Bryce grunted. "No. Got a bit of work to do. Scribbling—it's my profession. Shan't get out of my room before noon, probably."

"You are a novelist?"

"Of a sort. Nice set of characters all handy in this hotel. All we need is a murder." He stood up abruptly. "I'm turning in. 'Night."

He went upstairs, leaving Mr. Lewker to smoke a final pipe in solitary meditation. Then he too went to his bed and dropped easily into sleep, without any premonition of tragedy to come.

CHAPTER SIX

CORPSE ON A MOUNTAIN

Mr. Lewker was being patient with Macbeth.

"Observe, Dalziel," he was saying to a black-jowled and rather sulky actor, "you have just committed your first murder. You have knifed your guest, the old King of Scotland, in his sleep. This you did because you believed it was your fate so to do. But the knocking on the door, whose first effect is to make you fear lest your guest should be awakened by it, suddenly drives home the realization that Duncan will never wake again. Keep that in mind and let me hear that curtain line again, the last four words forced from your horror-stricken soul: 'Wake Duncan with thy knocking! *I would thou could'st!*'

Right—Props! Do that knocking again, and make it urgent."

The knocking sounded obediently—a brisk *rat-tat-tat!* Mr. Lewker suffered the mild shock that accompanies transition from dreamland to reality. He was no longer rehearsing the Abercrombie Lewker Players but lying in bed at the Hotel Obergabelhorn. The knocking, however, had made the same transition. Dimly he realized that someone was knocking at the door of the room next to his. *Rat-tat-tat* it went again. This time there came Léon Jacot's sleepy growl of *"Ça va! Merci!"* and the apologetic voice of the knocker-up informed him that it was two o'clock.

From the bedroom next door came muffled clumping sounds and a low-voiced oath. Deborah's voice murmured something sleepily. Before he rolled over and pulled the bedclothes round his ears once more Mr. Lewker opened one eye in the direction of the window. Beyond the dark roofs he could just see a star or two shining steadily; at least the weather was fine for Jacot's solitary ascent. He closed the eye and was immediately asleep.

Three hours later he was awakened again, and again by knocking. This time it was a cautious rapping on his own bedroom door. There was a gray twilight in the room now, and Mr. Lewker, switching on his bedside lamp, saw that it was a quarter-past five by his watch.

"Come in—the door is open," he boomed sleepily.

A figure in a leather flying-jacket with high fur-lined collar tiptoed in hesitantly. It was John Waveney.

"Damned sorry to wake you, sir," he whispered. "Deb said I wasn't to. But I thought perhaps—the fact is—if you don't mind—"

"If there is anything you want, and it does not involve my getting out of bed, I do not mind in the least," said Mr. Lewker amiably.

"Thanks a lot, sir. We're just off for a dawn flight, and Deb's got no helmet. Going to be damned cold at fourteen thou', and she ought to have something. That odd woolen helmet of yours—I saw it yesterday—it'd be just the thing."

Mr. Lewker grunted his relief. The possibility that he would be asked to help start the car or swing the propeller of the plane had crossed his mind.

"Certainly," he said cordially. "Will you take it to Madame Jacot with my good wishes for a pleasant trip? It is in the middle drawer of the dressing table."

John murmured his thanks and moved across, still on tiptoe, to the dressing table. He opened the drawer and having got out the woolen balaclava tiptoed back to the door, where he hesitated. Mr. Lewker wished heartily that he would go. But John had something to say.

"Look here," he got out at last, in a hoarse whisper. "Deb's worried about Jacot. He started at two, you know. What's your real opinion, sir? You know your stuff on mountains—will he get back all right?"

"If conditions are reasonable, and if he does not sacrifice caution to speed,"

Mr. Lewker stirred himself to reply, "he should have no difficulty. In my opinion, for what it is worth, you have no occasion to worry about Monsieur Jacot."

John gave a short laugh. His whispered words sounded bitter. "Wouldn't worry me if he broke his neck, matter of fact. I'll tell Deb you think he'll be O.K. Thanks, sir."

He went out and closed the door softly behind him. Mr. Lewker switched off the bedside lamp and lay drowsily meditating. It almost seemed as though John's visit to borrow the balaclava had been for the purpose of getting a reassurance which he could pass on to his sister. That was not unlikely, for John himself had plainly no great affection for his brother-in-law. And the more one saw of brother and sister the more evident it was that a very close affection existed between them.

The throb of a car engine passed below Mr. Lewker's window as the pair set off for their dawn flight. Before its diminuendo hum had died away on the road to Täsch he was once more sound asleep.

As on the previous morning, bells woke him to the new day. They were not church bells this time, however, but the flat *cling-clang* notes of the little bells on the necks of a flock of shaggy goats passing through the narrow lane beside the hotel, on their slow way up to the pastures below the Altes Haupt. This is the enchanted music that pleases the climber's ear as he mounts to his hut before the climb and greets him from afar as he threads his way down the glacier at the end of the day's adventure. It brought Mr. Lewker out of his bed with a leap surprising in so Pickwickian a figure, for he remembered the training walk he had determined to perform as a preparative for the ascent of the Breithorn.

By half-past seven he was dressed and walking along the passage with his nailed boots in his hand. From behind one of the doors came the sound of a typewriter hard at work. He paused to read the name on the door (it was a custom of Simler's to insert a neatly written card bearing the name of his guest in a slot on each door) and learned that this early worker was Bernard W. Bryce, M.A. Praising his gods that he knew better than to bring his work with him on a holiday, Mr. Lewker passed on down the stairs, and presently, with coffee and rolls and a pot of Simler's cherry jam in front of him, was dividing his attention between breakfast and a tattered map. Outside, the sky was blue overhead and the life of Zermatt was astir in the streets. The barometer in the hall showed a substantial rise since yesterday. He felt his middle-aged blood run a trifle faster as his eye glanced from peak to peak on the map, skipping over blue-contoured glaciers and black-shaded crags. After the Breithorn, perhaps, a crossing to Breuil for the Matterhorn traverse from the Italian side; after that the Dent Blanche from the Schönbuhl, if Heinrich passed him as fit for it. After that—

" 'Morning! Mind if I squattay?"

Mrs. Fillingham's cheery shout interrupted his lofty progress. She flopped into a chair at his table and snapped her fingers at the waitress to call her attention to the need for more coffee.

"Hullo! Off for a hike?" she added, jabbing a thick forefinger at the map.

"Not exactly a hike," responded Mr. Lewker, who detested the word as being non-Shakespearean. "It is my intention—"

"I do a good bit of hiking at home," pursued Mrs. Fillingham. "My pal Mona Smith's very keen. Not much of Surrey we don't know. Like the poem— 'Who never to himself hath said Tum-tumty-tum my native land.' Know it? That's what I feel. Switzerland's different, of course—oh, thank you, Frawleen." She poured coffee from the pot which the waitress had set before her, but the operation did not interrupt the flow of her full-voiced conversation. "Always call 'em Frawleen. That's an old traveler's tip. One word of their own lingo puts you at home straight away. I get along anywhere on the Continent with half a dozen words and a pally smile. What were we talking about? Oh, hiking. I'm off somewhere—don't know where yet. Where are you bound for?"

Mr. Lewker, who had already noticed that his companion was wearing heavy boots and her very short skirt, took heed of the warning. The only chatter he proposed to listen to on his day's scramble was the endless babble of mountain streams.

"I had thought of the south ridge of the Plattenhorn," he boomed, omitting to mention that he had rejected the idea. "It depends, however, on whether I can find a practicable route up the first *arête*. The traverse above is somewhat exposed to falling stones, but once one has passed the overhang and the strenuous chimney the knife edge should present no great difficulty."

"Oh!" Mrs. Fillingham's sun-blistered countenance had become steadily less hopeful during this recital. "That sounds a bit stiff for your Aunty Bee. I think I'll stick to the paths myself. But I thought you didn't agree with solitary climbing judging by your remarks last night when Léon Jacot was holding forth. By the way, he's gone, I hear. Simler told me. And John Waveney and his sister were off early, too. Did you hear the plane?"

Mr. Lewker said that he had not.

"I did. Not going—I suppose they were away before I was awake—but coming back. Half an hour ago that was, so they ought to be—hullo, Margot. Had your beauty sleep? Squattay, my girl."

Margaret Kemp, looking, thought Mr. Lewker, as though she had spent a sleepless night, joined them at the table and greeted them with her usual quiet self-possession. Her face, which had character as well as good looks, was pale, and there were shadows beneath her dark eyes. Mrs. Fillingham repeated her finger-snapping gesture and rattled on.

"Bernard's not down yet, the lazy devil. Come to think of it, half the gang's not here. There's Lawrence Greatorex over the pass in Italy, Monsieur de Goursac up at some hut or other, Léon Jacot swarming up the Matterhorn— and let's hope he doesn't fall off it—and Deb and John gone all air-minded, ha-ha. Young Waveney seems to be developing a pash for you, Margot. Better look out."

Margaret smiled briefly at the waitress as her breakfast arrived.

"You're imagining things, Aunty," she returned without interest.

"Oh, no—not your Aunty Bee," said Mrs. Fillingham roguishly. "Can't mistake that little flicker of the eye when a man's smitten. Bernard seems to have lost it lately," she added tactlessly.

A dull color slowly flooded the girl's face.

"I think we'd better talk about something else, Aunty, please," she said in an expressionless tone and without raising her eyes from her plate.

"Oh, all right. But *fate attongshong*, as the French say." She turned to Mr. Lewker. "What d'you think of John Waveney? He flew you over in his plane, I hear."

"He is a very competent pilot," he responded cautiously. "I understand his war record is a very good one. As an actor, however—"

"And all actors are dangerous, Margot. Isn't that right, Mr. Lewker?"

The actor-manager, dodging the arch glance that accompanied this remark, finished his coffee and pushed back his chair preparatory to excusing himself. It was his firm conviction that badinage, even of the airiest, should be strictly forbidden at breakfast-time, and Mrs. Fillingham's waggishness was about as airy as Falstaff's. Until the after-breakfast pipe has been smoked, he felt, a man is insufficiently armored against the slings and arrows of outrageous females. Before he could escape, however, there was a rustle and swish at the door and Camille de Goursac came hurrying across the room towards their table.

The Comtesse's full but not unduly ample figure was attired in a negligee of billowing laces that sent Mrs. Fillingham's eyebrows up a good inch. But it had been carelessly put on, and the Comtesse had given scant attention to hair and complexion. Her eyes looked red round the rims, and were wide with frightened anxiety. Mr. Lewker relinquished his chair to her and she sank into it amid a waft of expensive scent.

"I have not sleep, I am so worry," she began at once, ignoring Mrs. Fillingham's attempt to greet her in polite French. "Monsieur Lewkair, you must do something. *Mon Dieu!* What may be happening up there? *C'est affreux! C'est affreux!*"

She wrung her scarlet-nailed fingers. Her tones rivaled Mrs. Fillingham's for carrying-power, and the half-dozen other people who were breakfasting in the big room were looking round enquiringly.

"Please calm yourself, Madame," boomed Lewker hastily. "There is no need, I am sure—"

"Nerves," interrupted Mrs. Fillingham. "That's your trouble, Comtesse. Can't miss your sleep without a *crease day nairves.*" She snapped her fingers imperatively. "Frawleen! Coffee for Madame here—and make it hot and strong. My pal Mona Smith always said that coffee should be hot as hell, black as night, and sweet as sin. Now you take it from me—"

The Comtesse beat her hands upon the table.

"You do not understand! I—I am at fault! I should have made him stay here. *Que faire, mon Dieu? Que faire?"*

Mr. Lewker, aware of approaching hysteria, grasped both her hands firmly.

"Attend to me, Madame," he said in French. "There is no occasion for this display. It is foolish to excite yourself in this way. I insist that you calm yourself."

His authoritative manner had its effect. The Comtesse relaxed her quivering tension a little and looked up at him piteously. In spite of the theatricality of her entrance the apprehension in her brown eyes was real enough.

"Mais voyez, Monsieur, yesterday I did not think," she moaned. "Only in the night I see what he intends. Oh, I should not have let him go!"

"You distress yourself without reason, Madame. He was determined to make this ascent, and I do not think your appeal would have stopped him. Besides, there is every likelihood that an Alpinist as competent as Léon Jacot will return in safety."

She stared at him. "But it is not of Léon that I speak, Monsieur. It is my husband. He—"

Sliding tires shrieked as a car was jerked to a halt outside the hotel. A moment later the door flew open and Deborah Jacot came in hurriedly. She wore a thick fur coat over her slacks and her fair hair was in wild disorder. She was very pale. Her brother, in flying-jacket and thick knee-boots, came in after her as she reached the table.

Deborah spoke to Mr. Lewker, her voice low but strained.

"It's Léon," she began.

A piercing shriek from Camille de Goursac interrupted her. The Comtesse was on her feet, both hands gripping at her cheeks.

"It has happened! I knew it! *Mon Dieu,* I knew it! Léon—"

"Camille—please!" Deborah said desperately.

"Will you take her upstairs?" Lewker said to Mrs. Fillingham.

She hesitated, plainly anxious to hear what had happened. Margaret took charge with swift competence.

"Take her other arm, Aunty," she commanded. "Now come along, Madame. Quickly."

Between them they got the sobbing woman to the foot of the stairs and began to help her up. Lewker looked at Deborah. She met his gaze bravely though she was obviously holding her emotions with difficulty. Her face was drawn and peaked.

"An accident," she whispered. "We saw him. It was—"

She paused, unable to continue. John, looking ten years older than his age, grasped her arm.

"Let me, Deb. Listen, sir. We'd circled the Matterhorn at fifteen thou'. Conditions were perfect—no wind at all—so I came down pretty close to the big ridge that runs down towards Zermatt and flew across it twice. No sign of Jacot. He'd have been hard to spot among those crags anyway. Then, for fun, I took the plane right down into that snow hollow under the north side of the ridge."

"The Matterhorn Glacier," supplied Mr. Lewker. John continued as though he had not spoken.

"We were about five hundred feet up. Deb shouted. She'd a pair of binoculars. There was a dark heap on the snow where it begins to slope very steeply up to the ridge. We circled and I went as low as I dared."

Deborah drew in her breath with a little hissing sound.

"It was Léon," she said tonelessly. "He must have fallen."

CHAPTER SEVEN

STRETCHER PARTY

To the reader of newspapers, if he is not himself a mountaineer, the report of a climbing accident brings a certain not unpleasant thrill. The atmosphere of romance is present: the sporting contest between man and mountain, the tremendous scenery amid which the contest is staged, the heroic efforts of the rescue party. It makes a "story." A fatal accident in the Alps will rate a quarter column in a newspaper when the thirty deaths on British roads that took place the same day will not get so much as a line. It is drama, but drama of the stirring sort; tragedy, but romantic tragedy. To the mountaineer on the spot when news of an accident is brought to the valley the tragedy is that the victims are so remote from human aid. And there is, to him, no romance in the fact that a fellow sportsman has been struck down in the pursuit of the greatest of all sports.

Mr. Lewker, who had twice before had to help in the bringing down of an injured climber, experienced again the feeling of impotence. Jacot was lying in an upper bay of the Matterhorn Glacier. He could not possibly be reached in less than four hours' hard going. It might be quite impossible to reach him at all. These thoughts crossed his mind quickly before common sense reasserted itself and told him that Jacot could not have fallen three thousand feet or more and still be alive. It was impossible. And yet the fact of his death could not be taken for granted.

He glanced round. At the other tables the breakfasters were whispering excitedly. One stout gentleman was starting to cross the room, napkin in hand, with the evident intention of getting the news from its source. Mr. Lewker grasped the elbows of brother and sister and gently urged them to the door.

"Simler's office," he murmured. "We must enlist his help."

The hotel proprietor's office was a small room with a glass-topped door leading out of the hall. Mr. Lewker led his charges to it and opened the door. Herr Simler was not there. He pulled the two inside, closed the door behind them, and pressed the button which summoned the proprietor. Then he looked keenly at Deborah, noting that she still had herself well under control—was, in fact, rather calmer than her brother, whose hands were trembling as he undid the buttons of his flying-coat.

"Forgive me, Madame," he said gently, "but I must ask you one question. Are you quite certain that it was your husband you saw? Rocks on a snow-field have often been mistaken for—"

"I'm perfectly certain," she broke in. "I wish—I wish I weren't. There was one thing that made me certain." She covered her face with her hands. "Tell him, John."

John gulped. "No mistake, sir. He had round his neck a bright red muffler that—that Deb gave him last year."

Deborah looked up quickly, her blue eyes misted with tears.

"Tell me quite frankly, Mr. Lewker," she said steadily. "Is there—any hope of his being—alive?"

"In my opinion, none. If I may presume to advise you, Madame, you should try to find comfort in the certainty that such a fall would mean instant death. But of course a party must go up to the glacier immediately. Please leave the arrangements to me."

She nodded her thanks and once more sank her head on her hands. John put an arm round her shoulders.

" 'Fraid I'm no mountaineer," he said to Lewker, "but if I can help—"

The door opened and Simler bustled in. His genial grin vanished at Lewker's first words, and the brief explanation brought not horror and dismay to his wrinkled face, but a grim alertness; for he had been a guide in his youth. He pushed a pencil and paper across the table at John.

"If you please," he said rapidly. "From above you see well where he lies. A sketch will help us."

John's shaking fingers traced a cross with a long vertical arm at the bottom.

"The summit's at the center. Here"—he drew two short lines at right angles to and on the right of the long arm—"are two rock ridges sticking out into the glacier. Mr. Lewker says it's the Matterhorn Glacier."

Simler nodded. "And the—Monsieur Jacot?"

"Here."

John made a mark with the pencil close to the vertical arm and just above the upper branch arm. Simler muttered something in German. And simultaneously Deborah Jacot gave a little moan and would have fallen to the floor if Lewker had not caught her.

"Lieber Gott, I am a fool!" exclaimed Simler. "I forget Madame. She must have restoratives."

"I'll take her up to her room." John took the limp figure from Lewker's arms and carried it towards the door. "Get some brandy, will you?"

"It shall be sent up to you at once."

Simler had barked peremptory orders into the house telephone before John and his burden had disappeared. He closed the door behind them and turned to Lewker.

"Herr Lewker. Your opinion, if you please. Is this report correct?"

"I am afraid there is no reason to doubt it." He explained how the body had been identified from the plane. "The red scarf clinches it, I think."

"So. And is Herr Waveney an accurate observer, do you think?"

"I should say his diagram is correct, if that is what you mean. He has noticed the two subsidiary ridges, as you see."

Simler grunted and frowned at John's sketch.

"You have a map?" he demanded.

Lewker pulled his map from his pocket and spread it on the table. Simler placed the diagram beside the representation of the Matterhorn and indicated, on the map, the spot John had marked on his sketch.

"Tell me from where he fell," he requested.

Mr. Lewker pursed his lips and scowled at the map.

"If the sketch is accurate," he said slowly, "he must have fallen from the ridge just below the Solvay Refuge, while he was still some distance from the Shoulder."

"So. That is what seems to me strange. For a *bergsteiger* like Monsieur Jacot that place should not have any danger. It is on the Shoulder, *mein Herr,* where Whymper's party met with accident, that one might expect trouble."

"Hum. Yet a falling stone, or *verglas* on the rocks, could have caused a slip." Lewker bent again over the map and straightened up suddenly. "We must get a party up there as quickly as possible, Simler. If he slipped there he would fall nearly the whole distance on snow and ice. There is just a chance—"

"Impossible, *mein Herr.* The Matterhorn does not give chances."

Nevertheless Simler was reaching for the telephone as he spoke. In a few seconds he was conducting one end of a conversation in rapid German. A pause ensued, and with the receiver still at his ear he turned to Lewker.

"I speak to Zimmermann at the police office. He it is who has charge of the mountain-rescue party. They are very quick. He asks that you will go with them, and any other good *bergsteiger* who is staying here."

"I will go, of course. I have only to put on my boots. I think Mr. Bryce is the only other climber staying here—"

"Ja, ja!" Simler was engaged with the phone again. In a few moments he replaced it on its stand. "All is arranged. Six men—two guides and four porters—will start in fifteen minutes with a stretcher. You have some food?"

Lewker nodded, thanked him briefly, and went in search of Bernard Bryce. There was no sign of him in the big room where breakfast was still being served, and the waitress had not seen him. Lewker hurried upstairs and knocked on the door from behind which the sound of a typewriter had come earlier that morning. There was no reply, and finding the door unlocked he went in. The room was empty. He was about to go out again when a thought struck him, and he paused to glance into wardrobe, corners and drawers. No ice-axe, boots or mountain clothing met his eye. It looked as though Bryce had gone out for the day, though it seemed odd that he had not stopped for his breakfast or ordered sandwiches from the waitress. However, he was clearly not available for the rescue party. Mr. Lewker got his own ice-axe from his room, crammed lunch, snow-glasses and a few other essentials into a small rucksack, and set off for the police office.

Half an hour later he was toiling up the bridle path that leads to the Schwarz-see, the tiny lake under the butt end of the Matterhorn's Northeast Ridge. He was at the tail of the party, and the six wiry Swiss in front of him strode in silence with the unvarying rhythmic pace of their kind. It is a deceptive pace, for it appears slow and easy and is so, when the going is smooth and the angle small; but the same slow easy stride is maintained over rough and steep ground, never pausing, never halting for breathing-space, never setting a foot out of place. It is in fact the fastest form of mountain travel, this "guide's pace," and hard is the lot of the untrained man who must yet keep up with it. Mr. Lewker, who for all his paunchiness possessed strong leg-muscles and a phenomenal endurance, was panting while their way lay still in morning shadow. By the time they had left the steep zigzags of the pine-clad lower slopes behind and were out in the sunshine of the grassy hillside above he was soaked with sweat and his calves were aching unbearably. He kept on grimly, step for step with the guides.

Perren, the senior of the two guides, set the pace, a gaunt man in tweed knickerbockers and a belted jacket, carrying his ice-axe with the long pick hooked round the back of his neck. Behind him trudged the other guide, and after him came the four porters, two of them carrying the aluminium-framed folding stretcher. At fifteen-minute intervals they handed over the stretcher to the other pair, without pausing in their stride or exchanging a word. Mr. Lewker found himself hoping that they would drop it, so that he might break, if only for a few seconds, the eternal plod. But their big brown hands made the accustomed movements without a slip.

The path brought them at last over a brow to see the placid Schwarzsee lying a little below them. The Matterhorn, almost overpowering in its majesty, soared above their heads into a sky of clearest blue, with the Northeast Ridge dividing the sunlit eastern face from the shadowed northern precipices. Perren spoke for the first time since they had left Zermatt.

"Two hours," said he. "Not good."

They skirted the shores of the lake, Mr. Lewker thanking his stars for the cessation of uphill grind. But in ten minutes they were climbing again, mounting the slopes under the little peak called the Hörnli that guards the northern end of the great ridge. The bridle path gave place to a rougher track twisting among boulders and scree. Rougher, but well marked, for along it have passed many and diverse adventurers on their way to the peak which they must climb for many different reasons; for love of the high places, for pay, to be able to boast of the feat, to prove to themselves that they could conquer fear. This way had come the first climbers of the Matterhorn, Whymper's party of seven, four of whom never came back; and this way (meditated Mr. Lewker, wiping the sweat out of his eyes) had Léon Jacot come that morning, while the rocks were still cold to the touch and the awesome ice slopes overhead were rosy with the glow of dawn. He too would never come back.

The abrupt crags of the Hörnli, close above on their right hand, fell slowly as they climbed. The path mounted steeply round a corner and gained the crest of the ridge. It was easy walking here on the broad crest, with the Matterhorn summit hidden far beyond the toppling upsurge of its buttresses, so close beneath it had they come. Snow lay here and there on the shady side of the rocks, and before long they were on a short snow-ridge sloping up to a point where the rocks rose steeply at the beginning of the ridge proper. Mr. Lewker's maneuvers as he cast from side to side for the prints of Jacot's boots attracted Perren's attention and impelled him to his second utterance of the day.

"No footmarks," he said. "When he pass, snow hard. Here," he added, "we descend."

The snow-ridge, a tiny saddle of which the Hörnli formed the crupper and the Matterhorn itself the gigantic pommel, fell away steeply on the left to the Furggen Glacier and on the right, rather less steeply, to the lower part of the Matterhorn Glacier. A long slant of snow ran down at a fairly easy angle to a narrow ledge like the tread of a stair, with a precipitous ice wall below it and above it a cliff of ice a hundred and fifty feet high poised on the top of a vertical face of rock. These two transverse breaks in the great scoop of the glacier were caused by the protruding rock ridges which John Waveney had seen from above. To reach the spot where he had seen Jacot's body they must get on to the glacier above the ice cliff.

Perren led off down the snow slope without pause. The surface, though still in shadow, was just soft enough to allow steps to be kicked, and they made rapid progress. For ten minutes there was no sound but the regular *thud-thud, thud-thud,* as the guide's boots made the holds in which each following man trod. Then, from high overhead, a report like that of a great gun sounded. The upper crags echoed and multiplied it, mingling in a kind of frightful fugue. Crash after crash, coming nearer with each report, followed. A hundred tiny wailing voices—the hum of rock fragments flying down-ward through space at tremendous speeds—made terrifying music for a few seconds. Then silence again. The party on the snow slope held on steadily; that had been a rockfall on the sun-warmed eastern precipice, no threat to them as they came closer under the frost-bound steeps of the north face.

Halfway down the snow slope Perren turned left-handed and began to traverse across it. Mr. Lewker was relieved; he had thought at first that the guide intended to force a way up the ice wall, and he could see a long shaft of sunlight resting on the crest of the wall, loosening with its warmth the icy pinnacles. Perren was making for the point where the rocky outcrop joined the steepening crags of the ridge on their left. Here the ice wall merged suddenly into a steep little ice slope, to gain the foot of which there was an easy traverse across rocks.

When they reached the ice slope Perren halted for the first time that morning, and the party tied on to the ropes both guides had carried slung across their shoulders: three men on the first rope, four on the second. This short pause was welcomed by Mr. Lewker at least, but it was very cold in the shadow of the ridge and he was actually glad when they moved on again. And now they moved less quickly. Perren, in the lead, rapidly cut small steps, which were enlarged by his followers so that a return journey with the stretcher would be possible. The rhythmic chink of the steel on ice, the slither of the fragments as they flashed down to the glacier, were like remembered music in Mr. Lewker's ears. His spirits rose, and the purpose of that morning climb was almost forgotten. Once he glanced back as he stood precariously poised on the roof-like slope, to see the chalets of Zermatt sunlit in the green valley five thousand feet below. The others, too, seemed to feel the exhilaration of high places, for they threw off their former grim silence and exchanged occasional remarks in patois.

The rim of the ice wall was directly below them now. In a few yards the angle of the ice slope eased and the surface became hard snow. Perren headed downward, kicking in his heels for hold, and led them at last on to the gently-sloping glacier above the ice wall.

"We halt here to eat a little, if you wish," he said, as Mr. Lewker came up with him.

"Would it not be better to wait until we reach the—Monsieur Jacot?" suggested Lewker. "Already the snow is getting softer."

"Perhaps you have no wish for food when you see him," the guide said grimly.

Admitting the possibility, Mr. Lewker took off his rucksack and got out his sandwiches. The Swiss did likewise. There was little conversation; neither the champagne-like air of ten thousand feet up nor the brilliance of sun and snow could remove the dark recollection that only a few hundred yards away lay the body of a man who had been killed on the great mountain that towered above them. Sandwich in hand, Mr. Lewker bent his head far back to stare up at the terrific precipices of the north face, whose detail of stone-swept gully and shelterless slabs looked ghastly through the green-tinted lenses of his snow glasses. He marveled at the mentality of the men who had forced a way up that face, a route that held no possible attraction for a mountaineer; he held, with the great mountaineers, that mountains were created for man's enjoyment, not as places where the spiritually unbalanced could obtain a dubious notoriety by displaying their contempt for life and death.

These meditations were interrupted by Perren's abrupt order to the porters to take up their burdens. The party set off again after a halt of less than ten minutes.

The passage of the ice slope had taken the better part of an hour, and the noon sun was now blazing down out of a sky of darkest blue. The surface of the snow was no longer crisp and firm; it had softened to a depth of five or six inches although the ridge above had kept it in shadow for most of the morning and had only in the last hour withdrawn its shelter. Perren, in the lead, probed with his axe as he moved slowly onward, sounding for the crevasses that might lie a few feet below the level surface. Seven tiny black dots in an immensity of white, they toiled steadily up the glacier, heading for the snowy bay at its upper left-hand end, where it merged into a great sweep of unbroken ice and snow that fell to it from the Northeast Ridge. They were

within a few hundred yards of this white precipice when the guide behind
Perren uttered a hoarse ejaculation. He pointed. Perren, halting, unslung his
rucksack and took out a Zeiss monocular. He stared through it in the direction the other had indicated and then passed it in silence to Mr. Lewker, who
had come up beside him. In the bright circle of the lens the dark heap, with
one knee stiffly upflung, was unmistakable. Mr. Lewker nodded and handed
back the monocular. They trudged on up the increasing slope towards that
dark heap.

Fifty yards from it they came upon a boot, and a few feet farther its fellow.
It is one of the grimmer jests of the mountain that it strips the feet of its
victims as they hurtle downward to death. Léon Jacot, when they reached
him, had only the remnants of stockings on his feet. His clothing was rent
into long strips, but there was no blood on the snow. He was dead, and as
stiff as a framework of steel.

Jacot's body lay under the central steeps of the great snow wall, and it was
plain that he had fallen from the crest that towered dark against the blue sky
nearly four thousand feet above. Round his neck, secured with a rather lumpy
knot, was the red muffler, its ends spread across the snow beside him like
ugly stains. Either by instinctive courtesy or from distaste, the Switzers stood
back to allow the Englishman who had known the dead man to examine the
body. Mr. Lewker knelt beside it. Jacot was dead, of course. That fall must
have killed him almost instantly. He lay on his back, his head pointing down
the slope and his face half-buried in the little pile of snow heaped up by the
last slide of his body. The limbs were stiff; the sun had not yet reached the
body.

Mr. Lewker, noticing that Jacot's hands were ungloved, looked round for
gloves and other items of equipment; he would carry a rucksack with food
and spare clothing, and of course an ice-axe. None of these were to be seen
on the smooth expanse of the glacier. There was no sign of them on the
terrific slope above, where the grooves of that swift descent could be seen
for some distance up. Odd—but of course Jacot might have discarded them
for some reason before he fell.

He turned again to the body, scraping the snow away to reveal the dark
handsome features. The face had received little injury from the fall, but it
was swollen and empurpled and the wide-open eyes protruded as though in
terror. It was not a pleasant sight, but Mr. Lewker scowled at it for a full
thirty seconds, rubbing his chin meditatively the while. Then something caught
his eye; a thin strip of color across the purple lips. He bent forward and with
his ungloved hand opened the mouth as far as its stubborn rigidity would
allow.

Perren touched him on the shoulder.

"Another climber on the ridge," he announced, pointing upward.

Mr. Lewker, craning his neck to follow the direction of the pointing finger, was in time to see a minute speck move among the rocks that jutted from the crest and disappear.

"Another fool," Perren muttered in German. "We must not stay here, *mein Herr,*" he added. "Each minute it becomes more dangerous. Already the sun begins its work."

As if to point his words, a little trickle of snow swished down the slope beside them. Its small voice was scarcely more than a breath in the vast sunlit silence, but to each of the seven mountaineers it spoke of the avalanche that might follow. The porters were already adjusting the stretcher beside the body. Mr. Lewker got to his feet and brushed the snow from his knees.

"Except to place the body on the stretcher it must not be touched, or the clothing tampered with, in any way," he said to Perren, and the guide's harsh features showed momentary surprise at the authority in the other's tone. "It must be taken to Herr Zimmermann's office as fast as you can. I shall go down with one man. You will follow with the stretcher."

Perren seemed inclined to dispute this sudden assumption of leadership, but Mr. Lewker was already unroping from the porters and giving instructions to the second guide. In two minutes he was retracing their footsteps of the morning with the second guide following on the rope.

The passage of the ice slope gave no trouble, though as they stepped off it on to soft snow Mr. Lewker felt decidedly glad that it did not fall to his lot to carry one end of a loaded stretcher across it. The long upward slant through snow that was now knee-deep, under a sun that smote down with relentless force, set the sweat running into his eyes again; but he did not slacken speed, and on the easier rocks of the ridge made a pace that caused his companion to wonder that this squat plump Englishman could move with such celerity after a grueling morning.

Zermatt shimmered in afternoon heat below them as they sped down the long path towards the scattered pines. A dozen fantastic thoughts were clamoring at Lewker's brain as he strode and twisted through the lower woods, but he refused to admit them to consideration; they must wait until the one startling fact—for fact he believed it to be—had been confirmed beyond any possible doubt. Then—but he closed his mind resolutely to the consideration of what must follow.

Parched and weary, they came at last into the sweltering lanes of Zermatt. In the cool office of the *Polizei Wache* Herr Zimmermann was dozing over a file of papers. Mr. Lewker marched in without ceremony.

"Perren follows with the body," he announced. "You can get a doctor here to examine it? Good. Please do so—it is important. I will use your telephone. Where is it?"

Zimmermann, flustered and somewhat indignant, indicated a small cabinet in the corner of the office. "But, *mein Herr,* this is not permitted. If you will tell me who—"

"I wish to speak to Herr Schultz, at Visp. I have his telephone number."

Zimmermann gasped. "Herr Schultz? The *Kriminal Kommissar?* This is not—"

But Mr. Lewker was already inside the telephone cabinet. In less than a minute he was speaking in German to the maid at the house of Herr Schultz's parents. After a short pause a guttural voice at the other end vibrated the diaphragm of the earphone.

"Herr Lewker? So. I am much pleased to speak with a friend of Sir Frederick Claybury. But I understood that you had been instructed to see me in person, not to use the telephone."

The actor-manager scowled. "Instructed." And a pomposity of tone equal to his own.

"That is true," he replied suavely. "This, however, is a matter for a Swiss policeman rather than an English tourist. Léon Jacot—"

"Names should not be mentioned," said the voice sharply.

"Indeed? I fancy this name is likely to be much mentioned in the next few days."

The voice was impressed. *"Potztausend!"* it exclaimed. "Something has happened to him?"

"Yes," said Mr. Lewker. "Murder."

CHAPTER EIGHT

HERR SCHULTZ TAKES CHARGE

"And now, sir," said Herr Schultz in measured tones, "you shall tell me why I am here."

He was a short man—no taller than Mr. Lewker—with a round head of similar baldness and a paunch of even more comfortable proportions. There, however, the resemblance in looks ended, for the *Kriminal Kommissar's* habitual expression was that of a Creator surveying his world. Moreover, he wore a gray suit of incredible smartness, in contrast to the actor-manager's worn mountaineering clothes, and a gold watch chain like a ship's anchor-cable was looped across his creaseless waistcoat. His pale and prominent eyes surveyed Mr. Lewker with severity from beneath hairless brows. Yet for all his irritating pomposity there was a certain air of efficiency about him, and he had certainly not wasted any time in reaching Zermatt.

Herr Schultz had driven from Visp in his own car. It was now six o'clock, less than two hours after Mr. Lewker's return from the Matterhorn Glacier; and the latter gentleman, partly revived after his exertions by judicious drafts of lager beer, had obtained the use of one of Simler's private rooms for his meeting with Schultz. Before complying with the Swiss police chief's request, he poured two tall glasses of lager and passed one to his companion, who took it with a murmur of thanks but without taking his eyes from Lewker.

"In the first place," began the actor-manager, "I must point out that my suspicions have as yet no official confirmation."

"I have seen Zimmermann," Schultz interposed. "The doctor was then making his examination. Zimmermann will send his report here as soon as it is ready. Explain, please, how your suspicion arose."

"Very well." Mr. Lewker sipped his lager and set it down. "Some years ago I helped to bring the body of a climber down from the snow slopes of the Lyskamm. The body had been out all night and was frozen stiff. I was struck at the time by the way in which the natural hues of life had remained in the dead face. When I came to look at the face of the late Jacot I found it swollen and purple, with the eyeballs protruding unnaturally. That struck me as odd, and caused me to look more closely. There was a thread of red material on the lips, which looked blue and bruised. I forced open the mouth, and found that the teeth and the inside of the lips were covered with fragments of red wool."

Schultz's plump white fingers tugged at his watch chain. He regarded Mr. Lewker frowningly.

"You assumed from this that the man had been murdered and then flung down from the ridge?"

"He wore a red scarf knotted around his neck. The wool in his mouth was, I believe, from the scarf. It appeared probable that he had been suffocated with his own scarf."

"Did it not occur to you that in the course of his fall the ends of the scarf might have been forced into his mouth? You will pardon me, Herr Lewker, but you have very slender evidence on which to base an assumption of murder."

This had also occurred to Lewker. Faced with this shrewd gentleman who probed so swiftly at the weak points of his theory, he felt slightly nervous. He took from his pocket the crumpled piece of paper which after some searching he had rescued from his dressing table drawer.

"There were other circumstances, among them this." He handed the note to the commissioner. "That was given to me by Madame Jacot. It was received by her husband in this hotel two days ago. She believes it to be a threat to kill him."

Schultz took a pair of tiny pince-nez from his breast pocket and propped them on his nose to read the typewritten message on the half-sheet of notepaper. He took a long time over it. Then he looked at Lewker over the top of his glasses.

"Did Madame Jacot know who sent this?"

"No. She hinted that it might have come from one of an organization called the Flambeaux, who have threatened her husband before."

He told briefly of the man Deborah had recognized on the road from Täsch, on the afternoon of his arrival, and her fear that he was following Léon Jacot with evil intent.

"I promised Madame Jacot that this should not be disclosed," he added. "Her husband was against enlisting police protection, it seems. I think the present circumstances release me from that promise."

"Natürlich." Schultz scrutinized the note again and read it aloud. " 'The path you are treading is a dangerous path. One more step, and you will not live to take another.' Herr Lewker. Did you find anything odd about this note?"

"I thought it strange that it should be in English."

"If it is a French political agent who writes to a French politician. Yes. The typewriter?"

Mr. Lewker beamed upon him. "Your department, *mein Herr*. I am not a detective."

"So?" The commissioner eyed him coldly. "Sir Frederick Claybury tells me you were once in his department of the British Secret Service. However, I can tell you that this machine was of a kind not in general use in this country. I notice also several peculiarities." He pocketed the note. "Herr Lewker, why did you telephone for me instead of reporting this matter to Zimmermann?"

"I thought it wiser. Jacot's death will have considerable repercussions in France. If this should turn out to be a political murder—"

A knock at the door heralded the entrance of the hotel proprietor. He handed an envelope to Schultz.

"This was brought by a police officer, Herr Kommissar," he said, and retired.

Schultz ripped open the envelope and read the message it contained.

"So," he nodded. "You were correct in your inference. The doctor finds that Jacot died from suffocation. You were perfectly right to telephone for me."

"Thank you," responded Mr. Lewker gravely.

"I shall take charge of the case myself. Zimmermann is efficient, but un-imaginative, and I have no wish to bring detectives from Basle. This murder, sir, may be a matter of international importance. Until we have brought home the guilt to the criminal it must be kept quiet. I shall telephone the Federal Government to this effect. They will doubtless give me the O.K."

Mr. Lewker, startled by this concluding phrase, saw that Herr Schultz believed himself to be using a correct English idiom. He smothered a grin in his glass of lager.

"I hope I can rely upon you to assist me in my investigations," added the commissioner.

Mr. Lewker choked. He had not anticipated this invitation.

"I am an actor, *mein Herr*, not a policeman," he observed with some hauteur.

"I am aware of it." Schultz became suddenly affable. "The name of Abercrombie Lewker is well known. On the English stage you are the big noise. But also I know, from Sir Frederick, of your other gifts. I ask for your cooperation. For you it should be interesting to watch my methods—and, of course, to assist me with your own suggestions. I cannot demand your help, but you may consider you have cause to find the murderer of Léon Jacot, *nicht wahr*?"

Mr. Lewker did not at once reply. Schultz was right, in a sense, however tactlessly he might phrase his invitation. For Lewker had undertaken, in no very serious spirit, to watch for any attempt on Jacot's life. Deborah Jacot could hardly blame him that the attempt had been made and had succeeded, but he could not rid himself of a feeling of responsibility. Besides, the thing had its attractions.

Insensibly he found himself looking at it in terms of the dramatic. The stage was nicely set: the French climber-politician—not particularly to be lamented—murdered on the Matterhorn; the hint of a political gang at work; the charming ex-actress wife, now a widow; the Swiss Crime Commissioner himself enlisting the aid of the English amateur. By all the rules the English amateur's was the fattest part. Could he cast himself for that part? Mr. Lewker's professional pride rose in him.

"The case," he boomed weightily, "has points. I shall accept your suggestion."

Herr Schultz nodded as though he had fully expected it.

"Gut," he said. "Your assistance may prove of greater value than you think. You are, I believe, a mountaineer. I am not. You will understand that although deaths upon the mountains are not rare in my district, a murder on a mountain is distinctly rare. Technical points may arise in the investigation upon which I should be stymied, as you say."

"No, no," murmured Mr. Lewker deprecatingly.

"But yes, sir. For instance, you may have climbed the Matterhorn yourself."

"I have. By the Northeast Ridge."

"On which Jacot was killed. Therefore you have special knowledge of the locality of the murder, the difficulties to be encountered by the murderer, the times involved. What is more, you, a competent observer, first examined the body before it was moved." Herr Schultz leaned forward impressively. "Now think carefully, Herr Lewker. Was it at all possible that this body could have been *placed* where it was? That the murder took place, not on the ridge, but on the glacier?"

The question struck Mr. Lewker as somewhat pointless, but he answered it meticulously.

"I would say highly improbable. The signs in the slope above, the boots torn off, the ripped clothing, all point to a fall. No doubt the doctor who examined the body could confirm that from its condition."

"We shall ask him to do so." Herr Schultz produced from the breast pocket of his perfectly fitting suit, as if by magic, an enormous notebook. "Very well. Let us descend to brass nails. Afterwards you will, I hope, dine with me. I have arranged to stay here for a few nights. You shall tell me, please, all you know of the circumstances surrounding Jacot's murder. When was this solitary ascent first proposed?"

Ten minutes later he laid down his pen and sat back in his chair.

"So. We have then a clear story of Léon Jacot's intentions." He adjusted his pince-nez and picked up the notebook, peering over the top of it at Mr. Lewker as he read out his notes. "The Matterhorn was said by the guides to be unsafe. Jacot, who had come here with the intention of climbing it, was impatient—his wife tells us that, and his own speech confirms it. On the night of your arrival, Saturday, he talked of climbing it on Monday in any case—Frau Fillingham's statement. At lunch on Sunday, according to Jacot's words, he informed the Comte de Goursac that he would climb the Matterhorn alone next day. On Sunday evening he repeated this to several people in your presence, and it is probable that others in the hotel overheard him. He said he had arranged to be called at two and although most of the party attempted to dissuade him he held to his decision. You yourself were awakened by the porter calling Jacot and informing him that it was two o'clock, and heard Jacot getting up."

He paused interrogatively. Mr. Lewker nodded.

"You see what we have there?" enquired the commissioner with relish. "Jacot had been talking of this projected ascent for at least twenty-four hours beforehand. One cannot doubt that such talk would be reported outside the hotel."

"So that although the mysterious gentleman who is feared by Madame Jacot may not have been in Zermatt, the news could have reached him."

"That is what I mean, sir. Allow me to continue. Jacot, then, left this hotel shortly after two. An assumption, but it can be confirmed by the servant who let him out. How long, in your estimation, would it take him to reach the spot whence he fell?"

"He claimed to be a fast climber. I should say at least four hours, at most five."

"So." Schultz picked up the doctor's report. "This doctor is a man of caution. The conditions in which the body was lying, he says, prevent him from estimating accurately the time of death. Certainly not more than sixteen hours before examination, certainly not less than ten. Bah!"

He threw down the paper and returned to his notebook. Mr. Lewker ventured another comment.

"The examination was made at five o'clock, I see. That gives us a time of death between one o'clock in the morning and seven. But we can fix it more closely."

"Please. I come to that now. You tell me Madame and her brother left here at about half-past five to make a trip in Herr Waveney's *flieger*. At eight, or just before, they return with their story of seeing the body. *Gut*. We may allow an hour at least for the return of the plane from the neighborhood of the glacier, the landing, the journey by car from Täsch. They saw the body, then, within a few minutes of seven o'clock. Jacot, therefore, was killed before seven. And, taking your estimate as approximately correct, Jacot could not have reached the fatal spot on the ridge before six. Inference, a strong probability that he was killed between six and seven o'clock this morning."

He threw down the notebook and removed his pince-nez with the air of a professor demonstrating the first proposition of Euclid to a backward pupil. Mr. Lewker registered respectful admiration.

"Excellent," he approved. "But—does that get us very much further?"

Herr Schultz looked slightly contemptuous. *"Natürlich.* We have now to prove two more things. First, that the man of the Täsch road, the man feared by Madame Jacot, could have been at that place on the ridge between six and seven this morning. Second, that it was he who typed the threatening note."

Mr. Lewker considered that this was too great a simplification; but he kept the thought to himself. He remembered that the shadowy background that lingered disturbingly in his mind was not known to Herr Schultz. The thoughts that had troubled him as he hurried down the path from the Schwarzsee, the confusion of scenes he had witnessed and words he had heard spoken— scarcely more than personal impressions—might have nothing to do with Jacot's murder. There was a clear line to follow and nothing to gain by introducing these irrelevancies—yet, at any rate.

He reached out and pressed the bell-push at the side of his chair.

"You will take another glass?" he enquired affably.

"If you please," replied the commissioner abstractedly, without looking up from his notes. "This climb, it requires a good mountaineer?"

"It is not at all difficult under good conditions. But a man who attempted it alone, even as far as the place where Jacot was killed, in doubtful conditions, would have to be a competent climber."

The waiter came in and took Lewker's order. When he had gone Schultz continued.

"You saw this man of the Täsch road. Would you say he was a climber?"

"He carried an ice-axe, at least."

"So. We may, perhaps, allow ourselves to conjecture. This man starts out before Jacot, knowing that he intends an ascent that day. He reaches a spot as high as it is safe for him to go. He waits there, hidden in the rocks, until Jacot approaches. Then—"

"Then," interrupted Mr. Lewker, frowning, "instead of braining him with a rock, or merely pushing him over, he suffocates him with his own scarf. I wonder why?"

Schultz, displeased at this comment, was about to make some rejoinder when Lewker, recalling that tattered body on the snow slope, remembered also another detail. He told of the climber they had seen on the ridge above.

"This is important," snapped Schultz. "At what time was this?"

"About one o'clock."

"You are certain you saw someone?"

"Perren, the guide, saw him also. However, it is unlikely to prove important."

Schultz raised hairless brows.

"Why is it unlikely? It was, you say, not the day for an ascent of the Matterhorn. Yet here is a climber on the ridge, at the very spot of the murder."

"At least five hours after it had been committed."

"*Ja whol.* But there may be a reason." Herr Schultz leaned forward impressively, pale eyes glinting. "Let us suppose that the murderer had to make certain that the body was discovered, and waited for that. Or—"

Simler came in, carrying two bottles of lager with an apologetic air.

"Herr Doktor Greatorex is here," he said to Lewker, as he placed the bottles on the table. "He asks to see you, *mein Herr.*"

"I thought he had gone to Breuil," Lewker observed. "Did he not cross the Théodule after all?"

"*Ja.* But today he returned over the Matterhorn."

The commissioner sat up with a jerk.

"So," he exclaimed. "I think, Simler, we will ask the Herr Doktor to join us here. You have another glass?"

The hotel proprietor brought a glass from a cupboard in the corner and went out again. Schultz turned to Mr. Lewker.

"Here, perhaps, is your man on the ridge. Tell me, Herr Lewker, who is this Greatorex?"

Lewker hesitated before replying. Certain words of Lawrence Greatorex, spoken two nights ago, echoed unpleasantly in his mind. Oddly as they seemed to connect with the death of Jacot, however, they appeared too insignificant to mention.

"Lawrence Greatorex is a mountaineer staying here on holiday," he replied. "I knew him fifteen years ago."

"A good *bergsteiger*?"

"I believe so. He has been climbing with Bernard Bryce, who is also staying here."

"You know of no connection between Greatorex and the man of the Täsch road?"

Mr. Lewker could not repress a grin at the eagerness in Schultz's tone. Before he could reply Lawrence Greatorex had entered the room. The bearded doctor had substituted slippers for his climbing boots, but had not changed the patched tweed jacket and breeches in which he had been climbing. The sun had caught his beak-like nose and blistered it severely. He threw a sharp glance at Schultz and addressed himself to Lewker.

"Is it true that Jacot's been killed on the Matterhorn?"

"I am afraid so. The body was brought down this afternoon. Er—this is Herr Schultz, a friend of mine from Visp."

Greatorex gripped the hand extended to him by the suddenly genial Commissioner, but he did not smile back. His square-cut face was grim, and beneath the bristle of black beard his mouth was tightly set.

"You are the *Kriminal Kommissar,* I understand," he said abruptly. "Does that mean there was some funny business about Jacot's death?"

Schultz gave a fair imitation of surprised amusement. "My dear Herr Doktor! Why should you think—"

"Oh, don't tell me if you'd rather not." He sank wearily into a chair. "Only that Fillingham woman's spreading the rumor. She saw you drive up and hurry in to secret conference with Lewker. She found out who you were from the waiter."

"Potztausend!" The Swiss lost some of his geniality. "This rumor must be stopped. Herr Doktor, I must insist that you mention the matter to no one. Has this Frau Fillingham spoken to others?"

"Don't know. She popped her head out of her room as I was passing and told me. Haven't seen anyone else since I came in."

"She will be in her room now?"

"Probably. That was a few minutes ago only."

"I shall send up a note." Schultz got up hurriedly and went to a writing-table by the window. "Pardon me for one moment."

Lewker poured a glass of lager and handed it to Greatorex. Then he gave the doctor a brief account of the finding of the body, omitting, however, any mention of his suspicions or the way in which they had been aroused, Greatorex listening attentively, frowning.

"I see," he said when Lewker had finished. "Well—won't pretend I'm sorry. He was a nasty piece of work. But I can't see Jacot falling from that place on the ridge."

Schultz, who had returned with a sealed envelope in his hand, overheard him.

"You descended that ridge yourself, Herr Doktor. It was not dangerous?"

"Not for a climber like Jacot. Look here, what's the mystery? Did somebody push him off?"

"We can answer that when we have more information." He rang the bell and seated himself in the armchair. "You yourself may be able to help us. You traversed the Matterhorn today—alone?"

"I crossed to Breuil yesterday. An Italian climber I'm acquainted with was on the point of leaving with his guide to climb the mountain by the Italian ridge. He invited me to join them. We went up to the hut that evening. This morning we reached the summit rather late—about nine o'clock. I examined what I could see of the Northeast Ridge and found it to be in better condition than I expected. I decided to descend by it. The others returned by the Italian ridge."

"So," purred Herr Schultz. "Then you took four hours to descend to the spot from which Jacot fell?"

Greatorex set down the glass he had been raising to his lips. His face darkened.

"What the devil are you getting at?" he demanded angrily. "How should I know where Jacot fell from?"

"Your pardon, Herr Doktor." Schultz did his best to look apologetic. "I forget you do not know. A climber was observed on the ridge about the time the stretcher party reached the body."

"Oh. That would be me, I dare say. I took my time coming down—no one else up there—and spotted a biggish party on the Matterhorn Glacier when I was some distance below the Shoulder. Looked as though they were stopping for lunch. Didn't give much thought to it, except to think it was a damn silly place to have lunch." He turned to Mr. Lewker. "That'd be you and the guides?"

"Yes," nodded the actor-manager. He was beginning to feel that it was time for the gifted amateur to put a pertinent question or two. "Did you by any chance see any traces of a struggle at the place where you paused to look down at us?"

The entrance of a waiter prevented a reply. Herr Schultz handed the envelope to him with instructions to deliver it to Frau Fillingham instantly. When the man had gone Greatorex stood up slowly.

"I disliked Léon Jacot," he said, scowling down at Schultz. "I disliked him enough to have pushed him off that ridge if I'd met him. If you're thinking I did push him off, you'd better think again."

"My dear Herr Doktor—"

"I reached the place where Lewker saw me some time between noon and two o'clock," the other went on heavily. "I saw no sign of a struggle or anything else out of the ordinary. I made a long halt for lunch a little farther down the ridge. I arrived in Zermatt about half an hour ago. The Fillingham's bit of gossip was the first I heard of Jacot's death. Sorry I can't be exact about times and all that—I believe detectives require every detail, however insignificant. Anything else I can tell you?"

"No—no, I think not." Schultz tugged nervously at his watch-chain. "You understand, Herr Doktor—"

But Greatorex was already outside the door. Herr Schultz looked at Mr. Lewker.

"That is a young man of quick temper," he observed. "Do you know, Herr Lewker, why he should dislike so intensely the dead man?"

"I have no idea."

The commissioner began to write in his notebook.

"I do not see," continued Lewker thoughtfully, "how he can have had anything to do with Jacot's death. If he reached the summit from the Italian side at nine o'clock, Jacot's murder was taking place on the Northeast Ridge while Greatorex was still some way down on the south side."

"I am aware of it." Schultz closed his notebook with a snap and stowed it away in his pocket. "Nevertheless, we have only his word for that."

"That can be checked. We can doubtless obtain confirmation from the Italian climber who was with him."

"Doubtless. And that may yet be necessary."

Mr. Lewker shifted impatiently in his chair.

"To me," he said, "the appearance of Greatorex on the ridge seems an irrelevant coincidence, at this stage. Your line, surely, is to find and interrogate this unknown man of whom Madame Jacot is afraid."

"Natürlich," replied Schultz tolerantly. "However, at this stage we take note of all such circumstances, especially when they are pushed, as one says, beneath our noses. But it is true what you say. We must find this mysterious gentleman of the Täsch road. Since he was walking towards Täsch in the late afternoon, it is possible that he is staying there or in one of the villages farther down the valley. After dinner we shall drive there in my car to enquire."

"If he is the murderer, he may be out of the district by this time."

"In such case he will not get far. You can describe him, I think?"

Lewker nodded. "I believe so. Madame Jacot could probably make a better shot at it."

"Good. Ah, Simler, I have a favor to ask. You can serve our dinner in here, privately?"

The hotel proprietor, who had entered silently, bowed and grinned his tooth-less grin.

"I anticipated it, *mein Herr.* It is ready to be served."

"Excellent. We will dine at once, if you please."

Simler departed. Herr Schultz, tugging at his watch chain, regarded Lewker meditatively.

"You were entrusted with a confidential enquiry, I think," he said. "It was on behalf of your Department Seven. This much only I know, but I can guess the nature of the enquiry. One might say that the information you obtained is now valueless to your Government, *hein?*"

Mr. Lewker shrugged his shoulders. "In any case, I had so far failed to discover Jacot's political leanings."

"From this typewritten note, however, and the murder of Jacot, one is led to believe that someone had discovered them with an absolute certainty."

"The Flambeaux, you mean? The Anti-Communists?"

"Or," said Herr Schultz softly, "the other side."

The door opened to admit their dinner.

CHAPTER NINE

THE OBVIOUS SUSPECT

Like most mountain-dwelling nations, the Swiss have a very highly devel-oped clan spirit. For a distinguished English guest Simler would have pro-vided a dinner as good as any to be found in Zermatt; for the distinguished visitor of his own nationality he served a dinner such as any hotel in postwar Europe could hardly have surpassed.

Herr Schultz, thawing with the first spoonful of soup, observed that it would amount to sacrilege to talk business over such a meal. Instead, he delivered a lecture to his companion on the subject of English detective nov-els. He was one of those conversationalists who consider that conversation is at its best when one man talks and the rest listen; always assuming that the talker would be himself. He had, however, a remarkable knowledge of the innumerable cases of Lord Peter Wimsey, Inspector Alleyn, Mr. Fortune and Hercule Poirot. Mr. Lewker, whose readings in detective fiction were limited to such of the stories as had been converted into drama, accepted his role of listener with resignation if not with contentment. He was as a rule a bad listener, but he considered himself to be, at the moment, studying his part as the Amateur Detective Who Makes Good In The End.

With the Benedictine and cigars the commissioner was still holding forth.

"The reader of these tales, Herr Lewker, may perform his own detection in two ways. He may make his deductions from the evidence provided for the fictional detective, or he may make them from the way in which the author treats his fictional suspects. The crudest and most obvious example of this latter method is to choose the person who is most unlikely. That is to say, the character whom the author is striving to pillow up——"

"Bolster," murmured Mr. Lewker involuntarily, but Herr Schultz did not hear him.

"——with all sorts of tricks of characterization as well as with apparently unbreakable alibis. An author who really dislikes the character he intends to reveal as the murderer will often give himself away. As for these ingenious alibis that are broken at the eleventh hour, they are rare in actual criminal practice."

"Yet there have been cases," began Mr. Lewker.

"Rare exceptions." Schultz waved them away with his cigar. "In real life, when we have before us a suspect who is the most likely person, he is usually the murderer. We do not find our murderers very subtle, I assure you. A trained mind, assisted by an efficient police force with modern resources at its command, has little difficulty——"

There was a click and a rustle, and Deborah Jacot had entered the room. She was wearing a plain black gown that emphasized the pallor of her piquant face with its crown of pale gold.

"This is Madame Jacot," Lewker murmured, getting to his feet.

Schultz rose and bowed stiffly. "Madame, you should not distress yourself by——"

"I'm all right, thank you." She came quickly to Lewker. "Is it true? Mrs. Fillingham said that there's something wrong about—about Léon's death."

Lewker glanced at the commissioner, who frowned and tugged at his watch-chain.

"It is true, Madame, that there are certain curious circumstances," be began.

"He was murdered, then," she said very quietly. "It was in my mind before. Mr. Lewker knows why. You've told him?" she added to Lewker.

He nodded gravely. Deborah swung round to face the police chief, her hands clenched and her body tense.

"Listen," she said in a voice that quivered with repressed emotion. "I know who you are—that you're here to investigate my husband's death. I'm certain in my own mind why he was killed—and by whom. It was that gang, the people who call themselves the Flambeaux, who've been threatening Léon."

"You say you are certain, Madame?"

"Absolutely." She was plainly controlling herself with difficulty. "You see, Léon was already in touch with agents of the Soviet. He was going to throw the weight of his new party on the extreme Left, if that's what you call it."

"He told you this?"

"Yes. One night when he'd had too much to drink. I was lying when I told Mr. Lewker I didn't know what his intentions were."

Schultz ceased to pull at his watch chain and regarded her keenly.

"I see. This shall be investigated. But—"

"Oh, I know," she said bitterly. "You'll have to take statements, ask us all questions and so on. We're all under suspicion, perhaps."

"My dear Madame!" Schultz was shocked. "Permit me to assure you—"

"Well, I'll tell you this now. I'd no cause to love my husband. He was a brute to me. And I'm the one that benefits by his death—all his money comes to me."

Deborah's voice was rising hysterically. She shook off the restraining hand Mr. Lewker laid on her arm.

"That's what you always look for, isn't it? Even when the person couldn't have had anything to do with the—the killing?" She seemed to control herself, and went on speaking through tightly clenched teeth. "I'm sorry. Anyway, I want Léon's murderer found. I want him hanged, or guillotined, or whatever they do. If I can help, with money—a reward, or—or—"

Her voice broke suddenly. She dragged a handkerchief from the neck of her dress and pressed it against her trembling lips.

"I was not—a good wife to him," she mumbled piteously.

"And now—and now—"

She turned and almost ran from the room. Herr Schultz caught Lewker's eye and coughed in some embarrassment. He was plainly impressed with Deborah's charm (or her tears) but anxious to retain his cold analytical manner.

"So," he said with an appearance of briskness. "Here is additional evidence. What do you make of the lady, my friend?"

Mr. Lewker grinned inwardly at this admission to the commissioner's friendship; it was, he suspected, due to Benedictine and emotion. He relit his cigar, which had gone out.

"Deducing on the lines of your fiction reader, we have now two more suspects. Greatorex, who admits he hated Jacot, seems to possess an alibi. Deborah Jacot benefits considerably by the death of her husband, and she could not possibly have killed him—which makes her even more suspect. Fictionally, of course."

"We will leave the question of fiction, if you please," said Schultz coldly. "This unfortunate lady will hardly be telling us fictions, I think. We learn from her that her husband was leaning very much towards the politics of Communism. If, as she suspects, the man of the Täsch road is an agent of the Flambeaux, here is one more little nail in his coffin. For no doubt the Flambeaux possess reliable sources of information. They would know that Léon Jacot was negotiating with Soviet agents."

Mr. Lewker rubbed his chin—gently, for the morning's work on the glacier had resulted in a sore face despite his precautions with glacier cream.

"It sounds," he boomed, "too efficient."

"How so?"

"I will concede that a political gang might include fanatics who would be ready to kill in such a case. But such fanatics almost invariably prefer a machine-gun or a revolver, a fusillade from a window or an attack point-blank in a crowded street. They are city rats to a man, in my experience. To send an agent into the Alps on the somewhat unlikely chance of getting Jacot alone on a mountain and faking an accident—that is out of their repertoire."

"Yet, my friend, you say this murder was efficient."

"It was. The staff work was perfect. The news of Jacot's intentions is picked up with surprising quickness by the murderer. He makes an efficient plan at once. He gets somehow to that high point on the ridge without Jacot suspecting his presence—which argues an efficient mountaineer. The murder is done efficiently also, if we consider that the murderer could not foresee that I"— Mr. Lewker tried to look modest—"would be one of those who went up to find the body. Had I not seen it, there would almost certainly have been another death by accident on the list of the Matterhorn."

Schultz was politely contemptuous. "You make much out of nothing here. Political agents may be efficient. Murders may be committed because the opportunity offers itself. This is of that kind."

Mr. Lewker crushed the end of his cigar into an ashtray.

"I sincerely hope that you are right," he said seriously.

"But you doubt it?"

" 'Modest doubt,' " quoted the actor-manager, " 'is called The beacon of the wise.' And there is one thing that puzzles me about this murder."

Schultz smiled tolerantly. "Only one, my friend?"

"One peculiar circumstance, let me call it. Why was Léon Jacot stifled to death with his own scarf? Why not kill him with a lump of rock, or even his own ice-axe? Either would have produced the effect of being hit by a falling stone—a perfectly possible accident. Or, again, why not simply push him over the edge?"

"These matters," explained the commissioner kindly, "usually prove simple of explanation. I myself can suggest one reason. What color is Jacot's scarf? Red. Assume that it is the agent of the Flambeaux who waits on the ridge. He is doubtless a fanatical type, a hater of Communism. Remember he comes to murder Jacot because the man is turning to Communism. He sees the red scarf as his victim approaches. In his warped mind, heated by the intention of murder, the color appears as a symbol. It shall be, he decides, that same hateful color that ends the life of this man. Does not that ring the bells?"

"It is ingenious," Mr. Lewker admitted.

The commissioner allowed himself a satisfied smile. He flung his cigar into a brass bowl and stood up, brushing the gray ash from his waistcoat with finical care.

"Come. There is no need of this amateur psychology for us who have facts to deal with. A suspicious character, a threatening letter in keeping with the suspicious character, a murder in keeping with both. You shall see that so close a sequence will end in a dull arrest."

Obediently Mr. Lewker, having obtained coat and scarf from his room, followed the commissioner out of the hotel. The only persons in the hall as they passed through were Mrs. Fillingham and John Waveney, the former flushed with excitement and the latter with wine, if the quarter-full bottle of Simler's Johannisberger on the table before him was anything to go by. John half-rose as if to intercept them, but Mrs. Fillingham clamped a large hand on his arm and made him sit down again.

Schultz's big Packard rolled them smoothly out of Zermatt, unwinding the coils of the descending road up which Deborah had driven Mr. Lewker two days ago. The little Swiss was of those who dislike talking when they are at the wheel of a car, and his passenger was occupied with his own thoughts. The silver beam of the powerful headlights, probing the powder-blue shadows ahead, swung a changing perspective of wayside chalets, pine woods and rocky corners before his eyes; but they seemed the creations of a dream. More real than these, though unseen because it was always behind him, was the immense presence of the Matterhorn. The mountain brooded over that valley like an idol of rock and stone carved by elemental spirits, thought Mr. Lewker. It was Sphinxlike in its vast inscrutability, and like the Sphinx it seemed to smile contemptuously, guarding its secrets. The resting-place of Lord Francis Douglas's body, fallen from the ridge nearly a century ago, was still the Matterhorn's secret. And the identity of the murderer of Léon Jacot—was that to be another? Or would it be, as Schultz appeared to think, solved by a mere enquiry at a hotel?

As he had told the commissioner, Mr. Lewker hoped that the murder would indeed prove to be the work of some political fanatic. He had not allowed himself to think of the slight but disturbing signs that had come to his notice during his brief stay at the Hotel Obergabelhorn, like eddies on the surface of a river showing the strong currents beneath. He had joined Schultz in treating the matter as a sort of after-dinner problem, voicing only his puzzlement at the manner in which the murder had been committed. But in his bones he felt that there was something wrong with Schultz's theory. Well, they would soon see, if the man Deborah had been afraid of was still staying at one of the hotels in Täsch or Randa or St. Niklaus. The murderer, if he was the murderer, could very reasonably assume that Jacot's death would pass as an accident. He would be more likely to stay on for a day or two than to leave immediately after his crime. Come to think of it, the man of the Täsch road had looked not at all unlike the type that produces political fanatics. That disproportionately large brow, those brilliant eyes—

Mr. Lewker had a sudden irrational feeling that the Matterhorn was grinning at him behind his back. He twisted round in his seat. But the great peak was invisible, hidden by the towering walls of the valley that rose black against the pale stars.

The Packard twisted its way through the narrows of the gorge and emerged into the starlit amphitheater whose center was the village of Täsch. Herr Schultz brought the car to a standstill in front of the largest of the three hotels, the Täschhorn.

"You have found a gold fountain pen lying in the road between here and Zermatt," he said as they got out. "The only tourist you had passed was— and here you shall give your description. So you come to Täsch to find him and return the pen he must have dropped. That will serve our purpose, I think?"

Mr. Lewker said that it would. They went together into the brilliantly lit foyer and found a polite and intelligent gentleman anxious to help them. Mr. Lewker told his story. The intelligent gentleman whipped a ledger from a shelf and ran a forefinger down the list of his guests. There was one young Englishman who might, he thought, answer the description; he had a forehead most intellectual, hair brown, eyes very bright, complexion sallow. He was in the lounge now, if they would wait a moment. In a few minutes a lanky and spectacled young man was brought to them. His first syllable proclaimed Oxford to the world; he was frightfully sorry he hadn't lost a gold pen, must have been some other bloke.

The manager, regretting that none of his other guests resembled the description, bowed them out.

"So," nodded Schultz undismayed. "If at the first we do not command success, try, try again—that is English wisdom. We will try at the Weisses Kreuz."

The Weisses Kreuz was only a few yards away, a smaller and older hostelry depending (Lewker guessed) on the Swiss rather than tourists for its custom. Its lace-curtained windows, with the orange-yellow light streaming out on to the darkness, looked welcoming. As they entered its carved-wood portals Franz, the young Swiss who had taken charge of John Waveney's plane, came forward to meet them. He recognized Mr. Lewker with a pleasant smile, but his squarish bronze face, whose faint wrinkles were those of laughter, looked worried. The actor-manager, remembering what he had seen and heard of Lisse Taugwalder, thought he knew the reason. He retold the story of the fountain pen.

"Pale, dark, big front of head, shining eyes," said Franz thoughtfully. "*Ja*—it is much like Monsieur Frey, who stays here. He is an *alleingänger*—he walks on the mountains alone."

"He is a Frenchman?" demanded Schultz sharply.

Franz turned his blue eyes slowly to meet Schultz's gaze. Mr. Lewker caught a fleeting glimpse of emotion in them—surprise, or, perhaps, fear.

"You are the *Kriminal Kommissar*, are you not, *mein Herr*? I hope there is nothing wrong?"

Herr Schultz was condescendingly affable. He leaned across the counter of the hotel office.

"I see I need not make pretence with you, Herr Imboden. I am Schultz of the Criminal Bureau. You will, of course, treat my visit as confidential. Herr Lewker's story was a fiction, to assist me in tracing this Monsieur Frey. I wish to put certain questions to him. Is he in the hotel now?"

"He is," Franz replied. "In bed."

"Indeed? He retires early, it seems."

"He has a sprained ankle," explained Franz. "He was descending from the Täschalp in the twilight last evening when he slipped on the path. Fortunately he was able to reach the hotel, in an exhausted state. We have a doctor staying here who attended to him."

The commissioner's plump features lost some of their affability.

"I must see this injured gentleman," he announced. "Please take us to his room, Herr Imboden."

Franz hesitated a moment. Then he nodded.

"Very well, *mein Herr*. Follow me, please."

"One moment," said Schultz suddenly. "Is there a typewriter in your hotel?"

"No. We are old-fashioned here, *mein Herr*."

"Perhaps one of your guests uses one?"

"So far as I know, none of my guests has brought one with him. Aufdenblatten at the Täschhorn has one, if you wish to use it—"

"No, no. Please take us to Monsieur Frey's room."

Franz led them up a wide staircase to the first floor. At a door half-way along the carpeted passage he paused and tapped gently. An irritable voice answered in bad German, demanding to know what was wanted.

"Two gentlemen are anxious to speak with you," said Franz, prompted by Herr Schultz. "It is urgent, Monsieur."

The voice bade them come in if they must. Franz pushed open the door and they followed him into the room. A bed-side lamp, the only illumination, revealed the sallow features and brilliant eyes of the man Lewker had seen trudging behind the herd of goats, the man of whom Deborah Jacot had been afraid. He was lying in bed propped on pillows, reading. As they came in he laid down the book and frowned at the newcomers.

"I do not know you, I think?" he said in ungracious tones.

"C'est vrai, Monsieur," nodded Schultz. His French was execrable, but he continued to speak it throughout the interview. "We give ourselves the pleasure of making your acquaintance." He turned to Franz. "Thank you, Herr Imboden."

Rather reluctantly, thought Mr. Lewker, Franz went out and closed the door. Schultz stepped to the side of the bed, unbuttoning his dust-coat.

"I am desolated to force myself upon you thus, Monsieur," he said in his suavest tones, "and I assure you I would not do so if it were not a part of my duty."

"Who the devil are you?" demanded the other petulantly. "I'm not feeling well, and I don't like—"

"I am Schultz, Commissioner of Police. You may refuse to talk to me if you wish, but I should advise you, Monsieur Frey, to help me by answering one or two questions."

So far as Mr. Lewker could see in the uncertain light of the reading lamp, the man in bed gave no sign of apprehension. He merely looked weary and increasingly irritable.

"I'll answer anything I can," he said flatly. "Ask away and go as soon as you can."

"Very well. Your name is Frey?"

"I thought you knew that. I am Baptiste Frey, of Paris, aged thirty, French citizen, profession, lecturer in physics."

"You are a member of the society calling itself the Flambeaux?" Schultz continued without altering his tone.

Frey's eyes flickered quickly from Schultz to Lewker. His thick lips curled in a sneer.

"The clever police know everything," he said. "I do not deny that. I am proud of it."

"Ah." Schultz's watch-chain clicked beneath his jerking fingers. It was plainly an effort for him to turn his questioning into a more oblique channel.

"You were descending from the Täschalp, close above this village, when you hurt your ankle."

"I was."

"That was last night, I understand. At what hour?"

Frey shrugged impatiently. "Nine o'clock—perhaps later. I did not look at my watch to see what time I hurt myself. The pain was intense—"

"Yes, yes. But you managed to get down by yourself?"

"Very slowly. I could only drag myself along and I met no one to help me, until I was nearly at the hotel."

"And you reached here—when?"

The Frenchman twisted his body resentfully and winced as he did so.

"What the devil is this?" he demanded with sudden suspicion. "What am I supposed to have done? How do I know what time it was—I, who was in pain and exhausted?"

"Before midnight or after?" persisted Schultz.

"You can ask the Scottish doctor, Macrae," said Frey sullenly. "I am tired of your questions. I have nothing to fear from you."

"No?" Schultz contrived to sound both suave and sinister. "If that is so, Monsieur, you will perhaps answer me one more question. You are acquainted with Léon Jacot?"

For the first time Frey looked startled. He hesitated before replying.

"I once visited him in Paris," he said at last. "It was in a matter of business."

"Monsieur Jacot was interested in physics, perhaps," nodded the commissioner with heavy irony. "You also know Madame Jacot?"

"No. I—" Frey stopped suddenly and his brilliant eyes swung round to fix themselves on Mr. Lewker. "That's it!" he said with animation. "You were in the car with her. I was unable to remember, then, where I had seen her before. It was in Jacot's flat, the merest glimpse."

"You saw her in Geneva also," Schultz put in sharply.

"I have never been to Geneva."

"May I examine your typewriter, Monsieur?"

Frey jabbed his elbows into the mattress, thrusting himself upwards with the energy of rage.

"Dix mille diables!" he snarled. "I am pestered by lunatics, I think! Jacot—Geneva—typewriters—what in the name of God are you talking about? I have no typewriter—search the room—anything you like! I answer no more questions until you explain to me—but no!" he was working himself into a passion. "Explain nothing. Only get out. Get out, do you hear!"

"Monsieur!" rapped Schultz angrily. "Léon Jacot has—"

The bedroom door flew open and a little red-faced man bounded in. He bristled like a terrier and his shaggy red mustache was so aggressive that Mr.

Lewker half expected its wiry hairs to discharge themselves like darts. Behind him Franz lurked, manifestly apprehensive.

"Oot o' here, the two o' ye!" barked the newcomer. "Oot ye go before I throw ye oot!"

The commissioner swelled like a bullfrog. *"Potztausend!"* he fulminated. "Do you know who I am, sir?"

"No, and I dinna care. I'm Dr. Macrae, and this is my patient ye're exciting. Oot wi' ye, now!"

Mr. Lewker thought it time to put in his word.

"I assure you, doctor, we intended no harm to your patient. This is Herr Schultz, of the Criminal Bureau in Basle. He—"

"I dinna care if he's Auld Hornie himsel'. Oot wi' ye!"

Schultz controlled himself and spoke suavely.

"I leave immediately, *Herr Doktor*, if you yourself will answer one question."

Dr. Macrae had pushed Frey back on his pillows, none too gently, and was already taking his pulse.

"What is it, then?" he snapped, without looking up from his watch.

"It is this. What time was it when Monsieur Frey reached this hotel last night? That is, when you were called to attend him?"

"Within a few minutes of eleven-thirty. Good night to ye."

"You are sure of that?—I intend no offense," Schultz added, as Dr. Macrae bristled fiercely at him. "The matter is most important. I—er—trust the sprain is not a bad one?"

"It is, sir—verra bad. The man will no' walk for a week. Good night."

Schultz consented to see Franz's imploring gestures and took himself out with what dignity he could muster. Mr. Lewker followed. Franz hurried them downstairs as though he were afraid they might take it into their heads to return. Evidently the Scots doctor was an exacting guest. Schultz went straight to his car, but his companion lingered to speak to Franz.

"You have heard of the accident to Monsieur Jacot?"

"I have heard that he is dead," returned the young man stolidly.

"Of course. You would hear it from Madame Jacot or her brother, when they returned in the plane. You saw them take off?"

"No, *mein Herr*. I had been spending the night with my uncle Hans, at Zmutt. I got up at five to walk back to Täsch, along the road. Herr Waveney in his car, with his sister, passed me, but they did not stop. I do not think they saw me. I saw the plane flying up the valley when I was a mile from Täsch. I was here to meet them when they landed, but they said nothing to me of Monsieur Jacot's death. Both of them looked very white, and I thought something must be wrong. But it was Perren of Zermatt who brought the news, an hour ago. He said also that he had seen the *Kriminal Kommissar* arrive."

"I see. Thank you, Franz. Good night."

Mr. Lewker got into the car and they drove off.

"It will be difficult," observed the actor-manager as the yellow lights of Täsch slid away behind them, "to conceal this murder. Jacot's death and your arrival in Zermatt were known at the Weisses Kreuz an hour ago."

"So." Schultz sounded interested. "I should have looked at that sprained ankle, my friend."

"You think—"

"Frey could have known that all was not well with his faked accident. He was in a position to add two and two before we arrived, *nicht wahr?*"

"You imply that Dr. Macrae and Franz would assist him to prepare a false alibi? Surely that is most improbable."

"Improbable is not impossible," snapped the commissioner, and relapsed into brooding silence.

The car rounded a corner and the Matterhorn swam into view, a great ghost of a mountain glimmering whitely against the stars. Majestical, like the Ghost in *Hamlet*, thought Mr. Lewker, and with the same secret to reveal if it could speak as fluently as the shade of the King of Denmark. Was it still possible that the second part in that little scene played out on the Matterhorn crags in the half-light of dawn, the part of Jacot's murderer, could have been filled by Baptiste Frey? If Dr. Macrae was to be believed—and Lewker could not bring himself to think otherwise—Frey had a sound alibi. And there would have been others who saw him brought into the hotel or assisted to his room. The obvious suspect was going to prove a difficult man to catch.

The car was slowing to pull up in front of the Hotel Obergabelhorn when a girl ran into the glare of the headlights, shading her eyes to peer at the car. Mr. Lewker recognized Lisse Taugwalder.

CHAPTER TEN

AT HOFFMAN'S

Lisse came straight to the side of the car where Mr. Lewker was sitting and laid a hand on the door, peering at him anxiously.

"It is you," she said in German, agitatedly. "They told me you would return soon. Please, have you seen my father?"

In the yellow light of the lamp that hung from the hotel porch her eyes glistened with unshed tears. She wore a hooded cape that shadowed her face, but her attitude and the frightened urgency in her voice spoke of nerves braced to breaking point.

"I have not seen Heinrich today," Lewker replied. "Why, my child? Is something wrong?"

The gentleness in his tone seemed to release her dammed-up emotions. She clutched his sleeve convulsively.

"Oh, it is so dreadful, Herr Lewker, so dreadful. I don't know what to do, I am so afraid. This afternoon I heard that Léon—Herr Jacot—was killed on the mountain. He had no guide, they say. Then, when I go home, I find my father hasn't come back. He got up very early this morning and went off into the mountains. He—he did not like Herr Jacot, you know. I was afraid that— I cannot say it. But I hoped he was with you."

A picture, clear in every detail, flashed into Mr. Lewker's mind: himself sitting in the sunshine outside Heinrich Taugwalder's chalet saying idly that Léon Jacot intended to climb the Matterhorn alone, and Heinrich's big carved pipe slipping from his fingers. He realized suddenly that Schultz, beside him, had heard every word that Lisse had said. It was too late now to evade the consequences of Lisse's outburst. He covered her nervously twitching fingers with his hand and turned to his companion.

"This is Fräulein Taugwalder, daughter of the guide Heinrich Taugwalder," he explained.

"So!" Schultz lifted the extraordinary white peaked cap he affected when motoring. "Your father is missing, Fräulein? That is bad. It may be that we can assist you to find him."

"Who are you?" Lisse asked tremulously.

"It is Herr Schultz, the *Kriminal Kommissar,*" Lewker told her quickly. He sensed the commissioner's disapproval, but he was not going to let Lisse say another word in ignorance of his companion's identity.

Lisse drew in her breath so sharply that it was like a stifled cry. Her free hand went to her mouth and she tried to draw the other from Lewker's grasp. He tightened his hold and spoke urgently to her.

"Listen, Fräulein. We—you and I—know your father would do nothing wrong. If he is missing, this gentleman can do more than anyone to help us find him. It is best for all of us if you can tell us everything you know."

"I—I cannot," she gasped. "I am supposed to be working at Hoffman's tonight. I got permission to come out for five minutes, but—oh, I must go back now."

"Excellent," purred Herr Schultz, getting out of the car. "We will all go to Hoffman's, Fräulein. There we can talk, *hein?*"

"Oh, no—you see—I have to serve the tables. And there are many people, and much noise—"

"So much the better." Schultz came briskly round the car. His prominent eyes glistened unpleasantly in the half-light. "Noise is an excellent screen for talk. I shall insist that Hoffman allows you to sit with us and tell your story."

Lisse shrank against Mr. Lewker, who had also got out of the car. He linked her arm in his protectively.

"We can avoid mentioning your identity, Herr Kommissar," he said with firmness. "Permit me to arrange matters. Fräulein Taugwalder is a very old acquaintance of mine. I knew her when she was four years old. I will see Hoffman myself."

"*So!*" Schultz contrived to sound suspicious. "Let it be so, then."

They walked together out of the narrow lane into the main street. Many people were about, for the night was still and starlit. Lights shone in most of the shops although it was past nine o'clock. The long red-curtained windows of Hoffman's restaurant glowed cheerfully, and as they approached the sound of an accordion played with zest came from within. Lisse clung tightly to Mr. Lewker's arm. She was trembling. He was not surprised at her distress; he was, indeed, rather relieved that she seemed to be more worried about her father's nonappearance than about the death of Jacot, which argued that her affair with the dead man had not gone very deep after all.

The swing doors of Hoffman's admitted them to an atmosphere of warmth and noise and tobacco smoke. Dim orange light filled a long low room with a bar at one end and a small dais, where a man in Swiss peasant costume was playing an accordion, at the other. There were wooden seats with very high backs along both sides of the restaurant, placed so that each pair made a kind of alcove with a small table between them. On the narrow strip of floor in the center a few couples were dancing, while waitresses in neat red costumes passed to and fro between bar and tables. Mr. Lewker, who appeared to have taken charge of the party, dispatched his companions to find seats and enquired at the bar for the proprietor.

Hoffman, a fat little man with close-set eyes, came somewhat reluctantly from an office behind the bar. To him Lewker explained that he had met by chance the daughter of his guide of many years ago, Fräulein Taugwalder, who, it seemed, was a *kellnerin* in Herr Hoffman's famous restaurant. If it could be arranged, he would like the Fräulein to be released from her duties for ten minutes so that they might talk over old times.

Herr Hoffman looked dubious.

"We shall naturally," added Lewker quickly, "require a bottle of your very best wine to celebrate this happy reunion."

Herr Hoffman's little eyes disappeared in the creases of an obsequious smile. He bowed, rubbed his hands, and announced that this could be arranged. The restaurant, he pointed out, closed in half an hour's time, and he would release Fräulein Lisse for the rest of the evening. Mr. Lewker thanked him and went in search of the others.

The thick blue wreaths of smoke and the poor light given by the heavily shaded lamps made it difficult to see the occupants of the seats. He walked along one side of the floor, dodging the revolving couples and glancing into the smoky shadows; in one alcove burly figures rapped ale mugs on the table and sang lustily to the accordion's music, in another the gleam of a white shirt front and the shimmer of a woman's gown told of visitors from one of the big hotels sampling the night life of Zermatt. An ice-axe, leaned carelessly against the arm of a seat in the next alcove, almost tripped him up. The clatter of its fall did not rouse the solitary occupant, who sat with his head on his arms sprawled across the table. Mr. Lewker paused, frowning, and then passed on.

He found Schultz and the girl on the other side of the room near the dais, and sat down on the opposite side of the little table. Lisse had slipped the cloak from her shoulders and the pale gold of her hair glistened dully in the faint yellow light. She half rose from her seat as he arrived.

"I've changed my mind," she said in a flurried whisper. "There is nothing I can tell you. It was a mistake—"

"Please, Fräulein." Mr. Lewker's hand on her arm pushed her gently back into her seat. "If you will only tell us why you are afraid, and why your father's absence should worry you so much, I think we can promise to find him for you."

Lisse shrank back into her seat, staring at him in an apparent agony of indecision.

"I—I cannot," she faltered at last.

"Very well," he said. "I shall begin the story for you."

A waitress brought a tall bottle and three glasses, and Lewker filled a glass for each of them in silence. Schultz handed one to the girl.

"You need this, Fräulein, I think," he observed with an attempt at benevolence. "It is plain that you have suffered much anxiety."

She sipped it absently, her gaze on Lewker. A burst of applause greeted the end of the accordion player's solo. Lewker waited until the instrument swung into a noisy waltz tune and then began to speak without looking at Lisse.

"You shall tell me if my guesses are at fault, Fräulein. Léon Jacot made— shall we say?—advances to you. He was handsome, rich, famous, and you found it hard to repulse him. Probably you met more than once in the last few days. Your father discovered this and was violently angry—he had learned something of Jacot's reputation where women were concerned. He forbade you to have any more to do with Jacot, and you defied him."

Lisse began to sob quietly. She pulled out a handkerchief and dabbed at her eyes.

"Forgive me if this causes you pain," Lewker said gently. "I have nearly finished. You tell us your father got up very early this morning and went off to the mountains. I know, for he told me, that he intended to make a long training walk today. But the news of Jacot's death, alone on the Matterhorn, puts a dreadful thought into your head. Suppose the two men had met, up there. Suppose there had been a quarrel, with a tragic ending."

"You are suggesting," interposed Schultz, "that Heinrich Taugwalder would by chance choose the Northeast Ridge of the Matterhorn for a training walk?"

"I am only suggesting that this is what Fräulein Taugwalder may have thought."

Lisse blew her nose violently and spoke with sudden determination.

"That is what I did think. I see now how foolish I was to imagine such things. My father would not kill a man—and besides, it was an accident. I—I have been very silly."

Herr Schultz reached for the bottle and solicitously refilled her glass.

"But of course, Fräulein," he said persuasively, "you would not jump to the conclusion that your father had been on the Matterhorn today unless you had some reason?"

She shook her head violently. "No. No. I had no reason. It was a silly fancy."

"You are quite sure? He told you nothing of his intentions?"

"Nothing."

"So!" Schultz fingered his watch chain. "But we have still to find him. At what time did he set out?"

Lisse was quite willing to tell him; she even became voluble. Even allowing for the tongue-loosening effect of the wine it seemed to Mr. Lewker that she was too voluble. She was concealing something, that was plain, something that might endanger her father.

Her tale was simple enough, and told them little that seemed significant. Heinrich had told her briefly that he intended to rise early and go for a long mountain walk. He would be back at the chalet, he had said, at three in the afternoon. He was always very punctual. She had heard him get up—her alarm-clock, which she thought at first had roused her, gave the time as half-past one—and had gone to sleep again. She had worked at Hoffman's from eight until noon that morning. The waitresses whose turn it was to work in the evening always had the afternoon off, so she had gone back to the chalet. Heinrich did not come back at three, and by five o'clock, at which time she had to leave in order to get back to the restaurant, he had still not arrived. She was a little worried then because he always kept his word about times. At Hoffman's she heard the news of Jacot's fatal accident. And then it was that the dreadful possibility of her father's having been concerned in it occurred to her. It had tormented her until she remembered that he might have called to see Lewker, and had run across to the hotel to find him.

"I see," nodded Schultz when she had ended. He fixed a penetrating gaze on her face. "But here is little to worry a sensible girl, who knows that her father would not push a man over a precipice. There was something else that led you to think—"

"There was nothing, *mein Herr*—I swear it," she cried in a hurry.

"No? And just because your father has not returned two hours after his appointed time—which, as you must know, can easily happen to the best of mountaineers—you imagine this monstrous thing of him?"

Lisse pulled the hooded cloak round her shoulders and stood up, erect and determined. She was no longer, thought Mr. Lewker, the frightened child who had darted across the glare of the headlights a little while ago. There was a wariness, a new composure, about her whole bearing.

"I have behaved very foolishly," she said with a certain dignity. "You have shown me my foolishness. I thank you. Now I must go—it is almost time for the restaurant to close, and I shall have to clear up."

"But your father, Fräulein?" persisted Schultz. "Are you sure there is not some little thing you have not told, something that might help us to find him?"

"I expect my father will have returned to the chalet by now," she responded quietly, though she could not conceal renewed anxiety at this reminder.

Mr. Lewker, feeling rather like an amateur conjurer performing a trick whose mechanism is certain to be detected by his audience, got up and held out his hand to Lisse.

"I will take you to your father," he said. "He is in this room."

She followed him without a word, Schultz close behind. The accordionist's final number had brought a dozen couples on to the narrow dancing floor, and they had to exercise some agility to get across to the seats on the other side. Mr. Lewker found the place where he had tripped over the ice-axe. The solitary occupant was still there, still relaxed in that abandonment of attitude which is common to drunkards and very weary men. Common also, Mr. Lewker thought suddenly with a quickened pulse, to the dead. That lanky form slumped forward across the table with its tousled head on its arms was the very picture that appeared on the jackets of a hundred crime novels. Could it be that this was another murder?

Lisse Taugwalder pushed past him unceremoniously and sank down beside the man. Her arms went round his shoulders. She did not speak; she seemed to be crying silently. Heinrich Taugwalder was certainly not dead. He raised a tired and haggard face to his daughter's.

'Liebchen!' he whispered hoarsely, and did not even look at the two men.

As though it had received its cue the accordion blared out a triumphant final chord, reminding Mr. Lewker of the musical effects that used to go with the old silent films. He turned away and grasped Schultz's arm.

"Come," he said firmly, and fairly hustled the unwilling Commissioner to the door.

Outside Hoffman's in the cool night air Schultz jerked himself free.

"And why," he demanded with scarcely repressed anger, "am I thus dragged away? This Taugwalder, he is an old acquaintance of yours also, perhaps? I may not question your friends, sir—is that it?"

Mr. Lewker remembered that this was the second time in an evening that Herr Schultz's dignity had received a serious ruffling, and made allowances accordingly.

"You must admit it was hardly the time to interrogate a possible suspect," he said mildly.

"So! You admit we have now a second suspect. Motive is there undoubtedly. Opportunity seems probable. Yet we are to give those two time to arrange what tale they shall tell—perhaps to arrange another alibi. This is not how we work in this country, sir!"

The departing clientele of Hoffman's was issuing from the restaurant with a good deal of laughter and jostling. Mr. Lewker took his companion's arm, more gently this time, and drew him out of the throng in the direction of the hotel. He had come to a decision. Schultz, with Frey's alibi presenting an apparent impasse, would not be slow to seize upon this second line of investigation. Strong as was Lewker's impulse to protect the Taugwalders, he knew that he could do no more than he had done. What he could do was to put Schultz in immediate possession of certain impressions of his own, all that he had heard and seen of Léon Jacot's acquaintances at the Hotel Obergabelhorn. He could do nothing to lessen the black shadow which Lisse's words had thrown upon her father; but there were other shadows, hitherto faint, which the discovery of Frey's incapacity to be on the Matterhorn ridge at the vital time had brought into sharper relief.

"The Taugwalders will not run away, *mein Herr*," he said. "Naturally the guide must be interrogated. But you, as a man of sensibility, will have observed that a father and daughter, who have been estranged, have found each other again. Give them a little time before the blow falls."

This appeal to the native sentimentality of the Swiss appeared to have its effect. The commissioner grunted, but allowed himself to be steered away from the restaurant.

"I have information about the Taugwalders—and other persons—which I think I should lay before you," continued Lewker. "I should have done so earlier, but I have not your experience of judging what evidence is relevant to an investigation of this kind."

"I see." Schultz was completely mollified. "Then I must hear this at once, Herr Lewker. Perhaps in your room we shall be sufficiently private."

They entered the hotel, and went straight to Lewker's room. There, while the commissioner frowned and scribbled in his enormous notebook, the actor-manager set forth all the impressions, nebulous or sharp, which had forced themselves upon him during his two days at the Hotel Obergabelhorn. He found it singularly distasteful to report Bryce's apparent infatuation with Deborah and Camille de Goursac's more obvious passion for Jacot, but he stuck to his purpose. He repeated the words in which both Dr. Greatorex and John Waveney had expressed their intense dislike of the dead man. He told, without undue emphasis, how de Goursac, after learning from Jacot of the latter's proposed ascent of the Matterhorn, had set off alone to spend the night at the Schönbuhl Hut; and of the Comtesse de Goursac's dramatic interpretation of this action. Nor did he omit a full statement of his talk with Heinrich, or his impressions of the position between Jacot and Lisse Taugwalder.

When he had finished, Herr Schultz shot a shrewd glance at him over the top of his pince-nez.

"So!" he said coldly. "I think you throw me many bones to worry lest I chew too hard upon this Taugwalder, *nicht wahr?* I find little meat upon them."

Mr. Lewker shrugged. "If you think we should ignore them —"

"I ignore nothing of relevance, Herr Lewker," said Schultz severely. He snapped his notebook shut. "These are impressions, possibilities. But, as you—somewhat tardily, realized, they may be relevant. I will see all these people."

He put the notebook into his pocket and rose to his feet. Somewhere a deep-toned clock struck the hour of midnight.

"Taugwalder I shall interrogate in the morning," said the commissioner. "But first we shall gather together all who knew Léon Jacot. At ten o'clock. For the present, Herr Lewker, *gute Nacht.*"

CHAPTER ELEVEN

"ALL PERJUR'D, ALL FORSWORN"

"This where I squattay?" shouted Mrs. Fillingham. "Righty-ho. Thanks." She flopped into the chair which Herr Schultz held politely for her and looked round the table. "Great Godfrey!" she added with determined cheeriness.

"We look like the Long Parliament—or was it the Rump, ha-ha?"

Lawrence Greatorex looked up from manicuring his nails.

"The Long Parliament," he observed, "ended with an execution. Very apt."

The careless comparison, thought Mr. Lewker, was not entirely inept. The room that Simler had placed at Schultz's disposal for this meeting (with the complete incuriosity of the perfect *hotelier*) was paneled in some dark wood, and on its walls hung shields and trophies and medieval-looking prize certificates. It was the room Simler kept for the periodical meetings of local sporting societies—the Marksmen, the Male Voice Choir and the like. He called it his back parlor. Into it, by ten o'clock of this sunny morning, Herr Schultz's portentous but still genial manner had persuaded six of the eight people he wished to collect. They sat at the long walnut table in varying attitudes; Dr. Greatorex idly plying a nail file, Bryce stiffly with folded arms, John Waveney leaning back with hands in pockets. Deborah Jacot and Margaret Kemp both sat composedly with their hands folded in their laps, but Mrs. Fillingham had produced from her handbag some knitting of a violent purple hue and was already hard at work. All of them, even Mrs. Fillingham, wore clothes of a dark color. A shaft of morning sunlight, striking across from the window to sparkle on the silver-tipped horns of a mounted chamois head, reminded Mr. Lewker of the high snows on which he had hoped to disport himself, and he sighed; this was Tuesday, the third day of his holiday. It looked as though the great peaks would have to be left to more fortunate climbers until the problem of Léon Jacot's murder had been solved.

Schultz was looking at his watch impatiently.

"We wait," he announced, "for Monsieur de Goursac and Madame his wife. I have sent them a message requesting their presence. I understand Monsieur de Goursac returned to Zermatt yesterday from an excursion?"

"He got back just before dinner," said Margaret Kemp. "He looked as though he'd had a pretty tiring day, so perhaps—"

"Half a tick, Margot," interrupted her aunt without pausing in her knitting. "Better hold on to the information until we're all here. This is going to be a sort of enquiry, if your Aunty Bee ain't mistook."

Margaret glanced swiftly at Bernard Bryce, who did not meet her eyes. She turned to Herr Schultz with mingled puzzlement and apprehension on her face, but before she could ask her question the Comte de Goursac and his wife came in. The Comtesse was heavily made up, but her eyes showed traces of recent tears. De Goursac, his heavy features reddened by the sun of the upper snows and his close-cropped head held stiffly on its thick neck, looked more than ever like the Prussian officer of caricature. He stood just inside the door, grasping his wife's elbow tightly, and darted a suspicious glance round the assembled party.

"I come here," he said loudly, cutting short Schultz's pompous greeting, "to say that I have but a few minutes to spare. We leave Zermatt this morning. My wife cannot longer remain in this atmosphere of tragedy."

"Monsieur le Comte," said the commissioner sharply, "I must ask you to be seated, and Madame also. You will see, when you have heard what I have to say, that there is still a duty you owe to your dead friend. I believe I am right in saying that he was your friend?"

Camille de Goursac gave a dry sob, and winced as her husband's grasp tightened on her arm. The Comte returned Schultz's pale glare with a look almost of defiance.

"He was," he declared. "But I do not see—"

"If you please." Schultz was holding a chair for the Comtesse. With a frightened glance at her husband she sank into it. De Goursac, after a moment's frowning hesitation, took the remaining chair. The commissioner returned to his place at the other end of the table and assumed an expression of lofty benevolence. He looked rather like the chairman of a charitable society's committee meeting, thought Mr. Lewker.

"I shall be brief, my friends," he said. "I have asked you to come here because I need your help—I and my colleague Herr Lewker, who most kindly gives me his assistance. To Madame Jacot I apologize, and to her brother, for causing them pain. It has, however, become necessary to ask the assistance of you, his friends, in throwing light upon the circumstances surrounding the most regrettable death of Léon Jacot."

He paused impressively. De Goursac interposed.

"I know nothing of these circumstances, except that he fell from the Northeast Ridge. I returned from the Schönbuhl only last night."

"I come now to the circumstances, Monsieur. All of us here know that Léon Jacot was killed on the Matterhorn. Not all of us know that he was— murdered."

Camille de Goursac stifled a scream by crushing her handkerchief tightly against her lips, and Lewker heard a sharp gasp from Margaret Kemp. He was watching the Comte, but de Goursac's ham-like face seemed to have regained its former mask of impassivity. Bernard Bryce muttered "Good God!" under his breath. In spite of the sudden increase of tension in the room Mr. Lewker had the impression that no one of those round the table had been greatly surprised by Schultz's announcement.

John Waveney broke the short silence, taking his hands from his pockets and sitting up with a frown on his good-looking face.

"I knew—Deb told me last night," he said. "And I'd like to know why you haven't—"

"If you please, Herr Waveney." Schultz raised a hand. "I shall explain. But first I ask all of you here to say no word of this to anyone. The police officer here in Zermatt, Herr Zimmermann, and the doctor who examined the body, they are ordered to preserve strict secrecy. I have had occasion to request officially that one of you who had stumbled on this sad truth should keep it to herself." Mrs. Fillingham went red and dropped a stitch. "If any of you here knows of some person to whom the matter has been divulged, I ask you to tell me now."

He paused enquiringly. There was no response.

"May I ask why this hush-hush is necessary?" drawled Greatorex with some contempt. "If this is murder, it's bound to come out."

"That is true, Herr Doktor. But listen for one moment."

Schultz, who had spent the early morning telephoning, explained concisely that he had been in touch with a highly placed personage in the federal government who in turn had been in communication with his opposite number in the French government. The result had been that the commissioner was confirmed in his decision to conduct the enquiry into Jacot's death with the utmost possible discretion. The French, it seemed, were greatly concerned lest the already delicate political situation should be rendered more difficult by accusations and counter-accusations between two violently opposed factions. Léon Jacot, alive, had made himself a storm center of French politics; Léon Jacot murdered remained dangerous so long as his murderer could not be named with certainty.

"There is a possibility, you see," Schultz added with a meaning glance at Deborah, on his right, "that this was a political murder."

"I'm certain it was a political murder," she said quietly. "I've given you proof of it. I can't understand why you don't follow it up."

"I ask pardon, Madame," returned Schultz with some resentment, "but the information you gave us, helpful as it was, cannot be called proof. We have, unfortunately, to make a wider enquiry before your husband's murderer can be discovered beyond doubt."

"But surely you've made some attempt to find the man I've told you about?"

Deborah looked in frowning appeal at Mr. Lewker as she spoke, but it was Schultz who answered.

"That, Madame, I can assure you is being done."

"Then why are we here?"

"You must understand, Madame, that this is not a simple matter. I comprehend with sympathy your anxiety to see this miscreant delivered up to justice. But a murderer is not so easily caught." He leaned back in his chair and surveyed them patronizingly. "That is why you are here—to tell me, of your kindness, any matters, however small, that may add to our knowledge and make a net for the person who killed Léon Jacot."

Lawrence Greatorex emitted a sound between a snort and a laugh. "Being tactful, eh? Why not tell us we're under suspicion—some of us, anyway? That's true, isn't it?"

Camille de Goursac gave a frightened squeak and her husband darted a venomous glance at the doctor. Schultz looked shocked.

"My dear Herr Doktor," he said reprovingly, "that is not the truth. I have not sufficient acquaintance with anyone here to justify suspicions."

"But we're possibly suspects—you can't deny that?"

"Well, why not?" broke in John Waveney with heavy cheerfulness. "No need to get in a flap, old boy. Bloke dead, someone killed him, police suspect everyone until the murderer's taped. Find a chap with motive, opportunity, means—that's the drill. I've read—"

"Please, Johnny," interrupted his sister in a low voice.

"Oh—sorry, old girl, sorry." John subsided, abashed.

Bernard Bryce spoke unexpectedly. His gruff voice betrayed no emotion, but the brown hands linked on the table in front of him twisted restlessly.

"Before we go further. We—I, at least—don't know when or how this murder was committed. Going to tell us?"

"*C'est ça,*" nodded de Goursac. "And I also have a question. What is the status of Monsieur Lewker in this affair?"

Schultz pursed his lips and tugged at his watch-chain.

"To the question of Monsieur de Goursac," he returned ponderously, "I reply that since I am to conduct this enquiry in person I avail myself of expert assistance when I find it to my hand. Besides, you will pardon my reminding you that you are, in this country, aliens. You will surely not object to the presence of another alien, who will see, as the English say, fair game. Also I am informed"—the slight emphasis brought the shadow of a smile to Mr. Lewker's grave features—"that Herr Lewker has some experience of crime detection."

"My experience," boomed the actor-manager, "has been extremely limited. I am in this matter a mere anatomy, a mountebank, as they said of Pinch the juggler. But I am prepared, as I trust we all are, to give Herr Schultz all possible assistance in his very difficult task."

He looked hopefully round the table, but only Mrs. Fillingham met his gaze, looking up from her knitting to nod brightly. The rest were unresponsive. The Comte de Goursac continued to stare at Schultz with an odd fixity of expression.

"As to the murder," continued the commissioner, "our police procedure does not permit me to spill the beans."

Greatorex grinned mirthlessly. "At last," he sneered, "we have it. All this chat means merely that we are suspects. We are here to give an account of ourselves. In short, our alibis, ladies and gentlemen, are required."

"Great Godfrey!" exclaimed Mrs. Fillingham. "And here's me, a poor widow-woman, that was alone all night—eleven to seven." She giggled. "My pal Mona Smith always said I'd be safer if I married again."

"The Herr Doktor exaggerates," Schultz said coldly. "One may ask for information without imputing suspicion. That is reasonable, surely?"

Deborah spoke quietly and without emphasis. "What Mr. Lewker says is quite right. We are here to help. As for being suspected, that's nonsense—or at any rate it's the same for all of us, including me."

"Good girl," approved Mrs. Fillingham. She threw an arch glance at Mr. Lewker, who was frowning to himself. "Here's a theory brewing, I'll bet— the whole case hangs on a bent pin, or something."

"On the very odd choice of stifling with a scarf," muttered Mr. Lewker abstractedly.

Schultz overheard him. "You would no doubt prefer the Shakespearean dagger, my friend," he observed.

"Oh, let's be cheerful, by all means," remarked Greatorex caustically. "Meanwhile, our alibis are awaited."

De Goursac sprang to his feet, his impassivity dropping from him like a cloak.

"*C'est vrai, ça!*" he cried excitedly. "We are suspect, as you say. This Monsieur Lewker, he has told all that he has observed of us, *sans doute!*" He leveled a shaking finger at Lewker. "Léon himself called him 'Monsieur l'Espion'—*ah, mais il avait raison*! But I, I have nothing to fear! I was far away when this murder was done!"

The man was shaking with anger—or was it fear? Or was it, perhaps, an emotion altogether assumed? Mr. Lewker found himself unable to decide.

"Careful, Monsieur le Comte," Greatorex drawled ironically. "You are not supposed to know when the murder was done, remember."

"I prove to you, Monsieur, I am not near the Matterhorn yesterday," continued the Frenchman with vehemence, ignoring the doctor. "In the evening I reach the Schönbuhl Hut—you know where it is, *n'est-ce-pas*? I sleep there. I get up *de bonne heure* to see the sunrise. I make a promenade on the glacier. I am at the hut again by midday and then I walk back here to Zermatt. The *gardien* of the hut, he will tell you this is true, Monsieur."

"And why, Monsieur le Comte, should you imagine that you need an alibi?" demanded Schultz acidly. "It is surely most unlikely that you, an old friend of the dead man, should be the murderer. There is no reason why—"

"Ah, bah! You will find a reason!" De Goursac, still at the white heat of excitement, swept on as though the torrent of words was forced from him by some inner demon. "Envy—jealousy—hatred—are not these reasons enough for a policeman? Has not 'Monsieur l'Espion,' there, told you of my shame?"

The Comtesse, suddenly on her feet at his side, was hanging on his arm, incoherently tearful. He shook her off roughly.

"*Tais-toi!* All the world knows, except these imbecile detectives. I shall tell them—"

"*Non!*"

Camille de Goursac's deep contralto flung the word at her husband. She drew herself up, facing Schultz and Lewker proudly, her eyes flashing like those of an angry Valkyrie.

"I shall tell them myself," she said. "I am not ashame', me. Messieurs, Léon Jacot had been my lover. That is all."

A kind of smothered gasp ran round the table. The Comtesse took no notice. With admirable dignity she turned and walked to the door. Schultz frowned, but said nothing, and she made her exit in a taut silence.

"Well!" said Mrs. Fillingham, as the door closed. "Of all the brazen—"

"Please!" Schultz said sharply. He faced de Goursac. "How long have you known this, Monsieur?"

De Goursac seemed to have shrunk. The angry color had receded from his face and neck, leaving him very white. He raised his head slowly.

"I suspected for a month," he answered tonelessly. "On Sunday morning I—I knew."

"That was before you left for the Schönbuhl?"

"Yes. Now, Monsieur, you will permit me to go?"

"I must ask you not to leave Zermatt, Monsieur le Comte. For the present you may of course leave this room if you wish."

"*Merci, Monsieur.*"

The Comte turned away. Halfway to the door he paused, hesitated, and then faced the room.

"I swear to you all," he said in a low voice, "that I did not kill Léon Jacot."

The door closed behind him, leaving a rather embarrassed silence into which Lawrence Greatorex's harsh laughter fell like a stone into a pool.

"More fun and games for our twin 'tecs," he gibed. "I don't know how many other suspects you've got—I suppose this political mystery man's one—but that makes two good ones out of our little bunch."

"What do you mean?" demanded Margaret quickly.

"Well, can't rule out old de Goursac, can we? Motive—he had it. Means—a push. Opportunity—the Schönbuhl hut's separated from the Northeast Ridge by a couple of glaciers, I admit, but what's that to a mountaineer like de Goursac? As for his earnest oath, I seem to remember Shakespeare having a knock at the oath-takers. 'Methinks he doth protest too much'—isn't that it, Filthy?"

"You said there were two suspects," persisted Margaret. "Who—"

"The other?" Greatorex placed a hand on his chest and sketched a bow. "Who but your humble but homicidal servant? I disliked Jacot—forgive me, Madame Jacot—intensely. I was actually clambering up the Matterhorn at the very time he was killed. It's true that I was on the Italian Ridge at that time and I can prove it, so my alibi is as solid as de Goursac's will no doubt turn out to be. But an alibi's a mere nothing to a really efficient 'tec."

Herr Schultz, who had been following the doctor's words impatiently but with close attention, pounced upon him.

"I think, Herr Doktor, that you most thoughtfully warned Monsieur le Comte that he was—I use your words—'not supposed to know the time of the murder,' " he remarked suavely. "May I, perhaps, point out that this also applies to you?"

"Well, of course I assumed—" began Greatorex. He stopped abruptly and his mouth closed like a trap. "Very well," he said, jutting out his black beard defiantly. "Ask Signor Luigi Villanova, at the Hotel Mont Cervin, Breuil. He'll no doubt tell you how I left his party halfway up the Italian Ridge, traversed round the mountain by an unclimbable route to the Northeast Ridge, and there performed my fell work."

"Don't be a fool, Lawrence," said Bryce sharply.

Greatorex turned to grin mirthlessly at his friend. *"Et tu, Brute?* Come to think of it, why should you be left out of our merry gang, Bernard? What were you doing at the time—but of course you don't know the time—of the murder?"

"He was typing in his room long before breakfast-time," Margaret Kemp said swiftly. "I was up at half-past six and I heard him. I looked in and saw him, too, but he was busy and didn't see me."

Mr. Lewker caught the quick exchange of glances between Bryce and the girl; there was something that might have been surprise in his look, in hers an appeal urgent and unmistakable.

"I heard the typewriter at work in Mr. Bryce's room myself," he said, watching Margaret. "It was then half-past seven."

There was relief in the look she flashed at him. She dropped her eyes instantly. Dr. Greatorex snapped his fingers.

"Ha. Here, no doubt, we have another alibi." He was carrying this pose of banter too far—almost, thought Mr. Lewker, as though he were concealing other emotions. "Bernard was typing at six-thirty, so he couldn't have done the deed, eh? Well, what about this? Bernard steals out, steals Waveney's plane, and steals up. Heaves a brick at Jacot from above and steals back to his typing. Bernard can't fly a plane? All right—what about Waveney himself, then?"

"Here—lay off me, Greatorex!" John sat up, genuinely annoyed. "What are you trying to do—laugh yourself out of it? Pull a few more of us into your own tight spot?"

Greatorex flushed. "Can't you take a joke?"

"Not that sort of joke—from you."

"Oh, of course. Mr. Waveney doesn't consort with suspects. Mr. Waveney never said, in my hearing, that he'd like to break his dear brother-in-law's neck—"

He pulled himself up sharply. Deborah Jacot had risen to her feet. Greatorex began to mutter an apology, but she ignored him and addressed herself to Herr Schultz.

"I don't think I should be asked to listen to this," she said quietly. "My husband—" Her voice trembled and seemed about to break, but she controlled it. "May I go, please?" she finished.

"Certainly, Madame, certainly." Schultz, flustered, tugged hard at his watch-chain. "I am very sorry that you should—"

"Will you come for a walk, Bernard?" Deborah said composedly. "I need a lot of fresh air."

Bryce got up with alacrity and escorted her to the door. She made her exit with a dignity that reminded Mr. Lewker that she had had a stage training. Bryce stole a hurried glance at Margaret before he followed Deborah out.

Mrs. Fillingham bundled up her knitting and stowed it in her handbag.

"Well, well—you seem to have broken up the party, Doctor," she remarked loudly. "Can't say I approve of your methods."

"It was damned bad manners," said John Waveney, glaring at Greatorex, who was resting his head on his hands.

"Hear-hear from your Aunty Bee. Do we ooze away now, Mr. Commissioner?"

" 'Ooze'? I do not—" Schultz's wrinkled brow cleared.

"Ah, it is an English idiom. Yes, I think the meeting may, as you say, be declared shut."

"Righty-ho. Come on, Margot."

The girl rose obediently. John hastened to accompany them.

"Waveney," said the doctor, looking up. "I'm devilish sorry. Apologize to your sister for me, will you?"

John mumbled something and followed the others out.

"It's my blasted temper," said Greatorex penitently, with a shamefaced glance at Lewker. "Never could control my tongue. Fact is, I can't stand feeling I'm under suspicion. No excuse, I know."

He got up and went out of the room with quick, nervous strides. Schultz added a flourish to the notes he had been making and turned to Lewker complacently.

"You observe, my friend," he said, "how much information we have gained by simply letting our gathering talk for themselves."

Mr. Lewker had received the impression that the meeting had got out of Herr Schultz's control, but he did not say so.

" 'The rattling tongue of saucy and audacious eloquence' certainly served us well," he agreed. "There was, however, one tongue that did not rattle."

"Herr Bryce?" Schultz said keenly. "He is a novelist, *nicht wahr?* He had a pretty Fräulein to speak for him. And she did not speak the truth."

"That is what I thought. I believe I can confirm that in a matter of minutes."

"Then do so, and with discretion," said the commissioner patronizingly. "I also have a guess, a conjecture, which can be put to the test at once. But there is much to discuss in what we have heard. Shall we meet in your room, perhaps, in ten minutes?"

This arrangement concluded, Mr. Lewker sought the hotel proprietor. He had little to go upon except that Margaret Kemp, a bad actress, had almost certainly been lying when she said she had heard Bernard Bryce typing at half-past six in the morning. It needed no great powers of observation to see that Margaret was in love with the man and apprehensive on his behalf. She had hastened to give him what she thought would be an alibi; and Bryce had accepted it, albeit with surprise. To draw the obvious conclusion was not proof, but proof might be found.

Simler was in his office writing bills. To him Mr. Lewker put his question.

"Those who rose early yesterday?" Simler repeated slowly. "There was of course the unfortunate Monsieur Jacot, who was called by Bertrand."

"Bertrand is one of the waiters, I think?"

"Yes, sir. My staff take it in turns to remain on duty at night, in this office."

"He would let out anyone who wished to leave the hotel in the small hours, I suppose?"

"Yes. On that morning there were two. Monsieur Jacot first, and later Mr. Bryce."

"Ah. And would Bertrand know at what hour Mr. Bryce went out?"

"I know that myself, for Bertrand told me. It was at five minutes past three. Bertrand offered Mr. Bryce the special lunch packet which Monsieur Jacot had ordered but had not taken, but Mr. Bryce refused it, saying he was going for a walk because he could not sleep, and would be back for lunch."

Mr. Lewker fingered his chin. "He was in mountaineering kit?"

"Yes, sir. And he took lunch in the hotel."

"Thank you," said Mr. Lewker. He had opened the office door to go when a thought struck him and he turned. "Wasn't it rather odd that Monsieur Jacot did not take his lunch packet?"

Simler nodded energetically. *"Ja.* So I thought, sir. Bertrand tells me that Monsieur Jacot seemed in a great hurry. He passed very quickly through the hall and would not stop when Bertrand called out to him that the packet was here ready for him."

It was not, pondered Mr. Lewker, unnatural that Jacot should be in a hurry. But that he should neglect to take the food which he had specially ordered, when he was about to undertake a long and possibly hazardous climb, seemed strangely careless in so experienced a mountaineer.

"Bertrand," continued Simler, "thought that perhaps Monsieur Jacot was feeling unwell. The morning, here, was not cold, and yet he wore the red scarf twisted round his neck, and his windproof jacket and hood."

It is not unusual for volatile people like Jacot to feel cold and ill-tempered at two in the morning, reflected Mr. Lewker as he went slowly upstairs. But to leave his food behind, when venturing alone upon one of the highest peaks in the Alps—that was the act of a madman. For all his undeniable charm, Léon Jacot had from the first impressed Lewker as being of an unbalanced type of mentality. Could it be that he had indeed gone mad? Could it be possible, after all, that he had managed in some horrible manner to take his own life, up there on the shattered ridge? The idea was, of course, ridiculous. And anyway, here was Bernard Bryce allowing someone else to provide him with an alibi which had been proved false.

Herr Schultz, however, scarcely commented upon Lewker's brief account of his conversation with Simler. He appeared to be bursting with self-congratulation. Keeping one hand behind his back, he held out to Lewker the half-sheet of notepaper bearing the familiar threatening message.

"Tell me," he commanded, "what defects you observe in the lettering, my friend."

Mr. Lewker examined the note once again. The only peculiarities he could pick out were the slight blobbing of the o's and the faulty alignment of the t's. He said so.

"Gut!" Herr Schultz whipped the hand from behind his back and held out a second piece of paper. "Compare, please."

Lewker did so. The same nineteen words had been typed on it, and the defects corresponded exactly with those of the original.

"The second sheet," announced the commissioner triumphantly, "I have just typed on the machine in the room of Bernard Bryce."

CHAPTER TWELVE

DISTRESSED DAMSEL

About an hour after the breakup of the gathering in Simler's back parlor, Mr. Lewker was sitting on a warm gray boulder eating his "elevenses." Five hundred feet below his dangling legs the Zmuttbach roared in its terrific gorge, its white torrent sunk so deeply beneath pine-clad precipices that it caught no light from the brilliant sunshine that beat upon Mr. Lewker's handkerchief-covered bald head. On the opposite side of the gorge the trees rose, to peter out on mounting pastures which in turn gave place to rock and scree; above this shone the blue ice of the Matterhorn glacier, and finally, crowning this whole uptilted countryside, the Matterhorn itself towered tremendous into the blue overhead. Mr. Lewker, comfortable in breeches and shirtsleeves, gave thanks for his deliverance from the petty lower world of men.

That he was on this sunlit path leading to the big glaciers, with Zermatt an hour's climb below him, he owed to the zeal of Herr Schultz. Mr. Lewker had no liking for the commissioner, and had hitherto formed no very high opinion of his capabilities. The man seemed almost childish in his vanity, and far too apt to attach paramount importance to the most recently discovered piece of evidence. The actor-manager, who was beginning to form his own ideas about the interpretation of the evidence, had nevertheless been content to sit back and watch his pompous colleague; for (as he put it to himself) he did not yet know his lines. But he had to admit that the twenty minutes they had spent in Lewker's room after Schultz's typewriter discovery had given him a greatly increased respect for the little man.

Dropping his pompous manner, Schultz had detailed with swift conciseness the form of his investigations. Zimmermann was already well on the way to tracing, through the police of Paris and Geneva, the antecedents and travels of Baptiste Frey. In Zimmermann's hands was the seeking of further confirmation for Frey's alibi, and he was also trying to contact Signor Villanova at Breuil to obtain from him every possible detail of Lawrence Greatorex's movements on the morning of the murder. Schultz himself was to undertake the following-up of what might be called the Bryce angle: the typed note and the false alibi. Mr. Lewker had been detailed for the visit to the Schönbühl Hut, where he was to obtain from the hut warden, and any other witnesses there might be, statements regarding the movements of Paul de Goursac during his stay there.

A suggestion of Mr. Lewker's had also been adopted, though without much enthusiasm. This was that a party of guides including Perren should go up to the spot on the Northeast Ridge whence Jacot had fallen, to examine that area for possible clues. In particular, they were to look for Jacot's ice-axe and rucksack, whose nonappearance anywhere near the body struck Mr. Lewker as at least worthy of note.

Heinrich Taugwalder had not been mentioned. But Lewker knew that he had been sent for and was to be interrogated at the police office at eleven-thirty. Schultz no doubt preferred that he, Lewker, should be out of the way when he made his examination. Mr. Lewker had an uneasy feeling that, in spite of the typed warning and its origin, Schultz's main suspicions had shifted from Frey to the guide, who on the face of it did indeed appear to have the motive, opportunity and ability to commit murder. Was it possible, he asked himself as he munched one of Simler's cream cakes, that Heinrich—honest, quick-tempered, determined as Lewker well knew him to be—would kill a man as a means of protecting his daughter's honor? He had to admit that it was just the sort of thing that a Swiss peasant brought up in the stern beliefs of an earlier generation would do. And Schultz's list of suspects did not make this any the less likely.

For the commissioner, in those few minutes, had drafted with amazing speed a list of those persons who might be considered as having any possible interest in the murder of Léon Jacot. He had set forth all that was so far known of their motives and opportunity, and noted the steps to be taken in each case. A copy of this document, hastily scrawled, was in Mr. Lewker's pocket. Now, having finished his lunch and lit a pipe, he got out the sheet of notepaper and unfolded it.

Before giving it his consideration he glanced at his watch. It was ten minutes to twelve. He had ample time in which to get up to the hut, interview the hut warden, and return to Zermatt in time for dinner. He could afford to sit in the sun and meditate on murder for a while.

Schultz's brief observations had dealt with motive and opportunity in each case. The means, as he had pointed out, were available to anyone who could have been on the Northeast Ridge at the fatal spot between six and seven; though, as he admitted, this presupposed considerable strength on the part of the murderer, strength sufficient to overcome the resistance which Jacot must have made.

The list was as follows:

DEBORAH JACOT.—*Motive:* gains fortune and freedom to marry again; appears to be in love with Bernard Bryce. Admitted did not love husband and gained by his death. *Opportunity:* none. Was with brother in plane and car 5.15 a.m. to 8 a.m., covering time of Jacot's death. Improbable that she could have climbed alone to spot.

JOHN WAVENEY.—*Motive:* none, unless on behalf of sister. Admitted to A. L. that he did not care if Jacot broke neck. *Opportunity:* none. In A. L.'s room at 5.15 a. m.

LAWRENCE GREATOREX.—*Motive:* not known, but volunteered statement that he would have killed Jacot if opportunity offered. *Opportunity:* confirmation of his own statement, if obtained, will give alibi.

PAUL DE GOURSAC.—*Motive:* Jacot was wife's lover. Admits to hatred of Jacot. *Opportunity:* was at Schönbuhl Hut over period of murder. Could have reached Northeast Ridge. (*N. B.* Asserts he has alibi. This to be checked by A. L.)

BERNARD BRYCE.—*Motive:* in love with Jacot's wife. *Opportunity:* left hotel an hour after Jacot. Lied, or acquiesced in lie, about this. Note: threatening letter was typed on his machine. (*N.B.* Would he have been able to overtake Jacot, who was out to make fast time?—A. L.)

BAPTISTE FREY.—*Motive:* member of organization which had previously threatened Jacot (admitted by Frey and confirmed on phone by Paris Sûreté). *Opportunity:* alibi apparently sound.

HEINRICH TAUGWALDER.—*Motive:* to protect daughter from Jacot's advances. *Opportunity:* left his home at 1.30 a.m. No evidence yet of where he went. If to Northeast Ridge, could have reached spot before Jacot.

LISSE TAUGWALDER, CAMILLE DE GOURSAC, BEATRIX FILLINGHAM, MARGARET KEMP.—The foregoing have no apparent motive. Three of them have motives for wishing Jacot alive, in fact. On the morning of the murder Lisse was working at Hoffman's by 8 a.m. (confirmed by Schultz) and the others were having breakfast in hotel shortly after 7.30.

Mr. Lewker, when he had finished rereading this list, remained staring at it rather blankly. There was here, he felt, something of an *embarras de richesse* in the way of suspects. Even if one discounted altogether—for lack of motive—Mrs. Fillingham, Margaret Kemp, Lisse Taugwalder and Camille de Goursac, who all appeared to lack both motive and opportunity, there still remained seven names to which some sort of motive could be attached. And here was a point not without interest: of those seven, five had deliberately admitted that the death of Jacot was not an unwelcome event to them. Not only that, but Bryce and Heinrich, the remaining two suspects, had quite obvious motives for wanting Jacot dead and seemed to have taken no steps to conceal them. All, then, turned on the question of opportunity, assuming that the list of suspects was complete.

Mr. Lewker considered the question of opportunity. Deborah and John had none, on the evidence available. Greatorex and de Goursac appeared sure of their alibis, and if the former proved to have been in the company of Signor Villanova until 9 a.m., and the hut warden was able to confirm the latter's statement, they would both be clear on the score of opportunity. Frey's alibi seemed unbreakable. That left Bryce and Taugwalder, one with a false alibi, the other—at this moment Heinrich might be undergoing the subtle questioning of Herr Schultz, committing himself, perhaps, beyond help. . . .

With a muttered oath Mr. Lewker thrust the list of suspects into his coat pocket and strapped the coat on top of his rucksack. Long companionship on the high hills breeds a friendship that dies very hard, whether it is between two amateur mountaineers or between guide and "Herr." Lewker knew that he would rather find any other of the seven guilty of Jacot's murder—even Greatorex, whom he had known as a youth—than his old guide. As he had once before discovered, a strict impartiality is an ideal very difficult for an amateur of detection to attain; especially when the end of the hunt means death for the guilty. He began to wish that he had firmly refused to take any part in the hunt—that he had left Zermatt as soon as Schultz had arrived to take charge. But that, of course, would have been impossible. The thing must be seen through to its end now, whatever that end might be.

He had tapped out his pipe and was shouldering his rucksack when a loud *'Coo-ee!'* made him turn. Up the rough path below him a solitary figure was hurriedly scrambling, a girl in a dark blue skirt and jersey. He recognized Margaret Kemp. Mr. Lewker waited for her to come up to him. She was flushed and panting when at last she reached him and flung herself down on a patch of grass at the side of the path.

"My dear young lady," said Mr. Lewker severely. "To walk about on this sort of path in high-heeled shoes is unwise. More than that—it is not done."

"Well, I—haven't got—any others," she told him breathlessly. "And I had—to catch you."

"Why, may I ask? Not, of course, that I object to pretty girls trying to catch me—"

"Don't laugh about it, please," she begged. "I'm deadly serious."

Mr. Lewker regarded her closely.

"Yes, I believe you are," he sighed. "And of course you are right. It is a sad, sordid, serious business. We shall have to be solemn and earnest until it is all over." He sat down again on his boulder. "You want me to relieve your anxiety about Mr. Bryce, I take it."

Margaret gasped. "How did you know?"

"I guessed. Detectives, especially amateur detectives, do a lot of guessing, but not all of them are so frank as myself. To be candid, Miss Kemp, your interest in Bernard Bryce is fairly obvious."

She lifted her chin defiantly.

"I'm not—interested in the way I think you mean, Mr. Lewker. But we used to be friends, and I'm not going to see him being suspected of a crime he couldn't—he wouldn't—commit."

"And what makes you think he is suspected, any more than anyone else?" demanded Mr. Lewker sharply.

"Oh, that Swiss policeman—Schultz, isn't it?—he got hold of Aunty and was asking questions about Bernard. How long we'd known him and all the rest of it. She told me. Besides, I—I saw you looking at him."

"Did you indeed? In a moment I will tell you what caused me to look. First, however, what makes you think Mr. Bryce would not have committed such a crime as this?"

Margaret hesitated.

"I know he looks big and tough," she said at last, "but—well, I got to know him fairly well and he just wouldn't kill anyone."

"That is scarcely evidence, you know," he said gently. "Can you not tell me anything more convincing?"

"Oh—there's his writing, and he's fond of music, and—and once he went for a big brute of a man and nearly killed him because he was ill-treating a horse," said Margaret ingenuously. "He's four centuries too late, really—too chivalrous for these times."

"I see," murmured Mr. Lewker thoughtfully. "I also see that he has a valiant champion."

"I stick up for my friends," she said proudly. "Or," she added quickly, "people who've been my friends."

"An admirable quality, Miss Kemp. But it can be carried to extremes."

"What do you mean?"

"My dear child, why did you have to lie for him?"

The question seemed to take Margaret's breath away. She sat open-mouthed, staring at him with frightened eyes.

"You—you know that, too?" she whispered at last.

Mr. Lewker sighed and shook his head.

" 'Let me have no lying; it becomes none but tradesmen.' There's Shakespeare for you. And, my dear—if you'll pardon me—it was a very poor lie."

"But it was the truth," she cried desperately. "Bernard will tell you—"

"Listen, Miss Kemp. Bertrand, the waiter who was on duty in Simler's office at the time, saw Bernard Bryce, and spoke to him, as he was leaving the hotel at a little after three o'clock that morning."

The girl drew a long shuddering breath and covered her face with her hands.

"He was not worth that lie, if he sat there and let you tell it for him," Lewker said softly. "But you have not helped him by it. You have only brought suspicion on him."

"I'm not going to say anything more," she said without looking up. Then, suddenly, she lifted her face from her hands. "You said yourself that you heard him typing in his room at half-past seven," she accused.

"I said that I heard a typewriter at work. And I think you can tell me who the typist was, Miss Kemp."

He waited. It was some time before the girl spoke.

"I've been an idiot," she said at last, with a touch of defiance. "Hanging on to something I've lost. Well, I did lie—of course you found me out easily. I'm not much good at it, am I?"

"Frankly, no. And why did you lie?"

"Because—well, you see how he's fallen for that woman. That's obvious, if you like—even Mr. Schultz must have seen it. I supposed you'd think that was a—a motive. And I knew Bernard hadn't an alibi."

"Ah," said Mr. Lewker softly.

"You see, I was awake very early. I haven't been sleeping very well just lately. And I heard Bernard go out of his room. It was three o'clock, because I looked at my watch. And at six o'clock I did peep into his room, as I said. He wasn't there."

"And the typewriter?"

"He'd asked me to type some of his manuscript for him," she explained uncomfortably. "I'm a better typist than he is. So when I couldn't get to sleep again I thought I'd do some of it. I typed for an hour and a half."

"Yes. Now we have it." Mr. Lewker nodded to himself and then frowned. "I wonder now. I wonder why friend Bryce—"

Margaret looked up quickly. "Is he—do you think he did it?"

"Listen to me, please," Lewker commanded with some severity. "I am bound to assist Herr Schultz in his investigation. That means he trusts me to do nothing without his knowledge and permission. Miss Kemp, I have already, in a sense, betrayed that trust by telling you of our discovery that your attempt at providing Bryce with an alibi was a lie. I cannot tell you anything more. You understand that?"

She nodded dumbly.

"Good. And I am trusting you to tell no one of our conversation—no one, with the exception of Herr Schultz. I want you to go straight back to Zermatt—and if you don't you will be late for lunch—and tell Schultz what you have just told me. You must also tell him, with my compliments, that I thought it wisest to tell you about Bertrand's destruction of your story about Bryce. You agree to that?"

"Yes," she said dully.

"Thank you, Miss Kemp. By the way, Bryce must have left his room door unlocked that morning, I suppose?"

"Yes."

"Does he often do that?"

"Always. He never locks doors. He—he's awfully careless about things like that."

So anyone—anyone, at least, who knew of that carelessness—could have got at Bryce's machine and typed that threatening note without much difficulty or danger of discovery. Would Bryce, careless as he was reported to be, have been so reckless as to type it himself, on his own machine? It seemed unlikely, and yet—

A sudden disturbing sound interrupted his brief meditation. He looked up to find Margaret, her head in her hands, sobbing quietly to herself. Mr. Lewker cursed under his breath. It was a standing joke with his wife that tears, even crocodile tears, rendered him completely helpless, especially if the weeper chanced to be feminine and a brunette.

"Miss—er—Kemp!" he ventured. "Please do not cry. I had no intention of causing you pain."

The girl continued to sob. Mr. Lewker sought refuge in Shakespeare.

" 'These foolish drops do somewhat drown my manly spirit,' " he muttered; and tried again.

"Miss Kemp!" he said loudly. "For the love of heaven, blow your nose!" He pulled the handkerchief from his head. "Here—use this, and mind the knots in the corners."

She reached a hand for it and obeyed.

"I—I'm sorry," she said in a muffled voice. "It's all so wretched. It was sup-supposed to be a hol-holiday, and now—"

Her sobs overcame her once more.

"Now attend to me," said Mr. Lewker firmly. "I know the world seems a dark place at the moment. It will not remain dark for you, my dear. The shadow always passes. We shall end this wretchedness quickly, you will see."

It was, he knew, a crude sort of comfort; but it was having its effect. The voice that had stirred audiences a thousand times could bring comfort by the mere sonority and depth of its tone. Margaret's sobs became less. She looked up at him with wet gray eyes.

"Do you really th-think so?"

"Why, of course." He beamed at her and made a further effort. "I am on holiday myself, remember. I do not propose to spend it all in chasing a miserable murderer. Another twenty-four hours is all I can spare. At the end of that time, Miss Kemp—hear the words of the prophet Lewker—we shall have laid the villain by the heels."

"But—"

"Whoever it proves to be," he went on quickly, "you must remember that he deserves to pay for what he has done. Perhaps you have reason to dislike Madame Jacot. But her husband has been murdered—remember that. You must agree that when we find the criminal, whoever it is, it will be a relief for all of us."

"Y-yes," she said doubtfully. "I see that, but still I—"

"Then remember it when the time comes, my dear. Have you ever climbed a mountain?"

Margaret dabbed at her eyes. "Not in Switzerland. Bernard—Mr. Bryce said once that I should do an easy peak—"

"Then so you shall. As soon as this unpleasant business is done with."

"Not with Bernard," she said firmly.

"Perhaps with John Waveney, then?"

Margaret blushed and blew her nose violently.

"I shall take you up the Breithorn," continued Mr. Lewker cheerfully. "You will need some decent boots—not those ridiculous heels—and you must learn to walk. Select the place where the foot is to fall. Keep the stride steady, rhythmic, slow. To quote my fellow-prophet of Stratford, 'Wisely and slow; they stumble that run fast'—as you did coming up this path."

He held out a hand and she got to her feet.

"Thank you," she said, giving him back his handkerchief with a rather wan smile. "I'll remember that—all of it. Good-bye."

He watched her for a little while as she went down the path, and then turned to continue his uphill journey. His airy boasting, he reflected ruefully, had not much basis in fact. Twenty-four hours—but, after all, why not? If Schultz and Zimmermann did their parts, all the evidence within immediate reach should be in their hands by this evening. The Gifted Amateur, for which part he was cast, should be able to build that evidence into the grim shape of a Murderer, or he might as well throw up his part and walk out of the show. And Abercrombie Lewker had never done such a thing in the whole course of his career.

He trudged on doggedly, turning many things over in his mind. Among them were some words of Deborah Jacot's: *he's a brute to me sometimes.* And he frowned as he related them to a fragment of his conversation with Margaret Kemp.

CHAPTER THIRTEEN

EVIDENCE OF A PROFESSOR

The Schönbuhl hut, one of the two hundred mountain refuges maintained by the Swiss Alpine Club, has, like all its kind, an appearance of defense or even defiance. It stands high up under the butt of the long rocky comb that runs south from the Dent Blanche, its back to a precipice and its face turned stoutly towards the menace of the Matterhorn, the one tiny mark of human invasion in a sanctuary of giants. It has something of the fort in its construction; built to withstand the continual siege of Alpine storms, its solid walls might have been loopholed to enfilade the last zigzags of the rough path by which it must be approached. So thought Mr. Lewker as he toiled up the final steeps, to reach the sun-baked platform of rock on which the hut was built.

On his last visit to the Schönbuhl, in prewar days, there had been a crowd of cheerful climbers of half a dozen nationalities there, filling the little building with their various versions of mountaineering jargon. Today the hut and the rocky terrace in front of it were silent except for the snores of a young man, clad simply in bathing pants and as brown as an Indian, who lay sound asleep in the sunshine on a pneumatic mattress. He did not wake at the clatter of Mr. Lewker's boots, and the newcomer did not disturb him for the moment. It had been a steep pull up those last five hundred feet; he sat down on a rock and took a long drink from his water bottle.

In front of him the ground fell away to the glacier far below. It was the meeting place of three glaciers, in fact—a confluence of great ice rivers that wound in glittering folds from the snow peaks at their heads to form the mile-wide stream of the Zmutt Glacier. The Matterhorn was a fantastic cathedral on one side of the Zmutt, the Schönbuhl Hut a matchbox on its opposite shore; beyond the ice river a broken wall of rock buttressed the white cathedral close—the Matterhorn Glacier.

Mr. Lewker could survey, from his seat in front of the hut, almost the whole of the route which de Goursac must have followed if he had gone from the Schönbuhl to the Northeast Ridge on that fateful morning. Across the Zmutt Glacier, up the rock wall—there was at least one point where it was no more than a scramble—and on to the Matterhorn Glacier. Two hours, perhaps, for a good mountaineer; say two hours and a half in case there was difficulty in getting on to the ice. Then a walk, dodging the crevasses, across the easy slopes of the glacier and up on to the Northeast Ridge by the way the search party had used in descending to the glacier to look for Jacot's body. That might take another two hours. Therefore de Goursac would have had to set out from the hut no later than 1:30 a.m. in order to be on the ridge at six. Mr. Lewker frowned. The route was not a difficult one for a strong party in daylight, but for a solitary climber, in darkness or semidarkness for much of the way, it would be at the very least a singularly daring undertaking. Still, it was not impossible.

He drained the last drops of water from his bottle and got up. A noisy clatter of bootnails sufficed to wake the sleeper.

"Entschuldigen Sie, mein Herr," began Mr. Lewker.

"Ah, you're English," said the young man, sitting up.

Mr. Lewker, whose German accent was impeccable, looked surprised. The young man grinned. He was lean and fair-haired, with a thin intelligent face.

"I spot 'em by the clothes," he explained. "I'm getting rather good at it."

His English was the English of Oxford, but there was the slightest underlying gutturalizing of certain consonants to give the actor-manager's quick ear its clue.

"I can hardly perform the same feat in your case," he said gravely, "but you are either Swiss or German, lately of Oxford—at a guess, Trinity."

"Swiss," said the young man quickly, "but pretty work, sir. The accent, of course. But it's not bad, is it?" He stood up and held out his hand. "Adolf Venetz, professor of languages, Zurich."

"I am Abercrombie Lewker," returned that gentleman, shaking hands. He glanced at the hut, which, with its door, shutters and windows wide, looked empty. "I came up here to see the hut warden."

"You see him," said Venetz, grinning. "I've taken the job for a week. I was born in Zermatt, you see, and the hut warden's my uncle. He's on vacation and so am I. Look here—are you *the* Lewker? The Shakespearean actor?"

"I am indeed." Mr. Lewker endeavored to conceal complacency. "I wonder how—"

"I saw your *Lear* in London, three years ago. *Kolossal.* Sit down, sir—bench under the window there. This must be celebrated."

Mr. Lewker obeyed. Venetz bounded into the hut and emerged with two bottles of beer and two glasses.

"Off the ice," he announced, as he poured the amber liquid. "I keep a boxful and renew it from the glacier. *Prosit!"*

The actor-manager raised his glass politely and took a long drink.

"I expected," he remarked, "to find the hut more populous. Where are they all?"

Venetz shrugged bony shoulders. "The spell of bad weather's frightened them, I suppose. I had two English climbers here last night—they started for the Col d'Hérens early this morning—and the night before last there was a Frenchman, Comte de Something. He was alone, like you. You don't contemplate any solitary ascents, I hope?"

"Far from it, Herr Professor. With so recent an example—but perhaps you have not heard."

"Of the accident to Léon Jacot? The Englishmen brought the tale, yes. A plane making a morning flight spotted his body, they said, and he had fallen from the Hörnli Ridge, the easy route. That seemed to me rather strange, for I remember very plainly the afternoon—two years ago—when Jacot arrived at this hut after traversing the Dent Blanche in record time. It was that day René Lescaut was killed." He lifted a bottle. "Allow me to top up—delightful phrase!—your glass."

Mr. Lewker held out his tumbler. "I did not know, until I arrived in Zermatt—thank you; this is excellent beer—that Lescaut was dead. Fifteen years ago I took him and another young medical student, Lawrence Greatorex, on their first big climb."

Venetz slapped his knee. "Greatorex—that was the name of the man who had the row with Jacot. A tall fellow with a Mephistophelian look about him."

"That is he," nodded Mr. Lewker thoughtfully. He was remembering that brief conversation with Lawrence Greatorex in the hotel on the night of his arrival. "I wonder," he continued, "if you can tell me what this row was about. I have a particular reason for asking. Were you here at the time?"

"I was—taking my vacation as I am now." Venetz reached for a packet of cigarettes that lay on the bench and lit one from the match which Lewker was using for his pipe. "So far as I could gather, it was Jacot's idea that they should make this record time. Four of them left Ferpècle—Lescaut, Greatorex, Jacot and another Englishman whose name I forget. All were good climbers, accustomed to climb without guides. It appears that they climbed on two ropes, Greatorex going first with the other Englishman, Jacot following with Lescaut on his rope. The mountain was in good condition and they climbed very quickly as far as the summit. There Lescaut was taken ill. This much I learned from the man who was climbing on Greatorex's rope."

Mr. Lewker nodded. "Yes. And then?"

"Well, only three of them arrived at this hut, which happened to be unoc-cupied except by the warden, myself. Lescaut had fallen to his death from the South Ridge. He was unroped."

"Unroped? On the South Ridge of the Dent Blanche?"

"Apparently. The party of three were very tired and overwrought when they came into the hut here. But the first thing Jacot did was to request me to note the time of their arrival. He had, it seems, a bet of twenty thousand francs that they would make record time. Then Greatorex, in a towering rage, accused him of causing Lescaut's death. I gather that Lescaut, although he was feeling pretty bad, had insisted that he could keep up the pace. Half-way down the ridge, when the leading pair were out of sight below a steep break in the *arête,* Jacot had unroped from Lescaut. Greatorex asserted that Jacot had made his companion unrope on a very dangerous spot. Jacot re-torted that Lescaut had suggested the unroping so that faster progress could be made. Greatorex called him a liar and followed it up by calling him a murderer. They would have been at each other's throats if I and the other Englishman hadn't got hold of them." He blew a long cloud of smoke. "Not a pleasant tale, that."

"No," agreed Mr. Lewker. "A bad business. Did they stay here for the night?"

"Jacot stayed. The other two went on down to Zermatt to report the acci-dent. Two days later they took a party up to the Upper Ferpècle Glacier and brought down Lescaut's body. Jacot wasn't with them—he'd returned to Paris. I believe Greatorex tried to throw blame on Jacot at the inquest, but was disregarded. He and Lescaut seem to have been close friends. Have some more beer, sir."

"You are very kind. It will help to remove an unpleasant taste."

"*Nunc vino pellite curas,* eh?" chuckled the professor-warden as he disappeared into the hut.

Mr. Lewker, who had in his rucksack a bundle of those cheap and overpowering cigars beloved of the Swiss peasant, intended as a tongue-loosener for a surly hut warden, grinned a trifle ruefully. He had not expected to have Horace quoted at him by the warden of the Schönbuhl Hut. Nor had he expected to be presented with evidence that attached to Dr. Lawrence Greatorex a strong motive for the murder of Léon Jacot. For Greatorex was the type of man who would nurse that angry belief in Jacot's responsibility for his friend's death; a man in whom the interval of fifteen years would not lessen the desire for revenge. If the two men had met on the Matterhorn ridge, Jacot ascending and Greatorex coming down, the chances of something violent happening were a hundred to one.

Venetz came out with the beer and refilled the glasses.

"I am wondering," he said slowly, as he gave Lewker a brimming tumbler, "whether your object in coming here is now accomplished. You see, I happen to know that Dr. Greatorex is at present staying in Zermatt. And—it is certainly odd that Léon Jacot, a very good *bergsteiger,* should fall from the Northeast Ridge."

His eyes twinkled shrewdly as he regarded his companion. Mr. Lewker rubbed his chin.

"You are a great deal too perspicacious, Herr Professor," he observed. "And I am obliged to be so discourteous as to refuse to discuss that aspect of the matter. I am sorry, but it is beyond—"

Venetz raised a hand in protest. "Say no more, sir. You're welcome to any information I can give."

"Thank you. As it happens, my original object in coming to the Schönbuhl was to make an inquiry about the French tourist you mentioned—the Comte de Goursac. Did he, by any chance, make a solitary expedition from the hut?"

"I'd hardly call it that," returned the other, sipping his beer thoughtfully. "His behavior was rather peculiar, I thought."

"In what way?"

"Well, when he got here, in the early evening, he was very—morose, for a Frenchman. He refused to talk. It seemed to me that he was upset. After he'd made a feeble effort at eating his supper he asked me for writing materials. I took him into my room and gave him pencil and paper, and he stayed in there scribbling for half an hour. He had an early call—"

"What time?"

"I called him at four. He said he was only going for a walk up the Schön-buhl Glacier. I warned him to keep up on the left of the icefall and he set off."

"Did you happen to see which way he went?"

"I did. It was beginning to get light, so I didn't go back to my bunk. I messed about a bit, sweeping out and so forth, and then strolled outside to look at the sunrise. That was well over an hour later, but I could see the Frenchman on the glacier, only about half a mile away and standing perfectly still. He didn't move while I watched him, and when I had another look twenty minutes later he was still in the same place, just standing. Lord knows what he was up to."

"I think I can guess," Mr. Lewker said, frowning. "Was the glacier crevassed where he was standing?"

"Well, not to say crevassed, but there's one big crevasse about there—must be five meters wide and extremely deep. But only a blind man could fall into the thing, for it's visible even in the dark."

"Only a blind man—or someone afflicted in a somewhat different manner," murmured Lewker. "Would you mind," he added, "if we had a look in the room where Monsieur de Goursac did his writing that evening?"

"Not at all. Come along." Venetz put down his empty glass and led the way into the hut. "It's in a bit of a mess, but you'll excuse that."

The warden's quarters were a cubbyhole at one end of the building, furnished simply with a wooden bunk in one side, a chest of drawers, and a table. A zinc bucket under the table appeared to perform the office of waste-paper basket. Mr. Lewker, with a word of apology, drew out the bucket and began to sort through the screwed-up pieces of paper with which it was half filled. At the end of two minutes he had salvaged two crumpled pieces of paper obviously torn from a writing pad. He smoothed them out and laid them on the table. Both bore part of a message hastily scrawled in indelible pencil; the same message, but in different phrasings. The first began formally:

Madame,
  Quand vous avez reçu cette lettre je serai mort. Je ne peux pas

—the writing ended in a series of dots and squiggles. The second ran:

Camille, cœur de mon cœur, tu n'as connu jamais mon amour. Maintenant, tu m'as trahi. Pour moi la vie est finie. Demain

—and there it broke off. Mr. Lewker shook his head over the tragic fragments. The Comte, it appeared, had been sufficiently in love with his wife to contemplate suicide when he discovered her unfaithfulness; sufficiently in love, perhaps, to think of murdering the man who had seduced her, though that man had been his friend. But he had not committed suicide, nor—on the evidence to hand—had he killed Jacot.

"I see," said Venetz, at his elbow. "He was standing there wondering whether to jump, I suppose. Funny, but I'd have said he wasn't the suicidal type."

"I wonder," murmured Mr. Lewker, "whether Lord Clive was a suicidal type." He folded the crumpled sheets and put them in his pocket. "Herr Venetz, you have greatly obliged me. I hope you will dine with me at the Hotel Obergabelhorn if you should be in Zermatt during the next fortnight. I may be able to tell you the full story then. I have now, unfortunately, to hurry back to Zermatt."

Venetz accompanied him out of the hut into the glare and dazzle of the afternoon sunshine and escorted him as far as the top of the zigzags.

"You will, of course, count on me as a witness if I am required," he said, as they shook hands. "In a case of murder one must have no sympathies except with the law."

"Thank you. Good-bye, Herr Professor."

"*Auf wiedersehen, sir.*"

Mr. Lewker set off at a round pace down the path in spite of the heat. He had made good time coming up, even counting in his halts, and it was not yet four o'clock. He felt in excellent form physically apart from the slight soreness of shoulders which affects those unaccustomed to the straps of a rucksack, and he reckoned that by keeping up a steady pace he could be back in Zermatt well before seven, with time to confer with Schultz and have a bath before dinner. He was well aware of his good fortune in finding the young professor at the hut instead of his uncle. He had been enabled not only to get an intelligent and comprehensive account of de Goursac's movements but to acquire a valuable piece of evidence against Lawrence Greatorex, evidence which might—

He pulled himself up; literally as well as mentally. He halted on the path, frowning unseeing at the Rimpfischhorn that cocked its jagged crest above the deep valley below him. What state of mind was this, that led him to jubilate over the possibility of convicting one of his friends of murder? Was he falling into the pit that is dug for the professional detective, who, unless he is continually watchful, finds himself looking at all his fellow men with the eye of the hunter? Mr. Lewker continued his downward journey in a somewhat chastened state of mind, though at an undiminished pace. It was some time before he was able to tell himself convincingly that the job must be carried through to its end, that among the men and women he had met since his arrival in Switzerland, none of whom did he dislike, there was one who had killed a man and must be punished. He had covered half the distance to Zermatt before he could bring himself to consider the problem again.

It was possible that there was no problem to solve, of course. Though de Goursac must be allowed his indubitable alibi, there remained Bryce and Taugwalder, the former with a false alibi and the latter with none so far stated, and Lawrence Greatorex with an unproven one.

Mr. Lewker allowed himself a very un-detectivelike luxury: he eliminated, hypothetically and on psychological grounds only, the suspects as men and women in order of their improbability.

Heinrich Taugwalder he crossed off first. The guide was not incapable of killing a man, but he was incapable of killing a man secretly. He would not have used the method of stifling. He would certainly have expostulated with Jacot, at the hotel or elsewhere, before taking the drastic step of ambushing him high up on the Northeast Ridge. (Mr. Lewker could not be certain that such an interview had not taken place.)

Deborah Jacot he eliminated next. It was quite impossible to visualize her attacking and stifling her husband and throwing his body over the edge of a precipice. This was a man's crime. Deborah might have used poison—there was something secretive about her in spite of the dramatization of herself to which she sometimes gave way—but not the strong-arm methods that must have been used on the Northeast Ridge.

John Waveney? Mr. Lewker was not of those who believe that a man who has fought for his country is more likely to commit murder than one who has not. Yet he could conceive of John killing a man—if he had sufficient motive.

Bernard Bryce was, according to Margaret, psychologically incapable of a murder. But Margaret was probably psychologically incapable of saying or thinking otherwise. Besides, there were two significant things she had in all innocence told Mr. Lewker: that he was too chivalrous for his age, and that he had once nearly killed a man for ill-treating a horse. Could he have killed a man for ill-treating his wife? It was surely possible.

As for Greatorex, the circumstances of the murder were in keeping with his bitter humor. If, as was evident, he believed Jacot to be responsible for the death of his friend on a mountain, it would be poetic justice that Jacot in his turn should meet his end on a great peak. Reluctantly Lewker admitted that there was no incongruity here.

De Goursac; a man of strong if normally controlled passions, with a motive amply sufficient if those half-finished letters showed anything. And Frey, admittedly a member of a fanatical anti-Communist gang, a mountaineer accustomed to walk alone on the mountains—the use of the red scarf to kill Jacot might easily bear the psychological interpretation Schultz had placed upon it. These two were undoubtedly capable of this murder.

In order of psychological probability, then, he placed de Goursac, Frey and Greatorex equally, with Bryce next and John Waveney last. Of these only Bryce and Greatorex had no proven alibi, and if Greatorex's careless confidence was anything to go by it meant that the Italian climber at Breuil would confirm his story that he had been climbing on the Italian Ridge until 9 a.m. That left Bernard Bryce.

Two questions put themselves to Mr. Lewker in the matter of Bernard Bryce: why had Margaret assumed that Bryce had no alibi? Why, if Bryce had an alibi, had he not said so? The first question might be answered by saying that Margaret was by no means so confident of Bryce's innocence as she had tried to appear, that she had indeed suspected him of going out to follow and kill Jacot and had impulsively attempted to shield him. This, he thought, was not improbable. The second question could not be answered so easily. Bryce was no fool. He must have known that an enquiry, which was almost bound to be made, would reveal at once that Margaret's story was false. Well, no doubt a reason would emerge when Schultz questioned him. There was little to be gained by speculation here.

And the others—Margaret Kemp, Camille de Goursac, Mrs. Fillingham? On the face of it, none of them had opportunity or motive. If this was to be treated in the "fictional detection" manner, thought Mr. Lewker, with the least likely person turning out to be the murderer, Beatrix Fillingham was undoubtedly the one to watch.

By this time his steady pace had brought him far down the narrow track and into the cool shadow of the lower glen, with Zermatt little more than two miles away. He had covered fourteen steep and rough miles since eleven, and it was nearly six. The high-hung chalets of Zmutt were behind him, and he came now to a place where the path, unfenced and only a few feet across, skirted the deep chasm of the foaming Zmuttbach. It slanted across a mountainside steep as a cliff but clothed with pines and bushes. On his right the ground fell dizzily away to the torrent roaring in its gorge three hundred feet below, so that the path was in fact a broad ledge cut out of a precipice. Stony gullies seamed the pine-clad upper slopes, down which in early spring great boulders from the crags above sometimes crash to fling six feet of path into fragments and give work to the men of Zmutt and Zermatt. A chill moist air floated up from the awesome depths below. Mr. Lewker was fifty paces from the end of this section of path, where the ground eased its angle and the way curved away from the gorge, when he was aware of a most unpleasant noise of falling rocks above his head; unpleasant because it became rapidly louder and was plainly very close.

There was no time to spurt for the easy ground. No time, indeed, to do anything but what Mr. Lewker instantly did: plaster himself against the trunk of the nearest pine.

The quickness of his decision almost certainly saved his life. Crashing down through the thickets came three or four massive boulders, accompa-nied by an avalanche of smaller stuff. He felt the wind of one of the boulders as it whizzed past his tree, and there was a rattle of stones against the other side of the trunk. The whole furious cavalcade landed on the path with a frightful impact, shaking the ground beneath his feet, and bounded over into the gorge to thunder down from crag to crag in a devil's chorus of echoes.

Mr. Lewker stayed pressed against his tree until the last detonation had echoed and faded. Then, feeling rather sick, he stood up. A thick cloud of reddish dust floated in the sunlight. Through it he saw, two feet from his stance, a ragged edge of earth and a trickle of soil sliding from it into the chasm. A clear eight feet of the path had gone, and a few feet farther along a sizeable boulder, separated from its fellows, had cut another gap of four feet.

Stepping with exaggerated caution, Mr. Lewker made his way to the un-touched section of path beyond. His ears were humming with the noise of the rockfall, but it seemed to him that he could hear shouts coming from the steeps above. His scattered wits collected themselves and informed him that large rocks rarely fall across frequented Alpine paths in summer. He walked on, looking about him and listening. There was a sudden crackling of bushes on the left of the path. Mr. Lewker, expecting he knew not what, halted. A minor avalanche, consisting of dust, small stones and a human figure, slid on to the path in front of him. The human figure picked itself up and sneezed.

It was Mrs. Fillingham.

CHAPTER FOURTEEN

SPOTLIGHT ON BERNARD BRYCE

"Oy!" roared Mrs. Fillingham. "What's going on? Was that an avalanche, or what?"

Her blue-and-yellow check blouse was ripped across the shoulder and her large bare knees were sadly scratched. She spat out some fragments of earth, and then appeared to notice the havoc wrought on the path behind Mr. Lewker.

"Great Godfrey!" she ejaculated, staring goggle-eyed. "That's—why, it must have missed you pretty closely. What was it?"

"It was a fall of rocks, dislodged from above," replied Mr. Lewker slowly, his gaze on her flushed and rather stupid face. "It was indeed a near thing.

You did not see it, then?"

"Me? No—I was hooked up in a thicket. Only heard a sort of rumble and then a noise like the end of the world. I thought it was coming for me, so I tore myself loose and more or less fell down several small cliffs on to the path. Mercy I didn't go over the edge. I—great Godfrey, Mr. Lewker!" She clutched his arm suddenly. "D'you think someone might have shoved those rocks down—on purpose?"

If the mingled excitement and apprehension she displayed were assumed, thought the actor-manager, she was a much better actress than he had imagined.

"Why do you say that?" he asked.

"Let's move on," said Mrs. Fillingham urgently. "This place gives me the willies." She dragged him towards the safer part of the path. "I'll tell you. I've been doing a bit of sleuthing."

"Indeed?" Mr. Lewker frowned at her.

"Well, I have. You've been at it, haven't you? I don't see why your Aunty Bee shouldn't have a crack. I used to be a Guider, you know—got my Wood-craft Badge and everything."

"Was this why you were—hum—hooked up in a thicket, Mrs. Filling-ham? Did you by any chance see anyone up there?"

"Wait a bit. I'll start at the beginning, like the girl in *Death Walks Side-ways*. Read it? Super yarn."

They had emerged on to the open slopes above the valley. The chalets and hotels of Zermatt lay in front and below, bathed in the flood of rich golden light. The sound of cowbells, mellowed by distance, floated up from the lower hillsides where the huge shadow of the Matterhorn crept stealthily across pasture and stream. Mr. Lewker, who had recovered from the shock of his narrow escape, maintained his steady stride while Mrs. Fillingham, trotting along beside him, excitedly told her tale.

"We all had lunch together in that room where we had that meeting this morning—Simler thought it would be better. Herr Schultz came in and told us he might want to ask some of us questions this evening, but it would be all right for us to go for a walk in the afternoon if we wanted to. When he'd gone out Margot piped up and said she didn't think much of Schultz as a detective but put her money on you, or words to that effect. Said you'd told her the murderer would be in your clutches inside twenty-four hours. Did you?"

"I made some such unwarranted remark," he admitted, inwardly cursing Margaret's talkativeness. "You said, Mrs. Fillingham, that you were all lunch-ing together. Whom does that include?"

"Ah—you mean who heard Margaret say that, eh?" Mrs. Fillingham con-trived to look incredibly knowing. "Well, we were all there except Madame Jacot—she took sandwiches and went out somewhere. Don't blame her. I reckon she's taking this business pretty well. So there was me, Margot, John Waveney, the de Goursacs, Dr. Greatorex and Bernard Bryce—particularly Bernard Bryce."

"Why 'particularly'?"

Mrs. Fillingham became confidential. "Well, between pals and all that guff, I used to like him. Thought he and Margot'd make a pair. But I'm wondering. He's a dark horse, is Bernard. Nothing against him, of course, but—well, he was hanging round Madame Deborah from the minute they met. She had him taped from the word go—allure, they call it. So I was watching him, covertly, you know."

Mr. Lewker grinned—covertly. He had received a mental picture of his companion's covert regard.

"He went positively ghastly when he heard about your twenty-four-hour stunt," continued Mrs. Fillingham with relish, "and I could see he was in a hurry to push off somewhere. Now it seems to me you and this Schultz bird aren't doing nearly enough trailing people. After all, if we're suspects—and I suppose we are, even your Aunty Bee—we ought to be under surveillance, oughtn't we? Anyhow, I reckoned I'd put a spot of surveillance on Master Bernard to see what he was up to. When he went out of the hotel after lunch I shadowed him."

Again Mr. Lewker repressed a smile. "In those nailed boots?" he enquired gently.

"Oh, I kept well away behind him—too well away, as it happened. He almost spotted me after the first few seconds, when he was slinking past those old chalets behind the hotel, but I dodged behind a wooden post that happened to be handy. After that I kept my distance, and he zigzagged about through a lot of narrow lanes—I think he was messing up his trail—and in the end I lost him. Found myself in someone's back yard, and out came a massive Swiss woman and told me off at the top of her voice."

She hooted with laughter at the recollection, allowing Mr. Lewker to vent his own amusement without giving offense.

"But great Godfrey!" she exclaimed, quickly sobering. "It's no laughing matter, after all. Those boulders, I mean. If Bernard had 'em waiting for you—grrr!" she shuddered. "And he could have done."

"But I thought you lost sight of him."

"Well, I'll tell you what happened."

Here a very old man with a large pipe stuck in his mouth and a stately billy-goat attached to his wrist by a piece of string halted to let them pass him on the narrow path. He removed the pipe, lifted his round black hat to arm's length, and greeted them with a quavering *Gruss Gott!* as they tramped past.

"Quaint, aren't they?" shouted Mrs. Fillingham, delighted.

Mr. Lewker thought it likely that a similar comment, translated into Valais patois, would have occurred to the aged Swiss.

"What made you walk up this path?" he asked.

"Well, I cast about a bit trying to pick up Bryce's trail, and then I decided I was wasting my time. Margot had told me what a scenic sort of path this was, so I thought I might as well have a hike up this way. I got to just about where the trees begin and it gets very steep above and below, and then I happened to glance up, and—I saw a man."

She paused dramatically.

"Yes?" said Mr. Lewker patiently.

"Yes. There's a sort of little crag sticks out above the trees, not far above the path. He was standing on top of that. I only saw him for a jiffy—he bobbed down almost as soon as I spotted him. But he was about Bernard Bryce's build. Couldn't tell you what he was wearing, and I was too far off to see his face. Don't think he was broad enough for de Goursac, though."

"You thought it might possibly be Bryce. And then?"

"Well, the hunting blood of the Fillinghams was up. He'd behaved oddly at lunch and he'd diddled me in the village. I did a bit of scouting. Got into cover of the trees and started making up towards that little crag. But great Godfrey! What a place!" Mrs. Fillingham pointed to her scratched knees. "Talk about blood and sweat—look at that. It was all ravines and thorns. I never got anywhere near him. I'm not so young as I was, you know," she added candidly.

"You saw nothing more of the man?"

"Nary a sign. I was struggling through a sort of entanglement at an angle of forty-five degrees when that crashing started. It shook me—I thought it was coming my way. I yelled out something like 'Look out, up there!' and afterwards, when it had stopped, I yelled again to ask what the something was going on. Then—well, I cascaded down on to the path, and—that's all."

"I see," said Mr. Lewker. He pondered for a moment. "Did Miss Kemp mention at lunchtime that she had talked to me on this path—this particular path, I mean?"

"She did. De Goursac mumbled something about you going up to the Shern-something Hut to spy on him."

So any of those at the luncheon table would know that he would be returning down that path some time in the afternoon. It would not be a difficult matter, between two o'clock and four, to select a suitable place and arrange half a dozen rocks where they could be sent down at a push. No doubt the man—or could it have been Deborah in the slacks she sometimes wore?—had watched the upper path from his lookout crag; then, when he had seen his intended victim approaching, he would climb down to his pile of rocks and wait until the sound of footsteps told him the time had come. Bryce,

Greatorex and de Goursac were all familiar with the path to the Schönbuhl. But anyone with such a purpose in mind, and who knew he would be returning by that route, could have arranged the trap. At least Heinrich was out of it this time—unless the commissioner had finished his interrogation early.

Was it, then, Margaret Kemp's tale of Lewker's boastful twenty-four-hour limit that had led someone to decide that he would be safer put neatly out of the way? Or had there been something said in that extraordinary gathering that had been taken by the criminal as meaning that the actor-manager was on his track while Schultz was not? Bernard Bryce, John Waveney, Paul de Goursac, Lawrence Greatorex—which of them had it been? For this had surely been a man's work. None of them, as Mr. Lewker thought of them one by one, gave the impression of being the sort of villain who would deliberately send a rock avalanche down on to him, Abercrombie Lewker.

And then he remembered that it was no ordinary kindly human with whom he had to deal, but a man stripped of the veneer of humanity, a killer who had murdered one man already and now was in terror for his own life. It was a reversal of the train of thought that had halted him in disgust earlier in the afternoon. The idea of hunting down Jacot's murderer seemed much less repellent to him now. The attack upon himself had given him a less squeamish outlook on the business of detection. The man must be hunted without mercy. Or—was it a woman he must look for, after all?

There was, he recalled, only the story of the woman who walked at his side to substantiate this elusive rock-roller. She had tried to put him on the trail of Bernard Bryce; and Bryce, it appeared, had practically jilted her niece. Could Mrs. Fillingham—but no, it was ridiculous. And yet he had found himself thinking before now that the woman was not such a fool as she made herself out to be. She was a strong walker, too.

Mr. Lewker was startled out of these wandering fancies by a somewhat resentful voice at his elbow.

"Well, I suppose the great brain's deduced everything by now," it remarked loudly.

He became aware that he had not spoken for ten minutes. The path had reached the end of its descent and they were already entering the outskirts of Zermatt.

"My dear Mrs. Fillingham," he boomed apologetically, "I am afraid I have been rude. Pray forgive me."

"Don't mention it. Dare say having rocks bunged at one doesn't make one chatty. Sorry I couldn't spot who the bunger was."

"I think you made a very creditable effort," he told her.

Mrs. Fillingham blushed. They came into the lane behind the Hotel Obergabelhorn and approached the hotel porch. Simler was standing there surveying the quiet street, the inevitable cigar in his mouth.

"Not a word about the rockfall, even to Miss Kemp, please," Mr. Lewker warned his companion.

She nodded energetically and hurried into the hotel. Simler stepped forward as Lewker was about to follow.

"Your pardon, sir," he said politely. "Herr Schultz asked me to watch for you. He awaits you in your room."

"Thank you, Simler. You might send up two bottles of Pilsner. On second thoughts, make it four. And by the way—"

"Yes, sir?"

"How did the—er—party that lunched in your back parlor occupy themselves this afternoon?"

Simler showed no surprise. The perfect *hotelier* keeps himself unobtrusively informed of his guests' wanderings, especially in a mountain-surrounded place like Zermatt. His wrinkled face was impassive as he supplied the required information without the slightest pause.

"Madame la Comtesse retired to her room after lunch, and her husband also. I believe they are still there. The remainder went out. Miss Kemp walked down the road in the direction of Täsch, Dr. Greatorex I heard announce his intention of seeking a shady wood in which to sleep. Mr. Bryce set off to walk immediately after lunch after asking me if I knew where Madame Jacot had gone. I was able to tell him only that she had taken sandwiches and had walked towards Findelen. Her brother, Mr. Waveney, went out about ten minutes afterwards, also in search of his sister. Mrs. Fillingham I believe you met, sir."

"Yes. Have any of the others returned from their expeditions?"

"Not yet, sir."

"Hm." Mr. Lewker rubbed his chin. "Well—'marry and amen! Give me a cup of sack, boy.' "

"Certainly, sir," returned Simler without batting an eyelid.

Mr. Lewker passed through into the hall and went up to his room. Schultz was there, pacing up and down with a copy of the 1:50,000 map of the Zermatt district in his hand. He looked cool and neat in his fashion-plate suit compared with the actor-manager, whose face was begrimed with dust and sweat and whose open shirt revealed a good deal of hairy chest. The commissioner displayed satisfaction without geniality.

"Ha!" he snapped. "You have been quick. I am in need of you. But first, what is your news?"

Mr. Lewker, feeling suddenly tired, pulled a chair into the center of the floor opposite the open window and lowered himself into it with a long sigh.

" 'I am as hot as molten lead, and as heavy, too,' " he boomed. "Those are Falstaff's words, *mein Herr,* and I find myself too Falstaffian as yet for these mountain paths of yours."

"De Goursac, Herr Lewker, please. Have you—"

"De Goursac's alibi is as sound as an alibi can be. I have a reliable wit-ness."

Schultz nodded, his pale eyes gleaming. *"So!* I knew that it would be as you say. We shall find that all have good alibis except this rascal Taugwalder."

"Have you not interrogated him?"

Schultz compressed his lips. He looked dangerous.

"He—refuses—to—speak," he said, spitting out the words between pauses. "Yes, my friend, he will say nothing until you are present. He has the impu-dence—but it is like these stubborn peasants. You shall come to the police office with me and then perhaps Herr Taugwalder will condescend to ex-plain himself."

"You have kept him there?"

"Potztausend!" The commissioner gestured angrily with his map. "He sits there and will not go, he and that hussy of a daughter. Not, you understand, that I wish him to go until he has been questioned satisfactorily—and then, perhaps, we shall ask this obstinate gentleman to stay with us. *Ja*—in a cell!"

The arrival of the Pilsner soothed him. In his own glass Mr. Lewker con-cealed a grin. He thought he could understand Heinrich's refusal. The guide had realized from what Lisse would have told him that he was in a tight corner; also that he had, as it were, a friend in the enemy's camp. It was natural enough that he should want his old employer to be present when he told whatever story he had to tell.

"Have you heard from Signor Villanova?" he asked, refilling both glasses.

"I have. Zimmermann was on the telephone to him shortly after you left for the Schönbuhl. Signor Villanova confirms that he was attached to the Herr Doktor Greatorex by a climbing rope from four o'clock that morning until nine. Another firm alibi, *nicht wahr*? You shall see that Taugwalder—"

"You have not forgotten, I hope, that Bernard Brycc has as yet no alibi."

"I have not forgotten, my friend. I would have interrogated Mr. Bryce this afternoon, when I found I was wasting my time with Taugwalder, but he was not to be found. You will find, however, that Mr. Bryce is not our man."

"He allowed Miss Kemp to supply him with a false alibi, remember."

Schultz flung his map aside and sat down with a sigh of impatience.

"Yes, yes—I do not forget these things. But you do not mean to tell me that a guilty man would sit quietly while the girl told a story that could be dis-proved in five minutes? And here, Herr Lewker, I must tell you that I am displeased." He looked severely down his nose at Mr. Lewker. "You did very wrong to tell Miss Kemp of that discovery. She confessed to me, as you had instructed her, and I do not think any harm has been done. But you will please not to allow yourself in future to spill my beans."

"They shall remain unspilled," promised Lewker gravely. "Have you had a report," he added, "from the party that went up the Northeast Ridge?"

"I have. They found nothing—no sign of a struggle, no clue at all. Our murderer had been very careful."

"They saw nothing of Jacot's rucksack or ice-axe?" persisted Lewker.

"Nothing. Now, sir, if you will come with me to the police office, we shall question this obstinate fool Taugwalder."

Schultz got up. Mr. Lewker, doing likewise, caught sight of himself in the mirror over the washstand.

"Now by all the gods at once!" he boomed. "I do not stir until I have washed, even if I have to go without my dinner."

There was a knock at the bedroom door, cutting short the commissioner's protest. Mr. Lewker opened it. Bernard Bryce, looking hot and dusty, stood there.

"Got to have a talk," he announced, his glance going beyond Lewker to the commissioner. "Can I come in?"

"Most certainly, Mr. Bryce," said Schultz, coming forward quickly. "We have been anxious to see you."

Bryce came into the room slowly. His brown face was set impassively. Schultz waved him to a chair.

"Sit down, Mr. Bryce," he said with great affability. "You have enjoyed a good walk, I hope?"

"I have," returned Bryce stolidly, sitting.

"I saw you on the Schönbuhl path, I think," put in Mr. Lewker, watching him.

Bryce met his gaze coolly. "Not me. I've been up to Zumsee, other direction. For a purpose. Decided I'd better have a word with you both."

"I believe you went to find Madame Jacot," continued Lewker, to the annoyance of Schultz, who had been about to speak. "Did you find her?"

"I did," Bryce answered with a touch of defiance.

"But you did not stay long with her?"

"I don't see why you want to know, but I didn't. Madame Jacot was not far away when I found her—by the river south of the village. Her brother was with her. I stayed for five minutes and then went on. Anything else I can tell you," he added sulkily, "you've only to ask."

"That is amiable of you, Mr. Bryce," Schultz said quickly. "We are going to ask you to describe your movements on the morning of Léon Jacot's death."

Bryce showed no sign of perturbation. He nodded, frowning at the floor.

"I'd better tell you first," he said slowly, "that Miss Kemp was—mistaken when she said she saw me in my room that morning."

"We are aware of that," nodded the commissioner comfortably.

"She didn't tell you?" demanded Bryce, looking up.

"We had only to ask the man on duty in the hall, Mr. Bryce. You left at five minutes past three and returned to the hotel a little before lunchtime." Schultz leaned forward impressively. "Now. Will you say, please, why you did not correct Miss Kemp when she told us that—when she made that mistake?"

Bryce hesitated before replying, but his voice was perfectly cool when he spoke.

"Fact is, I realized I hadn't any too good an alibi. When Margaret— Miss Kemp—said what she did, I—well, you can see I had to choose between calling her a liar in public and at the same time making things awkward for myself, and just keeping quiet. I kept quiet. I see, now, I was wrong."

"You were wrong, Mr. Bryce," nodded the commissioner gravely. "But now you shall tell us the truth, *hein?* And you will see that matters will be O.K. in a brace of shakes, as you say."

The mountaineer folded his arms and seemed to collect his thoughts. The observant Mr. Lewker noticed that, although his set expression did not change, a tiny muscle at the angle of the jaw was twitching convulsively.

"I woke at ten past two," Bryce began. "I think it was Jacot going out that woke me. I knew I wouldn't get to sleep again—never can—so after a bit I turned out and got into climbing kit."

"You purposed a walk into high places?" questioned Schultz keenly. He had his notebook out and was scribbling rapidly.

"I thought I might get up high, yes. Took my ice-axe—suppose Simler's chap told you that. Idea was to go up to Findelen and scramble up to the Gornergrat from there. See the sunrise. After that I'd come down the ordinary path past the Riffel."

"You must have seen persons on this path, early as it was," observed Schultz.

"Wait a bit. I saw nobody on the way up to Findelen—too early, and dark anyway. When I got there I changed my mind. Instead of going up the Gornergrat I took the path that runs round above the Boden Glacier and climbed down to the ice."

"Wait," said the commissioner. He picked up the map and spread it out on the table. "I see. This route took you in the direction of the Hörnli, at the foot of the Matterhorn ridge, *nicht wahr?"*

"It did." Bryce's voice was expressionless. "My plan was now to cross the glacier, hit the little path that goes up to the Schwarzsee—that's the lake below the end of the Northeast Ridge—and go down to Zermatt from there. And that's what I did."

"You saw the plane, no doubt," remarked Mr. Lewker. "Did you notice the time when you saw it?"

"No, but I certainly saw it. I was a couple of miles below the little hotel by the Schwarzsee when it passed overhead, pretty high up, and it was just six-thirty when I reached the hotel. So it must have been sevenish when I saw the plane."

"When you passed the hotel," said Schultz, "did you see no one?"

"There were people getting up, I think, but I don't believe they saw me pass. The first chap I saw near enough to speak to was an old fellow who has a chalet in the woods near Zumsee. I had a glass of milk there."

"Aha!" Schultz beamed at him. "Then here we have something."

"Maybe. His name's Peter Knubel. He remembers my calling there, and the time. It was between eight and a quarter past. I know this because I've been up there this afternoon to find him."

Bryce made this announcement without any sign of triumph. He seemed, indeed, to be a little nervous, judging by the rapid twitching of that betraying muscle in his jaw.

Mr. Lewker, who had picked up the map to study it closely, eyed him thoughtfully.

"You say it was about seven o'clock when you were two miles below the Schwarzsee," he observed. "Yet you did not reach the chalet at Zumsee, which is a short three miles below the Schwarzsee, until at least an hour later. You took, in fact, an hour to do this mile of downhill path."

"I dare say I did," returned Bryce rather sulkily. "I kept stopping to admire the scenery and smoke a pipe. I suppose that's permitted?"

"In any case," said the commissioner quickly, "we need detain you no longer, Mr. Bryce. Thank you for this information."

He stood up. Bryce appeared puzzled at this abrupt dismissal. He looked from Lewker to Schultz.

"Don't I get any information?" he demanded. "Is it an alibi or isn't it? Remember, I don't know what time this damned murder was committed."

"I think you need have no anxiety," Schultz told him. He went to the door and opened it politely. Bryce got up, hesitated frowningly, and then went slowly out. Schultz closed the door on him and turned to Lewker, who was already stripping off his shirt as he advanced on the washstand.

"Now, my friend!" he cried. "You see that if this Knubel confirms, we have another alibi. For the spot whence Jacot fell, as Perren tells me, is two hours' climbing above the Schwarzsee for a fast climber. We may say, then, one and a half hours' down-climbing, *hein?* And if Mr. Bryce ran all the way from the Schwarzsee to Knubel's chalet, he could not do the distance in less than half an hour. Two hours—and that would be a superhuman feat. But if Bryce, as we know he did, left the hotel at just after three, he could not have been at the place of the murder before seven. Therefore, my friend, he could not have reached Knubel's chalet before nine o'clock. Yet he was there at a quarter past eight. This is an alibi, I think? You agree?"

Mr. Lewker took his face out of the washbasin.

"It is an alibi for a murder committed between six and seven o'clock," he said indistinctly through the folds of a towel.

"Gut." The commissioner glanced at his watch. "Now we shall go to see what Herr Taugwalder has to say to us."

Downstairs the dinner gong reverberated suggestively.

"Dinner we must miss, I fear," added Schultz cheerfully, "but Zimmermann will find us some coffee and cakes."

Mr. Lewker groaned.

CHAPTER FIFTEEN

LIMELIGHT ON HEINRICH TAUG-WALDER

Herr Schultz did not linger to watch Mr. Lewker finish his ablutions, but took himself off to the police office. The actor-manager was not long in following him. Much as the idea of substituting coffee and cakes in a police-station for Simler's excellent dinner repelled him, he was as anxious as Schultz to get this business cleared up. And he was a good deal more anxious than the commissioner about the welfare of Heinrich Taugwalder. He contented himself with putting on a scarf and sweater and changing nailed boots for shoes, and (looking more like Tony Weller in modern dress than like an actor-manager or an amateur detective) sallied out into the streets.

As he stumped along towards the police office he pondered that story of Bernard Bryce's. It was a plausible tale enough; it had a certain aimless inconsequence that truth sometimes possesses, and the alibi it contained was a closer thing than a guilty man would have devised. Even if Bryce had taken no time at all to meet, stifle and fling down Jacot, turning from his deed to race down the unstable ridge and the lower paths, he could not possibly have reached Knubel's chalet by 8:15. Knubel's reliability would have to be checked, of course; there was the possibility that Bryce had visited him that afternoon to bribe the man into giving him an alibi. But if he had, as he stated so ingenuously, been up the Schwarzsee path as far as Zumsee, could he also have laid the trap, on another path across two deep valleys, in which Mr. Lewker had so nearly been caught? It was possible, but it would entail furious speed and a taking of long chances.

As to that same trap, Mr. Lewker had intended to say nothing about it to

Schultz. He saw now, however, that the commissioner must be told. Who-ever rolled down those boulders, it had not been Heinrich Taugwalder.

The streets of Zermatt seemed strangely hushed, although there were many tourists and a number of cars about. Perhaps it was the effect of the great shadow that lay across the little town and its surroundings like a dark hand placed above the valley, the reminder of a mighty presence that had brooded over the place before ever Man came there and would be there, arrogantly blotting out the evening sunshine, when Zermatt and its inhabitants had crumbled into dust: the Matterhorn. The great shaft of rock and ice was dark now, though the distant snow crests were still tipped with gold. It seemed to nod contemptuously at the cluster of buildings nestling innocently in its shadow. Mr. Lewker experienced again the uncomfortable illusion that the mountain was laughing silently at his futile efforts to wrest away its secret. He was within a hundred yards of the police office when he met John Waveney, clad in blazer and flannels, hurrying towards the hotel with a parcel under his arm.

"By gum! Don't tell me you've had dinner!" John cried as he came up. "I know I'm devilish late—been shopping."

Mr. Lewker explained that he had some business to attend to in the town.

"Any luck, sir?" the other demanded eagerly. "With this murder business, I mean. It's wearing Deb out, this uncertainty."

"I may have something to tell you later," returned Lewker evasively. "Be-fore you go, Mr. Waveney, would you mind confirming a small point? You went to find your sister after lunch, I believe?"

"Yes, I did. She went off by herself with some sandwiches, you know. Found her down by the river about half a mile out of the town. Bit difficult for her, having to be with that gang, so she—"

"Tell me this, please. Did Mr. Bryce join you?"

"Not exactly. He turned up a few minutes later. He cleared off almost at once."

"What time would that be?"

"Oh—not much after two. Say quarter-past. But why—"

"Thank you, Mr. Waveney. I hope you will find some dinner left."

Mr. Lewker passed on before John could make any further remark. That part of Bryce's story was true, then. He wondered why he had hur-ried off—according to Mrs. Fillingham "looking ghastly"—to find Debo-rah Jacot after lunch. As for that lady's impression that Bryce had pur-posely dodged her in the Zermatt lanes, there was nothing at all improb-able in that. But what had he wanted from Deborah? Could it have been some information which led to his immediate visit to Knubel to assure himself of an alibi?

The green-painted door of the police office opened to his knock. A man in the gray-green uniform of the Swiss police admitted him to the large outer office. Here, at a table neatly stacked with papers, Herr Schultz was sitting with a coffee cup in one hand and a large cream cake in the other while he studied his open notebook. At a desk in the center of the room Zimmermann scratched busily in a ledger.

"More news," Schultz greeted him. He indicated a chair at the other end of the table, where a coffeepot and a large cup flanked a dish piled with indigestible-looking pastries. "Sit—eat—and I will tell you. It will not harm our friend Taugwalder to wait a little longer."

Mr. Lewker sat down and poured himself some coffee. It was excellent coffee, and gave him the courage to tackle one of the squashier cakes.

"Zimmermann has ascertained Frey's movements," said Schultz. He jerked his head at the police officer. "Let us hear, Zimmermann."

The policeman jumped and picked up a sheaf of telegrams.

"Frey arrived in Täsch eight days ago," he said rapidly. "He traveled from Paris via Belfort and Brigue without stopping. He—"

"He did not stop in Geneva?" queried Mr. Lewker.

"No, sir. He did not pass through Geneva at all. From Franz Imboden we have it that the man Frey arrived at the Weisses Kreuz with a sprained ankle at 11:26 on Sunday night. Dr. Macrae, who attended him, is a frequent visitor in Täsch and is vouched for by several English people. At 11:50—I transcribe our European time of 23:50 into the English form, so that—"

"Get on, man!" snapped Schultz impatiently.

"In brief, sir, the man Frey did not leave his bed between 23:50 and noon of yesterday."

"And that," murmured Mr. Lewker, "seems to dispose finally of our original 'most obvious suspect.' "

Schultz pretended not to hear. "Continue, Zimmermann," he barked. "We have much to do and I wish Herr Lewker to know all that we have discovered."

"Yes, sir. The enquiry we made to the English police through Basle has been answered by code cable. There is nothing against any of the English ladies and gentlemen except one—Frau Fillingham."

He looked up enquiringly as Mr. Lewker muttered under his breath, but the commissioner gestured impatiently and he continued.

"This lady, Frau Fillingham, was arrested last May for obstructing the police. She was taking part in a Communist procession in London. She was fined. That is all, Herr Kommissar."

"And that," said Schultz, "means nothing, of course."

"Do you remember, *mein Herr,*" Mr. Lewker said gently, "pointing out to me that the typewritten threat showed that someone had discovered Jacot's political intentions 'with absolute certainty?' And, when I asked if you meant the Anti-Communists, you said 'or the other side?' "

"Yes, yes," Schultz replied testily. "But this is old history. Our problem now is one only—Heinrich Taugwalder. And that little fool of a daughter of his. She is hiding something, that one. But first, Herr Lewker, I wish you to tell you the result of your visit to the Schönbuhl Hut so that Zimmermann may place it on record."

Mr. Lewker complied. Zimmermann took down his concise account of what Adolf Venetz had told him. Lewker, ignoring signs of impatience on the part of the commissioner, told also of Venetz's story of the quarrel between Lawrence Greatorex and Léon Jacot two years earlier.

"Ah," nodded Zimmermann when he had finished making notes of this, "I know this young man Venetz well. He is very clever and is undoubtedly a reliable witness."

"Do you also know Peter Knubel, who has a chalet near Zumsee?" enquired Mr. Lewker.

Schultz interposed. "I have made that enquiry myself. Zimmermann tells me this Knubel is a maker of clocks, a man of unblemished honesty. Also, for the purpose of his trade, he has in his chalet a very good clock which, as he boasts, is never wrong." He snapped his fingers. "I tell you, Herr Lewker, that alibi is sound as are all the others—Taugwalder only remains."

Mr. Lewker helped himself to more coffee and a fifth cream cake.

"I have one thing more to tell you," he announced, "I will be brief. It is scarcely worthy of Herr Zimmermann's record, I think."

He described the rockfall that had taken place on the Schönbuhl path and related the story told to him by Mrs. Fillingham. Schultz listened with restrained but obvious impatience. As the recital drew to a close his sharp eyes twinkled and he permitted himself to chuckle.

"Well, my dear Herr Lewker," he said benevolently, "I am a little surprised that you should fall into an error of this kind, though it is true that more experienced detectives have been known to make it. You assume that every unusual incident that occurs during an investigation must bear some relation to the crime that is being investigated."

Mr. Lewker stiffened. "You consider this rockfall to bear no relation to Jacot's murder?"

Schultz smiled and glanced at Zimmermann, who obediently smiled also.

"You surely do not imagine," he purred, "that anyone would go to such trouble to kill Herr Lewker? Why should they?"

"Then you think the rockfall was an accidental, that is to say a natural, rockfall?" asked Mr. Lewker with dangerous meekness.

"Of course. Such things are by no means uncommon on the path above the Zmuttbach. I am right, Zimmermann, am I not?"

"They are not unknown," replied the police officer cautiously.

"There! You see, my friend? Coincidences do happen outside your English detective stories. As for this tale of Frau Fillingham's, you may ignore it. The woman is quite unreliable. Also, she has probably a grudge against Bryce, who appears to have given her niece what you call the chuck."

Mr. Lewker restrained his rising annoyance. "It was surely a remarkable coincidence," he observed coldly, "that a number of large rocks should pass with extreme velocity over the exact spot where I had been standing a second before. In winter such an occurrence might be put down to chance, but in summer—"

"Ta, ta, ta!" Herr Schultz waved a podgy white hand in tolerant amusement. "I advise you, my friend, to think nothing more of the matter. Had it been myself—and you will agree, I think, that the *Kriminal Kommissar* is a more probable target for an assassin—I would have reported the matter to the authorities responsible for keeping paths in good repair, and that is all."

Observing, at this point, that Mr. Lewker's lips were pursed ominously and that he tapped with one finger on the arm of his chair like one whose patience is sorely tried, the commissioner became conciliatory.

"It is understandable, this fear of yours," he said soothingly. "You English live in a safe and easy land. Here in Switzerland a trickle of stones across a mountain path is an everyday occurrence."

That phrase, had he only known it, sealed his fate; his last chance of getting the credit for solving the problem of Léon Jacot's murder vanished. '*A trickle of stones!*' Mr. Lewker, a number of very Shakespearean oaths crowding to his lips, restrained himself with difficulty from venting them. One thing was very clear: the commissioner should henceforth receive no benefit from the brains of Abercrombie Lewker. The nebulous and rather fantastic theory that was already forming itself in his mind should be kept to himself. The Gifted Amateur would play his traditional part of confounding the officials in the last act. This decision taken, he instantly recovered his good humor.

" 'Silence; no more; go closely in with me,' " he boomed. " 'Much danger do I undergo for thee.' " He helped himself to a sixth cream cake and stood up. "I think, *mein Herr,* we should join the Taugwalders."

"You are right." Schultz rose also. "I shall be surprised if we do not find the end of our problems there. Zimmermann, you will take notes, please."

He pushed open a door at the inner end of the office and led the way into a small bare room where Heinrich and his daughter sat together on a wooden bench against the wall. Two empty coffee cups and a plate of rolls on a small table before them showed that the police had not been unmindful of their bodily comfort. Lisse's hand was clasped in her father's, and she had been crying. The guide's face looked more than ever like a face carved in dark wood, but it was haggard and sullen; his deep-set eyes lit momentarily when he saw Mr. Lewker, but his expression did not change.

"Now, Taugwalder," Schultz began aggressively.

"Well, Heinrich, my friend," interposed Mr. Lewker cheerfully, pulling up a chair and sitting down, "here I am. Why have you not told Herr Schultz what he wishes to know?"

"Because he thinks I have killed a man, and you know I have not," said Heinrich bluntly.

Schultz, looking annoyed, sat down facing the two. Zimmermann settled himself with notebook and pen in the background.

"I will remind you, Taugwalder," the commissioner said severely, "that you are in a police office. I have been very patient. You gave me your word that when Herr Lewker arrived you would give me a true account of your movements on the morning of Léon Jacot's death."

"So I will, so I will," nodded the guide. "It will not take long. I wished only that Herr Lewker, who knows I do not kill people, should hear it also. I do not trust the police since they tried to make out I had been smuggling wine from Italy, which the good God knows I never—"

"That will do!" rapped Schultz. "Let us have your story."

Lisse squeezed her father's arm urgently. He frowned at her and began to speak, framing his words with care.

"I left my house at a quarter to two in the morning. The night was clear. I intended to make a little walk on the glaciers to train myself. I wished also to speak with this Frenchman, Jacot, and it was my purpose to make my walk accordingly. I knew he was going to climb alone up the Northeast Ridge that morning. So—"

"How did you know this?" demanded Schultz sharply.

Heinrich hesitated. He raised a bony hand and tugged at his drooping mustache.

"Well?" pressed the commissioner. "How did you find out, eh?"

"I heard in Zermatt," began the guide hesitantly.

"Wait!"

Lisse sprang to her feet, her blue eyes fixed in tearful appeal on Mr. Lewker's benign countenance.

"It was my fault!" she cried. "It was the note he sent me, that night—"

Mr. Lewker, suddenly remembering a small incident of Jacot's last night alive, interrupted quickly.

"He sent you a note from the Hotel Obergabelhorn? About ten o'clock, it would be?"

"Yes. I was cleaning up at Hoffman's, and a waiter brought it across. You see, he had arranged, two days before, that—that we should meet very early on that morning. He was to pretend that he was going for a climb and I was to give myself a day off from Hoffman's." Lisse had gone very red, but she went bravely on, keeping her gaze on Lewker. "Then, you see, we would spend all the day together without anyone knowing. I suppose he decided not to. The note said he had undertaken to climb the Matterhorn by himself next day, and we must meet some other time."

"Your father saw this note?" demanded Schultz keenly. "How did that happen?"

Heinrich answered roughly. "I found it on the floor after she'd gone to bed. She dropped it when she took off her things, I suppose. Leave her alone, and I'll tell you what you want."

"I must ask Fräulein Taugwalder one question," said Lewker suddenly. His mind was a little confused; the new facts he had heard in the last half-hour were seething there, and something was beginning to take shape from them. It was nebulous as yet. He needed time to examine it, for he was not sure how many of the facts already established would fit into that shape. Also he wanted to see how many more facts would emerge to support it. "Tell me, Lisse," he said gently. "You say this meeting was arranged two days before you received that note. Had you, perhaps, told Franz Imboden of it?"

Lisse buried her face in her hands. "Oh, I have been a little fool!" she sobbed. "I did tell him—I wanted to make him jealous. He—he didn't seem to care—"

"This is irrelevance," snapped the commissioner. "Continue, Taugwalder, with your story."

Then Franz knew. Lewker's busily churning thoughts flung that also into the vat. Franz, who was able to fly a plane. Franz, who had been away visiting an uncle at Zmutt and had not returned until seven in the morning. The times did not fit, but—

With an effort he forced himself to listen to Heinrich.

"I knew, you see, *mein Herr*, where I could meet and talk with the French-man," the guide was saying. Like his daughter, he addressed himself to Mr. Lewker, a circumstance which visibly annoyed Schultz. "I had thought al-ready of going to see him at the hotel. The mountain would be a better place. One can speak one's mind on a mountain."

"You intended to threaten him? To force him to stop seeing your daugh-ter?" barked Schultz.

Heinrich went on calmly, answering the question but as though it had not been asked. "I was going to put it to him, as one man to another, that he was doing us both a great wrong in behaving towards my daughter as he had done—he, a married man, *ja wohl!* There was no need of threats and vio-lence in such a matter. Well, then. I was on my way early, as I told you. I made for the Hörnli. It was dark, but I climbed down to the Boden Glacier and crossed it—I know the way well, me."

"This is the same route taken by Bryce?" Schultz whispered to Lewker.

"Yes. He was some hours later, of course."

"I walked up from the glacier to the Schwarzsee," Heinrich continued. "There all the paths meet, as you know. I went a little way up the path under the Hörnli rocks. It was near the dawn. I sat down under some rocks above the path, in a place where I could see anyone who should approach to climb the Northeast Ridge, and I lit my pipe."

Lewker put in a word for Schultz's benefit.

"Any climber approaching from Zermatt must pass this spot where you were sitting—that is so, Heinrich?"

"Nobody but a fool would try any other way when there is a good path," replied the guide shortly.

"Well?" demanded Schultz impatiently. "What happened when Jacot arrived there? Speak up, man!"

"I sat there smoking my pipe," Heinrich went on stolidly. "I watched the dawn. It was very fine. I thought my thoughts, as one does. You are perhaps a father yourself, and—"

"*Potztausend!*" The commissioner waved clenched fists in the air. "Will you tell us what happened?"

"The sun sent its light over the Jägerhorn ridge, *mein Herr,* and still there was no footstep on the path. Then I saw the rim of the sun come over the ridge, and I knew it was after six o'clock. I waited still, though I began to think the Frenchman was not coming. Then, perhaps half an hour afterwards, I heard steps on the path below. There was a man coming up, walking very fast."

"The time," Lewker interrupted, "would then be about a quarter to seven?"

"A little more or a little less, *mein Herr.* I had not my watch. Well, then I got out my Zeiss glass, which was given to me by an English Herr whose life I saved on the Lyskamm in the year—"

"Who cares for that, *Dummkopf?*" fulminated Schultz. "Get on! Who was this man?"

"He was about seven hundred meters away," said Heinrich with deliberation, "but I could see him well in my glass. It was a man I had never seen before."

"Ah, bah! You tell us it was not Jacot?"

"It was not the Frenchman. He did not come past me, nor did he see me. Instead, he looked at the Hörnli rocks and then left the path to climb up them. He was a good climber, that one—the rocks are difficult there. He was soon out of my sight. And still I sat and waited for a little longer. Soon I heard another noise, the noise of a *flieger.* It came very high overhead, shining in the sun, and flew over the Matterhorn, out of sight. I heard it buzzing for a little time and then I saw it going away down the valley again." Heinrich turned to the commissioner. "You should make a law about that. One day some fool of an airman will smash himself, playing round the Matterhorn, and then—"

"Never mind that. This was the plane that discovered Jacot's body." Schultz jabbed a finger at him. "And yet you tell us Jacot did not pass you!"

Lisse flashed an angry glance at the commissioner.

"My father does not tell lies, *mein Herr*!" she told him proudly.

Heinrich shrugged. "I tell everything I saw," he said. "And next I saw the same man again, climbing down from the Hörnli rocks very fast. He climbed without care. He slipped when he was near the bottom, and fell a little way. He was all right, for he stood up on the path, but I shouted to ask if he was hurt. He took no notice and hurried away down the path. Perhaps he did not hear me. Well, then I gave up waiting for the Frenchman and climbed round over the moraine on to the Théodule Glacier. All the day I walked there among the high snows, thinking my thoughts. In the evening, a little tired, I am in Zermatt. That is all, *meine Herren.*"

He turned to Lisse, who was clutching his arm anxiously, and patted her head.

"*So!*" nodded Schultz, pressing his thin lips together. "That is your story. You have noticed, no doubt, that it does not provide you with an alibi?"

"I do not know what that means," said the guide, stolid as ever.

"It means, Taugwalder, that I must detain you in custody for the present. You will remain here for the night. We shall endeavor to trace this climber you say you saw, and tomorrow I shall question you again."

Lisse stood up, twisting her hands. "You will let me see him tomorrow?" she begged.

"It can be arranged." Schultz turned to Zimmermann. "We should, I think, find accommodation in Zermatt for Fräulein Taugwalder."

"My aunt has a spare bed, very comfortable, if the Fräulein will accept our hospitality," said the police officer with unexpected sympathy, and was rewarded with a grateful look from the girl.

"I have one thing to ask," boomed Mr. Lewker, as the commissioner was on the point of rising. "Heinrich, you say you are certain this man you saw on the Hörnli was not Léon Jacot. What makes you certain? Did you see his face?"

"He wore the hood of his climbing-jacket pulled over his head," replied Heinrich slowly, "and I could see little of his face. But he was not Jacot."

"Tell me why you are so sure," Lewker persisted. "Was he a smaller man?"

"No. I think about the same height, though I have not seen Jacot many times. This man had broad shoulders, but Jacot has also broad shoulders. No, it was the look of him—I have it! When he turned to look up at the rocks there was a moment when I saw the little patch of his face. It was not dark, as the Frenchman's is. I will not be quite certain, but I think his mustache was of a blond color, Herr Lewker."

Mr. Lewker turned to meet the commissioner's frowning gaze.

"Now I wonder," he murmured, "what Bernard Bryce was doing on the Hörnli?"

CHAPTER SIXTEEN

MR. LEWKER IS CANTANKEROUS

"This much is plain," said Herr Schultz complacently. "Mr. Bryce's alibi holds good, whether Taugwalder saw him on the Hörnli or not."

He and Mr. Lewker were sitting in the outer office smoking cigars and sipping the fresh coffee which one of Zimmermann's underlings had made for them. Heinrich had been bestowed in one of the cells (there were only two, and both were rather more comfortable than an English hotel bedroom) and Lisse had been escorted to the house of Zimmermann's aunt by the police officer himself.

"If we accept that part of Taugwalder's story," continued the commissioner, "Mr. Bryce arrived on the Hörnli, at the extreme northern end of the Northeast Ridge, at a quarter to seven. It would take him at least an hour to reach, from there, the spot where the murder took place."

"By which time the plane had come, spotted the body, and departed," added Mr. Lewker. "It all links up very nicely, does it not? Either Mr. Bryce, for some reason best known to himself, lied to us this evening, or Heinrich Taugwalder, for some equally incomprehensible reason, lied about Bryce's being on the Hörnli. In both cases Bryce has an alibi for the time of the murder and Taugwalder has none."

There was one large cream cake left on the plate. He took it without hesitation.

"I fail to see what you mean, my friend," shrugged Schultz. "But we must not take it for granted, if we assume that Taugwalder saw a man there, that it was Mr. Bryce. The description was extremely vague. For my part I incline to the view that Taugwalder invented the whole incident of the man on the path. A man came, yes—but it was Jacot. And Taugwalder was waiting for him higher up the ridge."

"Ven waff—ahem. I beg your pardon." Mr. Lewker disposed of a mouthful of cake and began again. "Then what reason had Taugwalder to invent this incident? It does not appear to help his case."

"It is the sort of tale he would tell, my friend. He is anxious to make us think that there might have been someone else on the ridge, since he has had to admit that he was himself in the neighborhood. I fancy, by the way, that he was observed—or thought himself observed—on his way there. That is why he has had to tell us a certain amount of hunky-dory."

> "Herr Taugwalder's story,
> May be partly hunky-dory;
> But the part we don't believe
> Is intended to deceive,"

murmured the actor-manager with a levity that brought a scowl to the features of his companion. "In short, you are convinced that Heinrich is our man. Therefore his tale of Bryce's actions is untrue."

Schultz flicked the ash from his cigar with an irritable jerk. "What does it matter, in any case? The facts are plain. Here is a man with an admitted motive, an admitted opportunity, obvious means. No one else has all these. The story he chooses to tell, the movements of Bryce who has a double alibi, the fact that Franz Imboden also knew of this ascent—yes, my friend, I saw your interest there—what bearing can these have upon the plain evidence of the Taugwalders themselves?"

"None, *mein Herr.*" Lewker rose rather stiffly. "They pass me by as the idle wind. But it interests me to know how you account for the typewritten threat, the use of Jacot's scarf as a weapon, the lack of interest shown by the victim in his food, the absence of his ice-axe, the—"

"All these things, my friend, you shall know tomorrow morning," said Schultz pompously. "You shall see that they are to be very simply explained." He stood up. "Now I have an hour's work to do on the case. We shall meet in the morning in Simler's parlor. Nine-thirty. It is my intention to explain to all those who have been connected with this unfortunate affair how we have cleared them of suspicion and fastened the guilt upon the actual criminal. That should appeal to your English sense of fair game."

"It does, it does," Mr. Lewker assured him. "Also it appeals to my sense of drama."

The commissioner eyed him a trifle suspiciously; Lewker's broad face was Buddha-like in its placid impassivity but there was a mischievous gleam in his eye.

"Good night, Herr Lewker," he said abruptly.

"Sleep," returned the other gravely, "dwell upon thine eyes, peace in thy breast."

The uniformed Swiss let him out into the street. The lamps of heaven and of Zermatt were alight and the night air was cool and sweet. The Matterhorn, inescapable even in the dark, loomed like a toppling tower against the stars. It was nearly ten o'clock. Mr. Lewker, walking slowly and somewhat wearily towards the Hotel Obergabelhorn, reflected with misgiving that he had satisfied a notable appetite with cream cakes to the number of a dozen. Whether the effect of this orgy was already making itself felt, or whether the somber suspicions that haunted him were the cause, he was profoundly depressed.

For that nebulous and fantastic theory of his was now crystallizing into unwilling certainty; and it brought him no satisfaction at all. Mentally he shied away from it, for it seemed now like the betrayal of a friend. He tried to tell himself that consideration would prove that a dozen of the facts could not be fitted into it; but without success. In vain he sought to comfort himself, admitting its possibility, by the reflection that a number of innocent people would be freed from suspicion. His illogical emotions persisted in a manner he found extremely annoying. By the time he reached the hotel the combination of these mental qualms and the equally unruly cream cakes had produced an unusually bad temper. Simler, coming forward as he entered the hall to condole with him on his absence from dinner, was severely snubbed. Mrs. Fillingham, bounding at him from the direction of the bar, received a different treatment.

"Oy!" she shouted. "What's afoot, Mr. Lewker? Tell your Aunty Bee— between pals, eh? I've been writing to Mona Smith about you. Great admirer of yours, she is. Given her the lowdown on how great actors behave on holiday and all that guff."

"Madam," said Mr. Lewker peremptorily, "sit down. At this table in the corner. So. We can talk unobserved. These walls have no ears. They are also walleyed. What is your favorite color?"

Mrs. Fillingham stared at him, goggle-eyed.

"Well, I'm fond of purple, you know," she said doubtfully. "Though I must say I've got a soft spot for a really deep orange, but as for a favorite color—"

"Is it—red, by any chance?" he demanded in a bass whisper, fixing her with a penetrating glare.

She stiffened and drew back.

"What do you mean? What are you getting at?"

"Why, Mrs. Fillingham, did you not tell me you were a Communist?"

"I weren't—I mean I wasn't—I mean I'm not!" she retorted agitatedly. "Well—I was once, but I gave it up. What's the matter? I've done nothing wrong—I'm a Liberal now, anyway. Why—"

"Why, Mrs. Fillingham, did you push down boulders upon me from above?"

"Ooh! I never did!" She sprang to her feet, looking both angry and afraid. "Don't look at me like that! I—I refuse to stay any longer!"

She swung round, knocking over her chair, and hurried away.

Mr. Lewker watched her bundle up the stairs and out of sight with malevolent satisfaction.

"How great actors behave on holiday, part two," he muttered to himself. "Another eye-opener for Mona Smith."

Somewhat cheered by this piece of savagery, he got up and crossed the hall towards the staircase. Deborah Jacot and her brother were sitting at a small table near the bar with Dr. Greatorex. The doctor rose hurriedly and came to intercept him.

"Any news, Filthy?" he inquired. His bearded face was sardonic as always, but there were traces of anxiety in the narrowed eyes that searched Lewker's face.

"What news there is will emerge tomorrow morning," returned the actor-manager. "Herr Schultz is to reveal it to us."

"I know. We've all had chits asking us to attend. Is the—er—responsible party known?"

"The murderer has been discovered. Good night."

He passed on, leaving Greatorex fingering his beard uncertainly.

A hot bath restored some of Mr. Lewker's customary amiability. He had the grace to feel ashamed of his treatment of Mrs. Fillingham. He rang up Simler's office on the house telephone and the hotel proprietor answered.

"I am sorry, Simler, that I was a little abrupt just now. It was doubtless the lack of a proper meal that caused my indisposition. Is your waiter Bertrand available? Good. Will you send him up to my room, please?"

Bertrand, arriving within two minutes, found Mr. Lewker attired in dressing gown and slippers and very affable.

"Ah, Bertrand—sit down, please. *Vous parlez français habituellement, je crois?*"

Bertrand showed white teeth. "Yes, sair. But I like best to practice my English. It is quite good, I hope."

"Just as you wish. I understand from Herr Simler that you are an observant fellow. You saw Mr. Bryce go out of the hotel on Monday morning?"

"Yes, sair. At five minutes past three of the clock."

"Yes. He carried his ice-axe with him. No rucksack?"

"No, sair."

"Did he carry anything else?"

Bertrand considered for a moment.

"Yes, sair. He carried some looking-glasses in a leather case."

"Binoculars, Bertrand, is the word—or, if you prefer it, field-glasses. A looking-glass is *un miroir.*"

"Thank you, sair."

"Thank *you*, Bertrand. Now—I want you to answer this one very carefully. I want you to describe to me exactly what you saw and heard when Monsieur Jacot left the hotel that same morning. You were on duty in the office then?"

"Yes, sair. I am on duty from midnight until four of the clock each Monday. Monsieur Jacot—*ah, c'est dommage, ça!*—he was called at two of the clock. I called him myself, precisely at the hour, and returned to the office in the hall. Monsieur Jacot had ordered lunch to be ready, an especial one for a day of climbing. It was in the office awaiting for him."

"Yes?"

"In a very small time he came down the stairs. It was not much cold outside, but Monsieur wore his climbing coat with its hood over his head, and the red scarf he wore also. I told him good morning, and he answered me as he hurried to the door."

"He answered you? You noticed nothing strange about that?"

Bertrand looked surprised. "No, sair, except that he seemed a little—short of the temper. He said *'bon jour'*, very quick, like that. At that hour some gentlemen are not—*ils sont un peu maussades.*"

Mr. Lewker nodded. "That is unhappily true, Bertrand. And then?"

"I took up the parcel of lunch, sair, and called after him—for he was nearly to the door—saying that he must not forget it. It was a small surprise to me, sair," added Bertrand deprecatingly, "when Monsieur Jacot gave me a curse."

"Naturally. Can you remember his exact words?"

"It was the curse he often said. *'Sangdieu!'* he growl at me, and then, *'Je ne le veux pas!'* Then, sair, he went out quickly."

"I see. One thing more, Bertrand. Did Monsieur Jacot carry anything with him?"

"But of course, sair. His *piolet*—his ice-axe, and his rucksack. Nothing more.' "

"Then that is all I wish to know. My thanks for your information."

A note changed hands and Bertrand departed grinning delightedly.

Mr. Lewker sat for a while considering. Another small piece of the puzzle dropped into place. He got into bed and fell asleep at once. At three in the morning he was awakened by the ghosts of a number of cream cakes. They sat on his lower chest and pointed goblin fingers at him. The Gifted Amateur, they seemed to say jeeringly, shall not escape us. We are the Facts. Test your theory by us—fit us in—and we will let you rest.

Mr. Lewker sat up in bed and switched on the light. The internal discord that had awakened him appeared to have clarified his thoughts. He saw plainly that in failing to reason out his theory to its conclusion he had been guilty of moral cowardice. He set his teeth and reached for the pencil from the pocket of his coat beside the bed. There was a book on the bedside table— Chesterton's *Flying Inn*. On the flyleaf he made a list:

The typewritten note was in English.
Jacot was stifled to death.
Baptiste Frey did not pass through Geneva.
If Heinrich is speaking the truth, Bryce lied about his movements.
Jacot refused to take his lunch.
Reported statement of Mrs. F's pal Mona.
Jacot took ice-axe and rucksack: neither was found on ridge or glacier.
Bryce (Heinrich states) climbed Hörnli rocks skilfully but descended carelessly, even falling.
Madame Jacot stated on Monday evening that she knew Jacot was in touch with Soviet.

He had jotted these brief sentences down as they occurred to him. Now he studied them, and the last of his doubts fled. Not only did they fit in with the theory he had built but they strengthened it beyond all possibility of error. And the times? They fitted in, too.

He switched off the light and lay back on his pillows. The ghosts of the cream cakes troubled him no more, but there remained one small point— perhaps it represented the cherry that had crowned one of the cakes—to keep him from sleep: had he enough proof to satisfy Schultz? Methodically he considered the places where the tangible and irrefutable evidence might be found. At the end of ten minutes he had come to the conclusion that there was only one place to look. In the morning he would look there. He slept soundly until seven-thirty and turned out to find a morning brilliant with reflected light from the high snows.

Few people were breakfasting when he came down into the hall, and no one that he knew. Herr Schultz, he suspected, would not appear until the hour he had appointed for his gathering had struck. Mr. Lewker, who wished to pay a visit to Täsch before half-past nine, toyed with the idea of borrowing Schultz's car and driving there by himself, but dismissed it when he realized that he would have to maneuver it out of the narrow alley behind the hotel, where the garage was situated. Mrs. Fillingham and Margaret came down while he was finishing his coffee and rolls, but went through the hall and out of the hotel without taking any notice of him; presumably they were bent on a pre-breakfast stroll. John Waveney was the next to appear, and him Mr. Lewker, making a sudden decision, buttonholed at once.

"I want your assistance," he announced. "When you have broken your fast, will you drive me to Täsch in your sister's car?"

"Hullo!" John exclaimed, eyeing him keenly. "On the trail again? Thought the sleuths had made a fair cop—some chap in clink already, they say."

"There is one last piece of evidence to be collected," returned Mr. Lewker gravely. "It is important, or I would not have asked you."

"Oh, I'm game, sir. But look here. We'll be late for this lecture of Schultz's, won't we?"

"I think we might just manage to get back in time."

"Hope so. Don't want to miss hearing how the job was done—sounds callous, I know, but there it is. Just give me five minutes for coffee and a roll, sir, and we'll buzz."

"Thank you, Waveney. Please do not hurry unduly."

While John disposed of a quick breakfast, Mr. Lewker visited Simler's office, returning therefrom with a pencil and a large sheet of drawing paper. With the latter rolled up under his arm he accompanied John to the garage, where Deborah's sports car stood next to Schultz's big Packard. As they backed out into the alley Deborah came out on to the projecting balcony of her room. She made a slight gesture in response to John's cheerful wave. Then they were roaring out into the main street and swinging left in the direction of Täsch.

"I hope your sister will not mind this use of her car?" remarked Mr. Lewker, hanging on to the side as they swirled round a bend.

"Not a bit," shouted John above the snarl of the exhaust. "Twins, you know—everything in common since we were kids. I say, sir," he added, "what's the roll of paper for?"

"Can you draw?" Lewker enquired.

"Only planes. And blueprints, plans and so forth."

"That will do. If we divide the work we can get it done in half the time."

He relapsed into silence for the rest of the drive. The speed at which John hurled the car down the twisting road was outrageous. Mr. Lewker clung silently to his seat and closed his eyes during the passage through the rocky gorge where four days ago Deborah had almost crashed into the herd of goats. The narrow valley was in shadow, and the air blew up it moist and cool from the torrent; but when they emerged into the wider strath, where Täsch stands, the morning sun was touching emerald meadows and red-brown chalets into brilliant color.

"Stop at the Weisses Kreuz," directed Mr. Lewker.

John obeyed. The little inn stood back a few yards from the road, and as the car drew up Franz Imboden was industriously shaking carpets in front of his father's establishment. He greeted them with dignity but without enthusiasm; possibly their arrival at an hour when those who keep inns are usually busy accounted for this.

"What ho, Franz!" cried John, getting out of the car. "Plane all right?"

"Quite safe, Mr. Waveney."

"Herr Imboden," said Mr. Lewker, advancing, roll of paper in hand, "the *Kriminal Kommissar* has asked me to collect certain information in Täsch. Mr. Waveney has very kindly agreed to help me. One thing that is required is a plan of your hotel—the upstairs parts only—showing the relation of rooms and passages and—" here he lowered his voice—"and showing the room occupied by Monsieur Frey."

"Oho!" John raised an eyebrow.

"Yes. I want the position of the window shown, and I also want Dr. Macrae's room marked." He handed his roll of paper to John and turned to Franz. "Perhaps you will be so kind as to allow Mr. Waveney to use one of your rooms."

"There is a table in my office," said Franz with a trace of reluctance. A frown creased his forehead as he regarded Mr. Lewker's bland features.

"The reason for this I shall be able to tell you some day," Lewker thought it wise to add. "It need not take very long. The plan, Waveney, need not be to scale. And—one more thing—ascertain for me whether both rooms, Frey's and the doctor's, have balconies, please. Is that clear?"

"Clear as mud, sir. I don't see why—"

"The Gifted Amateur is always permitted his little mysteries. Oh, Franz—is the post office open at this hour?"

"It is, sir."

"Thank you. I will meet you here in twenty minutes, Waveney."

The two went into the hotel. A little red-faced man in climbing kit, who had just emerged from the door, stood aside to let them pass in.

"Good morning, Doctor!" called Mr. Lewker cheerily. "I trust your patient is still recovering?"

Dr. Macrae stared at him for an instant, blew out his bristle of mustache with an audible crackle, and marched back into the hotel.

"Another gentleman who is *un peu maussade* in the morning," murmured Mr. Lewker as he turned away to attend to more urgent matters.

These same matters occupied him for a full twenty minutes, and he was out of breath when he returned to the Weisses Kreuz. John was not outside the hotel, and Mr. Lewker did not go in to fetch him. He got into the car and sat perfectly still, with his eyes fixed on the distant sunlit peaks. An observer would have said that he was contemplating something extremely distasteful. However, he appeared cheerful enough when John emerged with his plan completed.

"Bit rough and ready," the draftsman apologized, "but I dare say it'll do. Both rooms have balconies."

Mr. Lewker studied the plan frowningly.

"Yes," he said at last. "This is quite good enough. Now, as it is approaching the time of Herr Schultz's meeting—"

"By gum! It is, too." John sprang into his seat and started the car. "If you're thinking of putting up this Frey bloke as a rival candidate to Schultz's man," he shouted as they roared away towards Zermatt, "you've got your work cut out, sir. He's on crutches now—I saw him—but he was in bed from Sunday night to Tuesday afternoon."

> " 'The eagle suffers little birds to sing,
> And is not careful what they mean thereby,' "

boomed Mr. Lewker enigmatically. "I have yet a little thinking to do."

They completed the drive back to Zermatt in silence. The pace at which John drove, indeed, demanded his full attention, for there were by now farm wagons and many pedestrians on the road. Once more the Matterhorn swam into view round a corner as they climbed out of the Visp gorge, gloriously lit by the morning sun and framed in a gentian-blue sky. That air of brooding, of secretiveness, seemed to Mr. Lewker to mar its grand face still. Would it ever, he wondered, nod to him in friendly fashion as once—before this dark business came to hang over the great mountain—it had been a fancy of his to imagine? The tremendous upsurge of the Northeast Ridge shone in the clear atmosphere as though it had been newly washed. And Mr. Lewker, who knew that now a stain had been removed from that ridge, felt comforted.

The car pulled up with a jerk in front of the Hotel Obergabelhorn. Simler met them as they hurried into the hall.

"Herr Schultz has been asking for you, sir," he told Mr. Lewker.

The actor-manager nodded. "For what he is about to receive," he said piously, "let us hope he will be truly thankful."

"What about this plan?" enquired John.

"Bring it with you. Come along. Time driveth onward fast."

Outside the door of Simler's parlor Mr. Lewker paused for an accustomed self-adjustment. He cleared his throat in a subdued manner, settled his jacket, squared his shoulders. Thus he had done times without number in the wings of a hundred theaters. The curtain was already up on the last act. The Gifted Amateur had received his cue. He opened the door and made his entrance.

CHAPTER SEVENTEEN

THE GIFTED AMATEUR TAKES THE STAGE

"—and it is understandable that this delay, and the resultant uncertainty, should have given some of you to be browned off," Herr Schultz was saying as Mr. Lewker and John Waveney entered.

The commissioner was seated at the head of the long table facing the door, with Deborah Jacot on his right and Zimmermann, with notebook and pencil at the ready, on his left. Bernard Bryce, Dr. Greatorex and the Comte and Comtesse de Goursac were ranged along one side of the table and on the other sat Mrs. Fillingham and Margaret Kemp, with an empty chair between the latter and Deborah. The sunlight, sending a reflected brightness through the window behind Schultz, twinkled on medal-studded shields and mounted chamois horns but brought no answering sparkle from eight grave and pre-occupied faces. Mrs. Fillingham had brought her knitting—the same hideous purple mass as before—and was busily engaged with it. The rest were sitting very still, and about them all there was an air of strained expectancy; presumably they had all heard (as John had heard) that a man had been detained in connection with Jacot's murder, but it was obvious that no one's apprehensions had been entirely quieted by the news.

"My noble lords and cousins all, good morrow," boomed Mr. Lewker, who, when his mind was heavily occupied, was apt to become Shakespearean at unsuitable moments. "For the tardiness of Mr. Waveney and myself I am to blame. I apologize."

Schultz nodded coldly. "We have scarcely begun, Herr Lewker," he said. "Please sit down."

John took the chair next to Deborah, and as the only remaining place was at the end of the table facing Schultz, Mr. Lewker lowered himself into it and placed his fingertips together with an air of polite attention.

"The presence of my colleague Herr Zimmermann," Schultz continued at once, "is purely a matter of form. I wish him to make a record of the full explanation I am about to give you." He smiled deprecatingly. "The whole matter is indeed very simple. But since I have been obliged to question you, ladies and gentlemen, and to keep some of you, perhaps, in suspense, I feel that this full explanation is the stuff to give you."

Here he nodded to Zimmermann, who began to write. The commissioner fixed his pale eyes on a large framed certificate that hung on the wall above Mr. Lewker's head and spoke as though dictating—which, indeed, he was. Zimmermann appeared more than once to be in difficulties with the English words, but on the whole he managed to get the sentences down in good time. Mr. Lewker suspected that the intention was to present him with a neatly typed copy of the dissertation.

"This case," began Schultz, "is an example of a crime with a primary suspect, a later-appearing second suspect, and a certain amount of apparently relevant but really irrelevant surrounding detail. To one who is not constantly in touch with the detection of crime such detail may prove misleading." His glance flickered as low as Mr. Lewker's bald head for an instant and then returned to the certificate. "We whose business it is to deal with a number of murders every year know well that the majority of murders are not cleverly planned. The mind that acquiesces in the taking of a human life is rarely a brilliant one. The murderer may seek, before or after his crime, to cover his tracks—not infrequently he fails even to attempt that—but in every case motive, opportunity and means have led us in a notably short time to the dirty dog."

Mr. Lewker, who was pretty certain that Schultz had prepared this little speech beforehand, very nearly interrupted to remonstrate at this sudden descent from the sublime. He could not, however, bring himself to shake the commissioner's faith in his mastery of English idiom, and so held his peace.

"It is a great comfort to me to know that our friends and neighbors the French"—here Schultz closed his eyes and made a jerky little bow in the direction of the de Goursacs—"will not be put to inconvenience by my solution of the little problem. This was not, after all, a political murder. By one of those chances which so often occur, Baptiste Frey, a member of an organization who were determined that Léon Jacot should not offer his political sword to Communism, was holidaying in a nearby village. Madame Jacot recognized him as a possible enemy, and a typewritten threat came into her possession which appeared as though it might have come from him. With that I shall deal later. Frey, then, was our primary suspect. He had motive—Madame Jacot informs me that her husband was in touch with Soviet agents, and Frey might be assumed to know this—and as a mountaineer he had the means of committing this particular form of murder. So probable did Frey appear, as the man we wanted, that even when it transpired that he was incapable of reaching the place of the killing at the fatal hour I found myself seeking a way round the facts. It is an unfortunate human tendency, my friends, and even police officials are human."

"Hear, hear," put in Mrs. Fillingham unexpectedly. Schultz compressed his lips and continued.

"Almost at once, however, I was presented with another line of investigation. At the same time my attention was called to a number of circumstances which, though I was convinced they were irrelevant, could not be ignored. Madame Jacot will pardon me, I trust, if I call the spade the spade?"

Deborah, whose piquant features showed more color than of late, smiled faintly.

"Please speak as plainly as you like," she said. "If it's about Léon—well, I knew his faults as well as his virtues, and the truth can't hurt him now."

"Thank you, Madame. I will only say that a man with the mental and physical gifts of Monsieur Jacot could hardly fail to make enemies in more spheres than the political. To be brief, it emerged from my investigations—

for which I must ask the indulgence of you all—that some of you here present had reason to bear malice towards him, to an extent that might be construed as a motive for murder. I shall not go further into this repugnant subject now, except to add that with the aid of Herr Lewker I was able to prove that it was quite impossible that any of you should have been concerned in the bumping off."

A slight ripple, hardly to be called a sigh, ran round the table. Mrs. Fillingham looked up from her knitting with a frown on her ruddy face.

"Very nice, I'm sure," she said loudly. "But what about Bernard Bryce's little tricks the other day? Who shoved the boulders down on Mr. Lewker?"

"Auntie!" protested Margaret in a whisper.

"A trickle of stones, madam," amended Mr. Lewker with dignity.

"Well, I want to know," said Mrs. Fillingham obstinately; her gaze dwelt accusingly on Bryce, who looked uncomfortable.

Schultz condescended to take notice of this interruption.

"Mr. Bryce," he pronounced, "helped to complicate a simple investigation by failing to produce an alibi until late in the day. However, when this alibi was examined it was found to be perfectly O.K. Although Mr. Bryce admits, or rather states himself, that he was not far from the Northeast Ridge that morning, having very naturally taken an early morning walk to the Schwarzsee, it is beyond all possibility that he could have been at the fatal spot between six o'clock and seven. In that he is in the same ship with you all. Herr Lewker will support me there, I think."

"Certainly," boomed the actor-manager affably.

"As for Herr Doktor Greatorex, whose motive was discovered to be possibly adequate—"

Greatorex made a sudden exclamation and then resumed his sardonic silence.

"—and Monsieur de Goursac," continued Schultz, "the most ingenious writer of fiction could hardly find a way round their alibis."

The Comte, whose hamlike face was very pale, bowed his head. Camille de Goursac gulped audibly. Mr. Lewker suspected that their hands were clasped below the table.

"In short, as you must admit, Herr Lewker, there was no difficulty in disposing of these false trails. The motives were not hidden, the alibis were easily proved. From the time when Heinrich Taugwalder came within the scope of the investigation the line pointed straight to him."

The commissioner took out his little pince-nez and stuck them on his nose while he hurriedly consulted the notebook that lay open before him. Then he looked severely over the top of them at his audience.

"Parental affection, my friends, is one of the strongest of all human passions. And like all human passions, it may become dangerous. Here we have a man brought up in the strict religion of his fathers, believing—and, I think with reason—that his daughter's virtue is threatened. He is simple, almost primitive, in his emotions. He sees, placed before him by circumstance, a primitive means of ridding himself and his daughter of this threat. Moreover, the killing which he contemplates may be done in such a way that it will be taken for an accident. We know, from his own statement, that Heinrich Taugwalder reached the northern end of the Northeast Ridge before dawn—before Jacot could have reached it from Zermatt. He admits that he went there to intercept Jacot. His assertion that Jacot did not come is manifestly a lie, since Jacot fell from a spot much higher up the ridge, which he could only have reached by the path near which Taugwalder was sitting. This man has a strong motive, an admitted opportunity, and also the means—for he is an active mountaineer and likely to be the victor in a struggle on a precipitous ridge. And, alone of all those connected with this case, he has no alibi."

Schultz sat back in his chair and relaxed his severity a little.

"Tomorrow," he finished impressively, "Heinrich Taugwalder will formally be charged with the murder of Léon Jacot."

There was a short pause, which was broken by Mrs. Fillingham.

"Well, good show, and all that guff," she said, dumping her knitting on the table and folding her arms aggressively, "but I want to know who shoved those boulders down."

Schultz, perhaps observing the puzzled expression on several faces, deigned to explain.

"There occurred a fall of earth on a path by which Herr Lewker was walking," he said lightly, ignoring the actor-manager's lowering countenance. "Herr Lewker thought it might have some connection with this case. That, I may add, is where we investigators must mind the step. There were other such little matters, easily to be twisted into the thread of clues but equally easy to explain in other ways. The typewritten threat, for example."

Deborah Jacot leaned forward interestedly. "I wondered," she said, "how you would explain that."

The commissioner beamed upon her.

"These things, to the layman," said he with gusto, "point only to one way, Madame. For you, because your husband had received other threats, from the Flambeaux in particular, it seemed certain that this note was from Frey, a member of the Flambeaux. To Herr Lewker, I think, it seemed certain that it must have come from the hand of Jacot's murderer."

Mr. Lewker grunted noncommittally. Schultz wagged a finger at him.

"Ah, my friend, the fact that the note was in English should have told you that it was from an English person. That the note was typed on Mr. Bryce's machine—"

"Good lord!" interjected Bryce, sitting up.

"—means little, except that it was probably typed by someone in this hotel. Consider the phrasing. *'The path you are treading is a dangerous path. One more step, and you will not live to take another.'* It was natural to assume that the "path" was the road to Communism, Madame Jacot, but— again forgive me—your husband was treading other dangerous paths. He gave a jeering laugh, as you told Herr Lewker, when he read it. In my opinion it is at least probable that this note was sent, in jest or earnest, by someone—I shall not even guess whom—who wished to frighten him from one of his—h'm—*affaires due cœur."*

Schultz's glance rested on Mr. Lewker with almost affable satisfaction. The actor-manager's face displayed respectful surprise.

"I concede your point," he remarked. "But if this anonymous terrorist was, as you say, an English person, we have to choose from Mr. Bryce, Dr. Greatorex, Miss Kemp, Madame Jacot, and Mrs. Fillingham. Mr. Waveney was not here when the note was received. Surely it is improbable that any of these should have written such—"

"Please, please!" Schultz waved a hand irritably. "This is a matter not worth pursuing. As must be obvious, the letter is an irrelevance, whatever its origin."

"Very well, *mein Herr*. But, if you will allow me to enquire, do you propose to dismiss the other awkward facts as irrelevancies?"

The commissioner removed his pince-nez with a gesture of annoyance.

"For example?" he challenged coldly.

"The fact that the murderer used the method of stifling as his—"

"Ja, ja," Schultz interrupted contemptuously. "This small matter has been the wasp in your bonnet, *nicht wahr*? Ask yourself, my friend, why such a method might be employed. The answer? Because the victim is prevented from making any sound."

"Exactly," approved Mr. Lewker. "And why should Taugwalder be afraid of causing a noise, on the Northeast Ridge at that hour?"

"Have you forgotten that between six o'clock and six-thirty Mr. Bryce was scrambling up from the Boden Glacier to the Schwarzsee? On a still windless morning sound carries far. Taugwalder might easily have heard the sound of distant steps—he might, indeed, have seen Mr. Bryce from his position high up on the ridge as he waited for Jacot. He dare not risk a shout for help. He makes certain that there shall be no shout."

Mr. Lewker beamed and nodded. "I see. It is all so plain when you demonstrate, Herr Kommissar. These mysteries are happily resolv'd. And the refusal of Monsieur Jacot to take his lunch? The strange nonappearance of his ice-axe and rucksack? You will explain these for us, I hope."

Schultz tugged at his massive watch-chain. He frowned disapprovingly and with a hint of suspicion in his glance. Before he could reply Lawrence Greatorex was speaking.

"This is great fun for you two professors, I dare say," he observed caustically, "but the rest of us don't know what you're nattering about. Also, it can't be particularly pleasant for Madame Jacot."

"C'est ça," agreed the Comte de Goursac. "It has been made clear that the murderer is found, that we at this table are freed from all suspicion. It is sufficient."

Mrs. Fillingham shook her fuzzy blonde head vigorously.

"Don't agree," she said. "It's a nasty business and wretched for Deb, and all that guff, but I want to hear it thrashed out to the end. Let's have it all and get it over. Seems to me Mr. Lewker isn't satisfied about some of it."

Lewker noticed that she carefully avoided looking at him as she spoke; he remembered his inexcusable behavior of the previous evening and resolved to make amends.

"I support Mrs. Fillingham," said Deborah suddenly. "As I've said before, I can take it, now I've got over the first shock. And I'd prefer to think there were no loose ends left over."

"I'm with you, Deb," nodded John, who was still nursing his roll of drawing paper. "I rather fancy there's more to come."

He glanced meaningly at Mr. Lewker, who studiously avoided his eye.

"Well, we're all out of the wood anyway," said his sister. "And I don't see why we should all look so funereal. Cigarette, please, Bernard. This meeting isn't a nonsmoker, I suppose?" she added, with a glance at the commissioner.

Schultz looked a trifle shocked at this unseasonable levity, but he smiled perfunctorily as Bryce lit her cigarette. John fingered his roll.

"You were going to give us the lowdown on the Problems of the Missing Ice-Axe and the Lost Lunch, Mr. Schultz, when we chipped in with this debate," he said. "Carry on—we're all attention."

"They are of no account," grumbled Schultz. "Herr Lewker makes difficulties out of nothing. However, it is perfectly plain that in a fall of many hundreds of feet an ice-axe and a rucksack may easily be separated from their owner. Doubtless they are in some cranny of the rocks halfway down the precipice. As for the reason why Jacot refused to take his lunch packet—which, my friends, was the case—we know from the evidence of Bertrand the waiter that he appeared indisposed that morning. Perhaps Madame can further enlighten us?"

Deborah took the cigarette from her lips and frowned.

"Now you mention it," she said, "he did complain of internal trouble that morning. It was two o'clock, you know, and I was only half awake, but I remember him grumbling about it."

"So!" Schultz nodded. "We remember also that if your husband completed the climb as quickly as he anticipated he would have been back here by three o'clock in the afternoon. Also he could have obtained food at the hotel near the Schwarzsee."

He looked at Mr. Lewker, whose pouchy countenance was as benign and inscrutable as that of an idol in some Indian temple.

"Sounds reasonable enough," said John. He glanced at Mr. Lewker. "What's the next question, sir?"

"Herr Schultz has answered all my queries," replied the actor-manager placidly.

John looked puzzled. He took out his cigarette-case and frowned as he lit a cigarette. Plainly he was wondering why the indictment of Baptiste Frey— for the plan that rested on his knees could portend nothing less—was being held back. The rest of the gathering stirred and looked at each other. Herr Schultz closed his notebook and nodded to Zimmermann. Mr. Lewker, who had been waiting in vain for his cue, had opened his mouth to speak when Deborah's calm voice broke the little pause.

"Let me get this quite straight, Herr Schultz," she said quietly. "This man, Heinrich Taugwalder, was incensed because my husband had been—philandering with his daughter. You have discovered beyond doubt that he was on the Northeast Ridge at the vital time. Hasn't he made any defense at all?"

It was Mr. Lewker's cue.

"Madame," he boomed, before Schultz could reply, "Taugwalder denies that he set eyes on your husband that morning. He says that he did not go farther than the rocks under the west side of the little peak called the Hörnli— that is, he did not gain the crest of the ridge or go high enough to look down on the place where your husband's body was found. But he says that someone *did* do this and that he saw him."

"A ridiculous lie," snapped Schultz, jerking angrily at his watch-chain.

"I happen to believe Taugwalder's story, *mein Herr,*" observed Mr. Lewker quietly. "But you, ladies and gentlemen, will see that a great deal hangs upon this point. For although Heinrich Taugwalder does not claim to have recognized this man, he says he could distinguish his features through his Zeiss glass, and they were not those of Léon Jacot. This man, whoever he was, was climbing the Hörnli rocks within a few hundred yards of Taugwalder at a quarter to seven, according to the guide's story. If this man were to come forward and admit the truth of the story, he would save an innocent man from paying the penalty he does not deserve. You see, Herr Schultz and I agree—at present—that the murder must have taken place after six o'clock. But if Taugwalder was near enough to the Hörnli to distinguish the features of a man climbing there, he must have been well over an hour's climbing from the fatal spot on the ridge. Therefore he could not have killed Jacot."

Schultz thumped the table. *"Potztausend!"* he vociferated, purple with rage.

"This is mad foolishness! You know well, Herr Lewker, that—"

"If this man," boomed Mr. Lewker, drowning the other's voice easily, "does not come forward, he dooms an innocent man to pay the penalty for murder."

His gaze ran slowly round the table and came to rest on Bernard Bryce.

"You can't mean that Bernard—" cried Greatorex angrily.

"But how could he have—" shouted Margaret, suddenly jumping up.

Bernard Bryce's voice interrupted both of them. He spoke as though he were summoning every effort of mind and will to force the words out.

"I was that man," he said.

CHAPTER EIGHTEEN

THE MATTERHORN NODS

Deborah gave a small horrified gasp.

"Bernard!" she exclaimed, stretching an arm across the table towards him.

He deliberately turned his face from her. It was, thought Mr. Lewker, the face of a soul in torment. Almost at once, however, he regained control over himself.

"I went as far as the summit of the Hörnli," he said evenly. "I watched Waveney's plane flying about overhead. I climbed down again to the path when it had gone. Had a bit of a slip coming down. Thought I heard a shout but didn't stop to see who it was."

"Heinrich Taugwalder has told us that he shouted to know if you were hurt," said Lewker. "And now, Mr. Bryce, why did you not tell us this before? Why did you state yesterday that you went no farther than the hotel by the Schwarzsee?"

Bryce opened his mouth as if to reply, and then closed it again with an audible click.

"I shall say nothing more," he said through his teeth.

Margaret Kemp's bewildered gray eyes flew from Bryce to Lewker.

"I don't understand," she began in frightened tones.

The commissioner slapped the table wrathfully with his palms.

"Nobody understands!" he barked exasperatedly. "Herr Lewker himself does not understand what he talks about! He misrepresents the matter, I think to attempt cleverness—to be a clever Dick, as you say!"

Mr. Lewker raised tolerant eyebrows. Herr Schultz was really angry.

"This new tale of Mr. Bryce's," he fumed on, "does not give Taugwalder an alibi—that we agreed last night, Herr Lewker! Heinrich is uncertain what time it was when he saw Mr. Bryce—and could he not have descended that ridge from the fatal place, expert guide as he was, between six o'clock and a little before eight? Again, why could he not have seen Mr. Bryce while he, Taugwalder, was still descending from the ridge? There is nothing proved here. Taugwalder still has no alibi for the time of the murder, though Mr. Bryce has."

Bryce shot a resentful glance at Lewker, who ignored it. The actor-manager was beaming at Schultz.

"Mr. Bryce has no alibi," he contradicted gently. "Nor have any of us here except Dr. Greatorex and Monsieur de Goursac."

"Potztausend!" The commissioner's round face was purple. "What foolishness is this?"

Mr. Lewker looked slowly round the table. Eight pairs of eyes were fixed upon him in bewilderment, anger, fear or a mixture of all three. As for Zimmermann, he was regarding his chief with the apprehension of one who finds himself sitting next to a bomb with a smoking fuse. Lewker's gaze came back to rest on Schultz. One might have fancied his lips framed the words *A trickle of stones.* He folded his hands on the table and addressed himself to the commissioner.

"Upon one point, *mein Herr,* we agree. The method used by the murderer, that of stifling his victim, points to one thing plainly. The murderer found it necessary to be quiet in his work. Nothing else would induce him to use so slow and awkward a means of killing—unless, perhaps, it was the absence of bleeding, or the fact that it happened to be, for some reason, the most convenient method. This, as you have so aptly said, *mein Herr,* has been a wasp in my bonnet. The sting, however, did not penetrate to this dull brain until after a little incident involving—to use your own pretty phrase—a trickle of stones across a mountain path."

Mrs. Fillingham looked up quickly. Lewker smiled at her.

"I owe it to Mrs. Fillingham's energy and initiative, and, I may add, her woodcraft," he said, "that I have a witness to prove that there was a man at the spot from which this trickle was dislodged."

A blush suffused Mrs. Fillingham's cheeks. From the glance she threw at him Mr. Lewker gathered that he was forgiven.

"There is no doubt in my own mind," he continued, "that the purpose of this rockfall was to assist me to shuffle off this mortal coil. It took me a little time to conclude that something I had done or said had led the guilty person to think that I, and not Herr Schultz, had got hold of a vital clue. I remembered then that at the previous meeting in this room I had mentioned my preoccupation with this very matter—the odd use of the stifling scarf—and that Herr Schultz had pooh-poohed it as of no account. If I was right, the key to the whole thing lay in this. And that meant that the stifling of Jacot had a particular significance. The murderer had depended upon it for some vital part of his plan. And what more likely than that it had been used to mislead us—to help in providing the murderer with an alibi?"

Schultz made a contemptuous noise. Lewker, fearing an imminent explosion, cut short his rhetorical pause.

"Now Mrs. Fillingham, who had but the briefest view of the man who must have engineered the rockfall, thought it at least possible that he was Bernard Bryce. Let us turn our attention to Mr. Bryce." Suiting the action to the word, he swung round and fixed his little eyes on Bryce's sullen face. "Mr. Bryce, will you not tell us why you climbed to the summit of the Hörnli, and what you saw from there?"

Bryce's hands, on the table before him, clenched themselves so that the knuckles showed white under the brown skin.

"I—I can't," he said after a moment; and bowed his head almost as though he were praying.

"Very probably that is literally true," observed the actor-manager gravely. "For the present I will ask attention to the fact that Mr. Bryce first of all allowed Miss Kemp to provide him with a false alibi, then—when he was forced to do so—he told another story which was, in part, also false. I will pass to what the Herr Kommissar has called irrelevant facts. First, the missing ice-axe and rucksack. At the point from which Jacot fell there is an almost uninterrupted slope of ice. It was more than likely that an implement like an ice-axe would have fallen with its owner and perhaps slid rather farther on to the glacier below. The rucksack also, but in a lesser degree of likelihood. Neither of these articles was to be found either on the ridge above or the glacier."

"The murderer might have thrown them down the precipice on the other side of the ridge," suggested Greatorex.

"To what purpose? To arouse doubt in suspicious minds? No, Doctor. Here was a mistake, a piece of carelessness on the part of the criminal. Then the neglected lunch packet—a lunch ordered specially by Jacot, who knew that he had undertaken a very difficult and strenuous feat. No mountaineer would dream of setting out on such an expedition without plenty of food. That lunch was left behind because it would have been dangerous to take it."

Once again he made a dramatic pause. The Gifted Amateur held the stage now, and (perhaps because he subconsciously dreaded the revelation which must come) he was making the most of his lines. Schultz, who had been listening with a scowling face, as though his attention was being held against his will, made an impatient sound.

"You give us nothing to make sense," he declared. "These are your opinions only. No doubt you have also an opinion about the typewritten threat."

" 'A plague of opinion! A man may wear it on both sides, like a leather jerkin,' " murmured Mr. Lewker. "Shakespeare has always an apt comment, has he not? Your opinion in the matter of the typewritten note, however, seems to me to be a very thin jerkin, *mein Herr.* Surely it was much more likely that such a note came from a man like Baptiste Frey than from anyone here, who would probably approach Jacot personally rather than by an anonymous threat."

"From Frey? Although it was in English?" Schultz countered with a curl of his lip.

"Frey might have used English to help conceal the note's authorship," put in Deborah, who was listening absorbedly, chin on hand.

"Then how, Madame, could he have typed the note on the machine of Mr. Bryce?" demanded Schultz. "Herr Lewker, I think you waste our time. We have been given no new facts—only your fantastic interpretation of the old ones. If you have anything to say that is worth our attention, please shoot the line."

"You haven't told us," added Margaret Kemp, with an anxious glance at Bernard Bryce's bowed head, "what you mean by none of us having an alibi for the murder after all."

"You are right, Miss Kemp," nodded Schultz. He glared defiantly at Lewker. "Your facts, sir—if you have any."

The actor-manager drew a long breath.

"Very well," he said slowly. "I have facts for you. This morning Waveney and I drove to the Weisses Kreuz hotel in Täsch. There Waveney drew a plan of the hotel's first floor while I made other investigations. The result was evidence, tangible and irrefutable, of my theory."

"Ah," said John. He tapped the roll of drawing paper and threw a reassuring glance at Deborah.

"This theory," continued Mr. Lewker, speaking with great solemnity, "accepts all the evidence and gives a meaning to all the facts. The evidence of the doctor who examined the body is that Jacot died between one o'clock and seven o'clock on Monday morning. The evidence of Bertrand the waiter is that a man with his head and most of his face muffled up left the hotel just after two, refusing to take the lunch packet that Bertrand offered to him. My own evidence is that Jacot's body fell down a steep ice slope and that he had been stifled to death with his own red scarf. Heinrich Taugwalder's evidence is that Mr. Bryce climbed the Hörnli just before the coming of the plane and climbed down again afterwards carelessly, falling a short distance and then hurrying away down the path. Here is what happened."

He paused. Every face was turned towards him. The tension in the room could be felt, as the climber on a storm-ridden peak feels the tingle of electricity in his very bones.

"Léon Jacot was killed between one o'clock and two. It was not he who left the hotel a few minutes after two, but an impersonator who could risk a word or two with Bertrand but dared not risk the closer approach to take a packet from Bertrand's hand. This impersonator was, I think, the actual murderer. It was he, not Jacot, who answered the knocker-up. But his accomplice was the deviser and instigator of the whole plan. The impersonator, having clattered away through the deserted streets, returned, probably in stocking feet, and reentered the hotel by means of a rope lowered by his accomplice from a balcony overlooking the alley that leads to the garage. In the bedroom he thus regained Léon Jacot was lying, dead. He had been stifled in his sleep with a red woolen scarf."

Camille de Goursac gave a short, sharp cry of horror. As though the noise released him from a frozen immobility, John Waveney half-rose from his chair, an incredulous smile on his face.

"Look here, sir," he said in a tone of forced lightness, "you'd better go easy. That sounds almost as though you're trying to pin this thing on Deb."

"Sit down, Mr. Waveney," Lewker commanded in the voice of Prospero addressing Caliban. John slowly obeyed, without taking his gaze from the other's face. "There was ample time," continued the actor-manager swiftly, "for what had to be done. The impersonator removed Jacot's climbing kit from his own body, and Jacot was dressed in it. The rope—the dead man's climbing rope—was used again for a descent to wheel the car out of the garage to a spot directly beneath the balcony. Jacot's body was then lowered into the rear seat and covered with a tarpaulin. His ice-axe and rucksack were also sent down. At a quarter-past five John Waveney came into my room to borrow a woolen helmet, thus establishing beyond doubt that he could not have been on the Northeast Ridge at six. He and his sister then went out of the hotel in the ordinary way and drove the car to Täsch. At that hour there was no one to see the unloading of the body, its conveyance—discreetly covered, of course—to the plane in the little hay truck, its bestowal in the luggage compartment with the ice-axe and the rucksack. That luggage compartment, in the underside of the fuselage, has sliding doors which are operated from the instrument board of the plane. And now we see, do we not, why Mr. Bryce tried to conceal the fact that he had been to the Hörnli with his binoculars that morning. We see why he climbed down so recklessly that he slipped. He had seen a thing that turned him sick with horror—and yet he could not bring himself to tell of it."

Bryce had sunk his face on his hands. John Waveney seemed unaware of the fact that he was twisting and crumpling the roll of drawing paper in hands that trembled. Deborah had lit another cigarette and was drawing fiercely and quickly at it; her eyes were closed and her face looked haggard.

"In the plane," went on Mr. Lewker, "was the woman for whom Mr. Bryce had recently conceived a violent passion. He had climbed up there partly, I think, to watch Jacot through his binoculars as he climbed the Northeast Ridge, but also to watch the flight. He saw—this. The plane, after circling high over the Matterhorn, came down like a dive-bomber—remember Waveney had been in bombers during the war—and as it banked steeply away from the upper part of the ice slope its underside opened to eject a crumpled figure. Bryce saw the body of Léon Jacot strike the ice slope high up and go sliding down and down on to the glacier. There, later that day, I and the guides found it."

The short silence that ensued was somehow more dreadful than Lewker's words. Schultz was open-mouthed; his pale eyes had a glazed look. Deborah, suddenly, laughed and crushed out her cigarette on the table.

"Mr. Lewker," she said coolly, "I'm sorry, but you've made an ass of yourself this time. Bernard"—she turned to Bryce, entreating and commanding him with eyes and voice— "tell him, Bernard darling. You didn't see anything like that, did you? You know you didn't—don't let him get away with a damnfool tale like that."

Bryce neither moved nor spoke; his lean hands clutched his face as though he tried to shut out her very presence from him.

John Waveney flung from him the crumpled roll of drawing paper and stood up, thrusting his hands into his pockets and glaring round him.

"You can't believe him!" he cried, trying in vain to sound confident. "Where's his proof? He hasn't—"

"Mr. Waveney!" Lewker's voice was like the measured tolling of a bell. "I have proof. To get it I used the deception of occupying you with that plan while I went to your plane. I looked into the luggage compartment. In it, jammed across a strut, were Léon Jacot's ice-axe and rucksack."

John seemed to lose his angry defiance. His lean face relaxed into a smile, and his eyes met his sister's.

"Deb," he said quietly, "he's pranged us."

Mr. Lewker saw the flash of intelligence that passed between them. He sprang up and set his bulk against the door.

"Achtung, Zimmermann!" he bellowed.

The police officer was only half out of his chair when John's fist took him in the stomach. He collapsed gasping. A chair crashed through the window. John picked up his sister as though she was a baby and flung her through the opening, instantly following himself. It was done in a few seconds of violent action and the others had scarcely moved.

"The hall!" Lewker shouted, dragging the door open. "His car—in front of the hotel!"

Schultz and he managed to jam each other in the doorway and for a moment the air was thick with oaths in two languages. Then they broke through into the hall. Zimmermann was spluttering at their heels as they reached the porch. They were in time to see the sports car rocking madly round the corner with a snarl of its exhaust.

"Täsch!" panted the commissioner. *"Schnell! Schnell!"*

"Telephone—" began Mr. Lewker. But Schultz was already running round the hotel to the garage. Lewker and Zimmermann followed. It was unfortunate that in backing the Packard out Schultz should ram the wall of the hotel, and, in accelerating with frantic haste, smash his radiator against the doorpost of the garage. In the end, however, it made no difference.

The Packard had almost reached the Visp gorge when its engine seized. The car stopped with a fearful grinding sound and Schultz leapt out in a state of frenzy dreadful to witness. He was still cursing his folly in not telephoning to Täsch when the drone of a plane silenced him. The Finster passed above them like a flash of silver light, climbing steeply into the blue air. They saw it wheel high above the Matterhorn Glacier, glittering in the sun; saw it hang like an insect, incredibly small, above the huge North Face of the Matterhorn; saw it move swiftly, as though drawn by an invisible thread, towards the mountain.

There was a tiny yellow flash, a far-off little report like that of a toy pistol. Then there was no sound in the sunlit valley but the murmur of streams and the distant lonely voices of the sheep.

Over the snowy summit-ridge of the Breithorn, on a morning six days after the deaths of John Waveney and Deborah Jacot, toiled three begoggled figures. The leader, a short stout man with a face tanned to the color of a brown boot, halted on the lovely blade of snow which was the highest point and extended an arm.

" 'I weep for joy,' " he declaimed, " 'to stand upon my kingdom once again.' Richard Second. A poor king, but mine own interpretation of his lines."

Margaret Kemp, slim and sunburned in blue ski-trousers and shirt, laughed at him as she came to stand by his side.

"I think you'll quote Shakespeare when St. Peter lets you into heaven," she told him.

"Not I. He will quote it at me—'the force of his own merit makes his way.' Come along, Aunty Bee!"

"I wish to goodness," panted Mrs. Fillingham, plodding valiantly up and tangling herself in the climbing rope as she came, "You'd drop the 'Aunty,' Abercrombie. I'm young enough to be your daughter if you only—great Godfrey! What a view!"

She sank down in the snow and the other two joined her; Mr. Lewker took off the rucksack he carried and extracted a slab of chocolate. They munched for a while in silence, surveying the tremendous array of glittering peaks that stood round them like an army of giants clad in dazzling armor. Far to northward, beyond and above the blue-green valley at their feet, shone the serried summits of the Bernese Oberland. To the west the Matterhorn, little more than five miles distant, stabbed the blue with its magnificent upraised finger.

"It's really rather a terrible mountain," said Margaret. And then, irrelevantly, "I wish Bernard were here with us."

Mrs. Fillingham scooped up snow to eat with her chocolate.

"He's better off with Larry Greatorex," she said with her mouth full. "Man needs a man pal when he's all down in the mouth. Not but what Bernard deserves to suffer—sticking up for that murdering woman as he did."

"Well, I admire him for it!" Margaret said defiantly. "She made a fool of him, I know, but just because he's chivalrous and——"

"All right, all right!" interrupted her aunt hastily. She addressed Mr. Lewker. "Haven't had a chance to ask you something. Was it Bernard who typed that threatening note?"

"My dear lady, why should he? No—it was Deborah Jacot."

"Deb!" ejaculated Mrs. Fillingham. "To her own husband?"

Mr. Lewker nodded, his eyes on the Matterhorn. He was remembering the tiny speck of wreckage, crumpled and charred, which he and Heinrich Taugwalder had seen from the Northeast Ridge when they traversed the Matterhorn two days earlier.

"She was a clever woman in her way," he said, "and something of an actress, too. She wanted to be rid of her husband, who treated her abominably, and she was in love with Bernard Bryce. I think she sent for her twin brother with her plan already half-formed in her mind. There was a very strong affinity between them and he would do anything to help his sister. My arrival led her into the mistake so many murderers make—over-elaboration. She decided to impress upon me that her husband's life was in danger. The chance presence of Baptiste Frey—whom, of course, she recognized at once as one of the Flambeaux—gave her the cue."

"She had her nerve with her," observed Mrs. Fillingham.

"You mean she used him as a sort of reserve in case her fake accident didn't come off?" asked Margaret. "Surely that was a risk?"

"It was a murderer's risk. In trying to provide for every eventuality she doubled the odds against her. As a further cover when she heard that the accident was known to be a fake she told us that her husband had gone over to the Communists, though she had previously said that he told her nothing. That is typical of the mind of a murderer. Daring and ruthless, but always handicapped by the fearful desire to cover up every loophole. You will find in every case——"

"Oh, bosh and guff!" said Mrs. Fillingham heartily. "What do you know about murderers' minds? I feel pretty murderous myself when I think of the scare you gave me. What's more, I could quite easily shove you over that edge a few feet away, and I've a jolly good mind to do it."

"Forgetting, doubtless, that we are still roped together," observed Mr. Lewker gravely.

Mrs. Fillingham made a snowball and missed him with it.

"The detective mind," she said, "is a darned sight more peculiar than the murderer's. How did you get on to those two, anyway?"

"First, Madame Jacot's insistence on Frey as the murderer, and the type-written note. It was in English, you know, because her French, as she told me herself, was very poor. That, when the reason for the stifling had penetrated my thick head, made me consider her as a suspect. For it is very awkward to stifle a man except when he is in bed and asleep."

"And it was John who pushed the rocks down?" Margaret said.

"Yes. Yet another attempt to cover up. He realized that I had seen that the stifling was the clue to the whole thing and decided—or his sister decided—that the risk of an attempt on my life was worth while."

"But I'm disappointed," declared Mrs. Fillingham. "There ought to have been one tiny clue that made the mystery plain in a flash, like in *Death Walks Sideways*—"

"There was," beamed Mr. Lewker. "And you gave it me."

"Me?" she cried delightedly.

"You, or your—hum—pal Mona Smith. She told you, and you told me, that during his brief career in Variety John Waveney's best act was the im-personation of various film stars, among them Charles Boyer. It would have been no very difficult matter, then, for him to impersonate Léon Jacot—so long as his face remained unseen. Once I had linked that with the rest—you see?"

Margaret stood up and brushed the snow from her ski-trousers.

"I see," she said. "Thank you. And now let's not talk about it any more. The air's clean again."

Mr. Lewker got up also. "It is time we were starting down," he boomed, pulling Mrs. Fillingham to her feet. "We shall have soft snow to plow through on the glacier."

They moved from the snow crest and began the long descent. Mr. Lewker, coming last with a watchful eye on his roped charges, lifted it for a moment to look up at the lofty crest of the Matterhorn. The great mountain, smiling in the sun, seemed to nod at him in friendly fashion. Mr. Lewker nodded back.

THE END

About the Rue Morgue Press

"Rue Morgue Press is the old-mystery lover's best friend,
reprinting high quality books from the 1930s and '40s."
—*Ellery Queen's Mystery Magazine*

Since 1997, the Rue Morgue Press has reprinted scores of traditional mysteries, the kind of books that were the hallmark of the Golden Age of detective fiction. Authors reprinted or to be reprinted by the Rue Morgue include Catherine Aird, Delano Ames, H. C. Bailey, Morris Bishop, Nicholas Blake, Dorothy Bowers, Pamela Branch, Joanna Cannan, John Dickson Carr, Glyn Carr, Torrey Chanslor, Clyde B. Clason, Joan Coggin, Manning Coles, Lucy Cores, Frances Crane, Norbert Davis, Elizabeth Dean, Carter Dickson, Eilis Dillon, Michael Gilbert, Constance & Gwenyth Little, Marlys Millhiser, Gladys Mitchell, James Norman, Stuart Palmer, Craig Rice, Kelley Roos, Charlotte Murray Russell, Maureen Sarsfield, Margaret Scherf, Juanita Sheridan and Colin Watson..

To suggest titles or to receive a catalog of Rue Morgue Press books write 87 Lone Tree Lane, Lyons, CO 80540, telephone 800-699-6214, or check out our website, www.ruemorguepress.com, which lists complete descriptions of all of our titles, along with lengthy biographies of our writers.